WHAT YOU'VE DONE TO ME

STEPHANIE ONEILSTRAIGHT

WHAT YOU'VE DONE TO ME

One girl's Life
Becomes
One Man's Obsession

TATE PUBLISHING
AND **ENTERPRISES**, LLC

Published by Tate Publishing & Enterprises, LLC
127 E. Trade Center Terrace | Mustang, Oklahoma 73064 USA
1.888.361.9473 | www.tatepublishing.com

Tate Publishing is committed to excellence in the publishing industry. The company reflects the philosophy established by the founders, based on Psalm 68:11,
"The Lord gave the word and great was the company of those who published it."

Book design copyright © 2016 by Tate Publishing, LLC. All rights reserved.
Cover design by Samson Lim
Interior design by Shieldon Alcasid

Published in the United States of America

ISBN: 978-1-68301-992-3
1. Fiction / Crime
2. Fiction / Psychological
16.04.05

1

"FIVE, SIX, SEVEN eight!"

Emily Connors quickly finished securing her long red hair up in a ponytail before busting out the first moves of her class's newest dance. It was eight o'clock Monday morning at Emily's high school, Kinley High, and she wanted nothing more than to be where she was in dance class. Emily was just starting her senior year and was thrilled when she discovered that all of her closest friends were with her in the advanced class. Emily had been in the advanced class the year before, but this year was much better now that she had all her greatest dance partners and best companions with her.

"Go, Kim!" Emily shouted as everyone froze, allowing Kimberly to perform her solo. Strands of her long, thick black hair fell around her face piece by piece as her hair tie slowly fell out of her bun. Kim was one of Emily's dearest friends. She had just come home from visiting her family in the Philippines and brought a nice new tan with her.

Once she finished, Emily immediately started her solo for one count of eight. It wasn't very long, but as her shoulders popped, her body rolled, and her hips swayed, she made her point that in dance, there was no room for dancing halfheartedly. Finally, three minutes later, the song ended. Emily, Kim, and Jasmine dragged themselves off the dance floor, sweat dripping down their bodies as they tried to catch their breath.

"I think I need more deodorant," Emily groaned as she flopped down on to the floor.

Kim laughed before collapsing beside her, followed by Jasmine.

"Anybody else feelin' like they're glued to the floor?" Jasmine asked as she attempted to raise her arms to retie her short black hair.

"I'd raise my hand if I had the strength," Emily stated before all three began giggling. The rest of dance class flew by as the trio worked themselves hard, giving each dance everything they had. Once they changed out of their dance clothes back into their regular outfits, they grabbed their backpacks before walking down the stairs to exit the dance studio.

"I'm gonna head down to the locker rooms real quick, but I'll see you guys at lunch," Emily stated as she hugged both her girls.

"A'ight girl, we'll meet you at the picnic tables. Stay black," Jasmine joked, causing all three girls to laugh. Jasmine and Kim then headed outside.

Emily smiled as she watched her friends go. She loved them both dearly and couldn't imagine dancing or keeping herself sane in life without them. She turned and moved around the corner before heading down another flight of stairs to the basement of the building where the locker rooms resided. She wiped her forehead with her sleeve, her entire body still overheated from dance. She walked past the metal double doors that lead into the school's weight room, then halted, and took a few steps back to peek inside. She needed to ask the gym teacher, Greg Riley, a question. Mr. Riley was definitely the right person to ask when it came to exercise. He was six and a half feet tall and weighed over two hundred and fifty pounds of pure muscle. With a body like that, he would definitely have all the answers to her questions.

"Mr. Riley?" she called out as she stepped inside. She made her way through the maze of equipment then stopped when she saw him working with the school's quarterback for the football team, Aden MacLean, who was also Emily's boyfriend. Her eyes scanned over Aden's body, fascinated as his large muscles flexed under the weight of the bench press.

Aden racked the bar then sat up and wiped his face and chest off with the towel that had been resting at the end of the bench.

"Now I don't know what Coach Bombay has you guys doing, and I don't really care. If you do every day what we did today, your body will be in perfect condition all season," Greg stated as Aden stood.

"Yeah, Coach has been kind of distracted with making better plays, so I'll be in here doing this every day, don't you worry," Aden stated as he slid the small hair tie from his hair to retie it. A few of his shoulder length auburn ringlets had come loose from his ponytail.

Emily sighed happily as she watched him. Aden was only eighteen years old but everyone always assumed he was in his twenties. His face was of pure masculinity with his high cheekbones and strong jaw. Aden turned and smiled when he saw her standing there.

"Hey, babe, how long have you been here?" he asked as he walked up to her.

"Not long, I just came to see Mr. Riley before I go to Gothic Fiction," she replied before accepting a small, sweet kiss from him.

"Came to see me, did ya?" Greg asked as he made his way toward them.

"Hi, Mr. Riley, I was wondering if you'd be able to help me tomorrow after school. For dance, I feel like I'm on top of my game, except when we do modern. It's a lot of holding up your body weight on your arms or legs, and I can feel them shake sometimes, like their ready to give out. So basically, I need to start working out more often and get my body into better shape. Do you think you could help me after school tomorrow?" Emily asked eagerly.

Greg smiled as he studied her in her tight blue jeans and white baby tee.

"You look fine to me, but that doesn't mean that your body is as strong as it should be. I'm free tomorrow, just stop in here after your last class. We'll figure out what you need to work on," Greg stated as he swiped his hand over his smoothly shaved head.

"Great! I'll be here," Emily replied excitedly.

Aden finished his earlier conversation with Mr. Riley before taking Emily's hand and heading out toward the boys locker room.

"Em, I think you should take it easy with working out," Aden stated as he leaned against the wall and pulled Emily into his arms.

She smiled up at him reassuringly.

"Don't worry about me. I know I already do a lot in dance, but if I want to be a better dancer, I need to make my arms stronger and especially my legs," she replied as she rested her hands on his chest. He placed a soft kiss on her forehead as he hugged her tightly.

"Just take it easy. I don't want to see you get hurt," he stated softly.

Emily looked up into his eyes before leaning up on her tiptoes to place a soft kiss on his lips.

"I promise I'll be careful," she replied. "But you need to keep in mind that I am not a porcelain doll. I've said it once and I'll say it again; if I don't leave dance class with bruises, then I'm not dancing good enough."

"I know, Em. I'm not saying you're made of glass. I know how it feels to work out as hard as you can, but you still want to do more. I just don't want you over doing it, that's all I'm saying," Aden clarified.

"I understand," she replied with a nod. They finally said their good-byes when the first bell rang, urging them to their next classes.

Emily hurried out of the building and headed toward the English building. Once inside the classroom, she took her seat and attempted to listen to her teacher's lecture when he began to speak but she just couldn't get Aden out of her head. They had been together since the middle of their sophomore year. It was, so far, the longest relationship either of them had ever had and they could only hope it would last.

"Emily…Emily!"

She blinked a few times to focus before smiling over at her friend, Jetta.

"What?" Emily whispered back.

"Get your head out of Aden Land before Mr. March notices," she replied with a friendly wink. Jetta giggled, her amber eyes sparkling as she turned her head back toward the teacher, flipping her long black ponytail over her shoulder. Jetta Johnston was a lot like Emily when it came to personality. They could be your best friend or your worst enemy, depending on how you treated them first.

Emily giggled softly before turning her attention to her teacher.

Everyone waited anxiously for Mr. March to let them all go to lunch. She tried to hold back her laughter when she saw everyone leaning so far off their chairs that it was a miracle no one fell over. He gave the entire class an exasperated look before throwing his arms up in defeat.

"Go to lunch," he finally stated.

Emily and Jetta immediately slid off their chairs and moved right out the door.

"So, I can tell that you and your man are doing good," Jetta stated.

Emily smiled brightly as they made their way down the stairs.

"Everything is going great. He's so open to me, ya know? We talk about everything. If anything is ever bothering us, we always talk about it."

"Awww, he talks about his feelings?" she mocked, batting her eyelashes.

Emily laughed and gently shoved her friend out the front door of the building.

"Not funny, but yes, he does talk about his feelings. I'd rather him talk about his feelings and be sappy than have him hide everything and say the words that every guy loves to say…'Don't worry, everything is fine.' Now that would get annoying."

Jetta agreed wholeheartedly. The two girls hurried over to the picnic tables where Jasmine and Kim waited.

When the final bell rang, signifying the school day's end, Jetta and Emily hurried out of the building toward the buses, wanting nothing more than to go home. Jasmine and Kim were waiting at the tree at the corner of the school's front lawn, which was everyone's normal meeting place.

"I need a shower," Emily stated with a laugh as she hugged Jasmine.

"Me too, girl," Jasmine replied before turning and hugging Kim.

"I'll see you guys tomorrow," Emily called out before she and Jetta hurried to their bus.

"How come Aden didn't come see you?" Jetta asked once they took their usual seat in the back.

Emily smiled dreamily as his beautiful face wafted through her mind.

"He has football practice, so he'd be late if he came to say bye. He calls me after practice anyway. I swear, he's so amazing. I've never felt anything like this before," she replied, a smile plastered on her dreamy face.

Jetta laughed and nudged her friend with her elbow.

"You two are so pathetic but so adorable," Jetta commented, Emily laughing along with her. They chatted while the bus jerked around, hurrying them home.

"I'll see you tomorrow, babe," Emily stated once the bus made it to her house.

"Sounds like a plan," Jetta replied before Emily made her way off the bus.

2

Emily fixed her backpack over her shoulder as she made her way up the driveway.

"Whatever you're selling, I'm not buyin'."

Emily laughed at her father's words as she tossed her backpack onto the ground.

"Very funny," she stated as she made her way over to him. He was tinkering away on one of his motorcycles, which he constantly felt the need to fix or add to.

Mark laughed as he tossed his long auburn hair out of his face. Mark and his daughter were a complete mirror image of one another, from their red hair to their emerald eyes. He leaned back and wiped his oil covered hands on a rag as he glanced up at his daughter.

"How was school?" he asked, a smile on his face.

She smiled back as she sat down beside him.

"Pretty good, dance class was awesome and English was great," Emily replied as she studied the tattoos covering her father's right arm. Both of his arms were sleeved with tattoos from wrists to shoulders and no matter how long he'd had them, she still loved to look at them.

Mark owned a motorcycle shop in town, was built of pure muscle, and was over six feet tall, which all made him seem intimidating to others but not to Emily.

"What about your other classes?" he asked with his eyebrows raised.

"I'm doing good but doesn't mean I enjoy them."

Mark laughed softly and watched as she hopped up to her feet, grabbed her backpack off the ground, then headed through the garage door into the house.

"Where are you going?" he called out.

She peeked her head back in.

"I have to go practice my dances."

"Haven't you been dancing all day?".

"Yup," she stated with a giggle before heading into the house.

"Dinner's at six," he called out as the door closed behind her. "As if you even heard me."

Emily hurried through the house then up the stairs to her bedroom. She tossed her back pack onto her bed before moving over to her CD player. Music immediately blasted through the speakers once she turned it on then hurried to the middle of her room to wait for her cue. Dancing was everything to her. She could never hear music without dancing, no matter where she was. She had done ballet when she was younger but it never quite caught her full attention. Once she hit high school, she not only found dance but also found her profound passion for the art of body movement and thumping beats of music that moved to the beat of her heart.

About thirty minutes later, Emily collapsed on to her floor as sweat slid down her forehead and chest, which moved up and down rapidly with her heavy breathing.

"Tired?" Emily heard from her right.

She turned her head and immediately jumped to her feet with excitement when she saw Aden leaning against her closed bedroom door, arms folded over his chest. His smile warmed her heart as he lifted her off her feet in a tight embrace.

"How was practice?" Emily asked as she tucked a strand of hair behind Aden's ear.

He laced his hands under her backside as he carried her over to her bed.

"Brutal…just the way I like it," he replied, making Emily giggle. He gently laid her down on her bed and rested his weight on his elbows as he hovered above her.

"Sounds good to me. I was just practicing the four dances we have so far. They all feel pretty good, but I keep getting out of breath really easily. That's not so bad, but when we do any kind of squats, I feel like my thighs are gonna explode. I can't wait to start that workout tomorrow," she explained before lifting her head to place a soft kiss on his lips.

"Working out is fine, but make sure-"

"I don't work too hard, yes I know. I promise I'm going to be careful. Mr. Riley won't let me overwork myself," she replied.

Aden nodded in agreement as he gently stroked her hair.

"You're beautiful," Aden whispered as he looked deep into her eyes, mesmerized.

"I love you," Emily whispered back, a smile playing on her lips.

"I love you too," he whispered in reply. Aden's lips lowered to hers, almost immediately melting Emily's entire body, his kiss so unexpected, yet so breathtaking.

She tilted her head up, pressing her lips closer to his, wanting to feel his love for her through their kiss.

Aden's hands gently slid into her hair, tangling her auburn locks around his fingers. All he wanted was to feel her against him, feel her breath on his skin and hear her melodic voice whisper his name.

Emily could already feel her heart pounding in her chest, her pulse quickening with each movement between them. Their sexual restraint wavered each time they found themselves locked in such a heated embrace, but they always held themselves back. Emily was adamant about saving herself for marriage. Aden had always respected her decision, never wanting Emily to feel uncomfortable.

They both knew most of the girls at Kinley High were extremely promiscuous because of all those teenage hormones, but Emily refused to end up like them. She was dying inside to be with Aden, but she knew the longer they waited, the sweeter it would all be.

"We better stop," Aden whispered, once he mustered enough strength to break their kiss.

Emily's chest rose and fell rapidly as she tried to calm her body, bringing herself back down to earth.

"Stop…right," she whispered as she nodded as if trying to convince herself that it was the right thing to do.

Aden laughed before kissing her forehead softly.

"Trust me, baby girl, it's killing me as much as it's killing you, but it's your decision and I think it's the right one," he stated as he stroked her hair lovingly.

She reached up to run her fingertips down his cheek before taking his chin between her fingers and pulling him down for another soft kiss.

"Thank you…and I know it's the right decision. Usually when two people in a relationship jump into sex right away, the relationship dies within weeks. I don't want that to happen to us, Aden. I really don't," she said softly as she twirled a strand of his hair around her fingers.

"I know honey, and I completely agree," Aden replied.

"You know, there are not many guys who would be so understanding about all this. Most would want it, and if they can't have it, then they'd leave," she stated softly as she studied Aden's beautifully strong features.

"I know but that just shows that they're immature assholes. But not me, I'm content with just laying here and holding you in my arms," he purred as he leaned down to nuzzle her neck.

Emily bit back a smile as she felt her body immediately reigniting.

"What else do you like?" she asked innocently, her hands slowly sliding up his back.

Aden smirked mischievously at her question before running his lips up her neck slowly, tantalizing her already frazzled nerves.

"I like giving you kisses…little ones of course," he said nonchalantly before nipping her earlobe.

Her body jerked in response, a soft whimper of pleasure escaping her throat.

"What else?" Emily whispered, her hands now clutching the back of his shirt.

"I like when I…" Aden began to whisper.

"Emily!" Mark's voice called up the stairs, interrupting Aden's husky words.

Emily groaned in annoyance, her father's voice bringing an end to the sensuous mood.

"Maybe that was for the best…keep us from getting carried away," Aden stated before kissing her forehead softly.

"Maybe…" she replied, a scowl on her face.

He laughed softly before carefully lifting himself off her, up onto his feet.

Emily stood and led Aden out of her room then down the stairs.

"What's up, Dad?" she asked when she reached Mark at the bottom of the stairs, his eyebrows raised.

"Are you two behavin'?" he drawled, leaning against the railing.

Emily smiled before walking into her father's arms.

"Yes, we are, Daddy," she replied.

Mark wrapped his arms around her and held her tightly as he stroked her hair.

"I know ya are, baby girl. I'm a parent though, ya know I gotta ask and be suspicious," he stated with a chuckle, making his daughter, as well as Aden, laugh. Mark trusted his daughter with all his heart and he knew Aden was a good kid, but he could easily remember the things he had done when he was younger, which was why he worried so much about the welfare of his little girl. Mark had been far from a bad kid, but he had been a curious boy, and the last thing he wanted was any curious boys sniffing around his daughter.

Mark glanced up at Aden. He was a good-looking kid, Mark would give him that, but usually with good looks came a cocky attitude, which was why he was so surprised when

WHAT YOU'VE DONE TO ME | 21

he had the chance a few months ago to sit down and talk to him. Aden truly cared about Emily, anyone could see that.

A smile curved his lips when he looked down at her after releasing her. The amount of similarities in their features was simply astounding. He felt pride swell in his chest at that thought. This girl was here to make a difference in the world in any way possible, whether it be through her dancing, her writing, or one of her other many talents.

"Something wrong?" Emily asked curiously as she studied the look in her father's eyes.

"Nothing in the world," he replied before kissing her forehead then draping his arm over her shoulders.

"So, Aden, are you staying for dinner?" Mark asked.

"I'd love to, and I really wish I could, but my mom is making a really nice dinner, and I promised her I'd be home. I can't disappoint her," he replied as he made his way down the last few stairs.

Emily smiled before moving into Aden's arms.

"We'll make plans for another time then," she stated hopefully.

"You know it," Aden replied before placing a small kiss on her lips.

"I should get going. I have homework left and after the way football practice went, I definitely need a shower."

"Okay, call me later. I'll be up until probably around ten," she stated, wrapping her arms around his waist in the process.

STEPHANIE ONEILSTRAIGHT

Aden gently cupped her face in his hands as he smiled into her eyes.

"I will…I love you," Aden whispered.

"I love you too," she whispered in return.

He kissed her once more before releasing her and turning to Mark.

"Sir…" he stated, holding out his hand.

"How many times do I have to tell you, boy? If you don't start callin' me Mark, I'm gonna have to create a new way for ya to remember," Mark replied as he shook his hand.

"Right…Mark," Aden stated with a wink. They both watched as Aden pulled his car keys from his pocket then headed out the front door.

"Did you hear that? He doesn't want to disappoint his mother! Now *that* is a man right there, and he's all mine," she stated happily, along with a few squeaks.

Mark chuckled and headed into the kitchen.

"Let me know when you're out of La La Land, darlin', I'll be over here," Mark called to her.

Emily followed him and paused in the doorway, hands on her hips.

"Are you making fun of me?" she asked with her eyebrows raised.

Mark turned to her with a pained expression.

"I would never, young lady. To do such a thing would be an abomination," Mark preached.

Emily tried not to laugh, but she couldn't stop herself. She was thrown into a fit of giggles as Mark innocently went back to preparing dinner.

"Get your butt upstairs and get that homework done. If Aden has some, then so do you," he said as he pulled a pot out from the far right cabinet.

"Actually, I have an essay due this Friday, but I finished it yesterday. That's what I was typing yesterday for the two hours you had to listen to my 'clacking on the keyboard', as you call it," she replied with a smug smirk before skipping her way back into the living room then up the stairs.

"Fine, then become president, and then paint the house," he shouted up to her. He chuckled softly when he heard his daughter's laughter from her bedroom.

3

EMILY AND MARK were sitting at the kitchen table a few hours later after Emily spent time up in her room, talking to Jasmine on the phone and running through her dances a few more times.

"So how was school? And this time I mean all your classes," Mark asked as he handed Emily the salad bowl.

"It was awesome. Dance was incredible, I mean I was tired at first since it was still early, but once we started dancing, I woke up. English class was good too. We're reading Mary Shelly's *Frankenstein*. It's getting really good," she explained as she made herself a bowl of salad then started making up her entree.

"How about math or history?" he asked before taking a bite of his food.

"Eh…boring," she replied before winking at him. Emily always had very good grades but that didn't always mean that she enjoyed the class. English and dance were the only classes that made her happy. She excelled in them and loved what they did for her life.

"I'm staying after school tomorrow. Mr. Riley is gonna help me work out. I need to keep everything strong for dance, and he practically lives in that gym, so I figured he would be the best person to ask," Emily stated happily.

Mark nodded in complete agreement.

"Greg's the man to see, all right. Just take it easy and don't overwork yourself," he admonished gently.

"God, you sound like Aden. Don't worry. Mr. Riley will warn me of all of that I'm sure," she replied.

"You know, I bet he wouldn't mind if you called him Greg. I mean, he's known you almost you're whole life," Mark said before continuing into his dinner.

"True, if he mentions it, then I will. But if not, then I'll stick with Mr. Riley," Emily replied. The two continued with their dinner, Emily inquiring as to how her father's business was as well as answering a few more of her father's questions about school.

"I'm gonna go take a shower," she said as she carried her dishes into the kitchen.

"Then do your homework, right?" Mark asked, not being quite subtle.

"Yes, Daddy, only my math though. Everything else is done," she called back as she made her way up the stairs to her bedroom.

"That's my girl," he stated with a soft chuckle as he cleared the rest of the table.

————◆————

Emily sighed as she stood underneath the hot spray of her shower, letting it wash away all the stresses of the day. All she could think about was what Aden had done to her body today. She had wanted to give herself to him in every way she could, but she wanted so desperately to wait until marriage. It was simply so hard to ignore the outcries of her body. She had never felt such an intense sensation of desire before, and she had to admit that she enjoyed it.

"But you're still waiting," she muttered to herself. She finished with her shower before dressing in a pair of black sweat pants and a black tank top then tossed her backpack onto her bed to begin her math homework.

"Damn it," she cursed when her cell phone started ringing. She hurried over to her door and grabbed her jacket off the doorknob before fishing her phone out of the right pocket.

"Hello?" Emily finally answered.

"Hey, angel face," Jetta replied.

"Hey, beautiful, God, am I glad you called," Emily replied as she hung her jacket back on her door.

"Why, what's going on?" Jetta asked, her interest peaked by Emily's enthusiasm.

Emily happily hopped onto her bed.

"Well, Aden came over here after football practice and…stuff almost happened."

"What!" Jetta exclaimed excitedly. "How did that happen?"

"Well we were just laying together, little kisses and stuff, and things just started to heat up . He started kissing my neck, touching my hips, my hands were running down his back…dear God, it was so hard to hold back," she stated before sighing heavily, a smile on her face.

"Trust me, honey, I know it's tempting, but you've wanted to wait until marriage for so long. Don't give that goal up," Jetta replied.

"I know, darlin', I won't. It's just so hard, ya know? Making love to that boy would be the sweetest thing life could offer," she said softly as Aden's cobalt blue eyes wafted through her mind's eye.

"I know, Em. It will be worth it to wait though. Especially if it turns out that Aden isn't the guy you're meant to marry," she replied softly.

Emily stared out the window across from her bed as she listened to her best friend's words.

What if he is the man I'm meant to marry? What if I'm going to spend the rest of my life with him? Emily pondered as she lost herself in thought. She knew that she could never find anyone better for her than Aden, but she couldn't help but wonder if Aden could find someone better than her.

"Em? Hello?" Jetta stated with a laugh. "Are you still in reality?"

"Sorry, I was just thinking," she apologized. "Do you think Aden will find someone better than me?"

Jetta sighed before laughing softly.

"Em, Aden adores you. You two match together better than any other couple I know. He loves you; I can see it in his eyes when he looks at you. He's not going to find anyone better for him than you."

"Thanks, J. That really means a lot to me," Emily replied, a smile lighting her face. They talked for a while longer before exchanging good-byes, both needing to do their homework.

Emily set her cell phone down on the bedside table before pulling her math book and notebook into her lap.

"I hate math," Emily sang softly to herself as she started solving equation after equation. She couldn't help but giggle at herself.

"I swear if people could hear me, they'd think I'm insane." Once she finished her work, she shoved her school materials back into her backpack before sliding it down on to the floor.

"Come in," she called out when a knock sounded at her door.

"Interrupting?" Mark asked when he cracked the door open and peeked inside.

"No, I just finished."

Mark nodded and moved over to sit down on her bed beside her.

"I wanted to talk to you about something," he said as his hands fiddled on his lap.

Confusion shadowed over Emily's face as she watched her father. She was almost certain that she had never seen her father so nervous.

"What is it?" she asked, her voice soft.

Mark took a deep breath before finally speaking.

"I just want you to know that I trust you. I know earlier I had made a comment about you and Aden behaving upstairs, but that was just a father's first reaction. Em, I trust you with Aden. You're not a child anymore and no matter how much I hate to admit it, you have the body and hormones of a woman. I just trust you to have good judgment and make your own decisions."

Emily smiled at her father's discomfort with discussing her hormones and sex.

"Dad, Aden and I haven't had sex yet, and yes I'm still a virgin. I want to wait until I'm married to have sex so I know that when it happens, it's right," she explained, hoping to ease her father's worries.

Mark smiled down at her, her words music to his ears.

"That's very good to hear, darlin'," he replied as he gently pulled her against his side and kissed the top of her head.

"Well you better get to bed, girl, it's getting late," Mark suggested as he rubbed her arm.

Emily sighed in contentment as she leaned her head against her father's chest. When she was younger, Mark had the tendency of letting Emily sleep on top of him, her ear above his heart. Now, even at the age of seventeen, Emily found extreme comfort and peace when her father would envelope her in his arms.

"I'm getting pretty tired so that doesn't sound like such a bad idea," Emily replied, her voice faint.

Mark smiled down at her as he stood slowly.

"Can you shut my light off?" she asked as she made her way under her covers.

"Of course, sweet dreams, baby girl," Mark stated as he flicked the light switch, sending her room into a comfortable darkness.

"Sweet dreams, I love you, Dad."

"I love you too, Em."

Emily listened as he closed her bedroom door then headed back down the stairs.

"Dear, God," she whispered softly, "please watch over my family, my friends, and my friend's families. Keep us all safe, happy, and healthy, and please bless mine and Aden's relationship. I love him so much…amen."

A smile played on her lips as her eyes slowly fluttered closed, her body relaxing as sleep swept her away.

School seemed to fly by with nothing exciting happening, except for Emily's favorite class, English.

"Now take it easy, and if he's working you too hard, let him know. Take breaks when you need to and keep hydrated," Aden admonished as he walked beside Emily toward the weight room.

She shook her head with amusement before stopping and wrapping her arms around his waist.

"I promise to be careful, but I'm definitely going to work my butt off. I'm not dumb, baby. I know it's just like dance. Be careful, don't overwork myself, and drink water. I have this under control," she stated firmly.

"Okay, now get your butt in there before he decides to go home."

She kissed him good-bye before pulling open the heavy door and heading inside.

"Mr. Riley?" She called out as she maneuvered her way through the different machines. Emily suddenly stopped dead in her tracks when her eyes finally located him. He was laying down on one of the bench presses, pumping weights that were probably three times heavier than her. It still amazed her how large he was and every ounce of him was muscle.

It would sure be a chore to find any fat on that man, she thought as she watched him. She had to admit that he was an attractive man. She had always preferred large muscles rather than too much bone and skin, and she always found herself crushing on older men, especially her favorite *Law and Order SVU* character, Elliot Stabler. However, having

Aden in her life directed all of her affections toward him instead of little crushes.

Greg glanced up when he felt Emily standing there.

"Hey, there," Greg stated as he racked the bar then stood from the bench. "Sorry about that. I was just getting in a quick workout for myself."

Emily smiled and couldn't help but let her eyes wander down his sweat-dampened chest. He had taken his shirt off to make his workout more comfortable.

Greg chuckled as he flexed his pectoral muscles, enjoying the way her eyes immediately looked elsewhere.

"Don't be shy on me now, Em. I don't see any punk teens in this school looking like this. So don't be embarrassed about curiosity," he commented.

Emily giggled nervously when he winked at her.

"You have a point there. Well I just have to go change and then we can get started." She quickly made her way to the women's locker room at the far back of the weight room then shut the door behind her. She took a few deep breaths to calm herself. She was a bit intimidated by Greg's strength and size, but she knew there was nothing to worry about. He had helped her by joking with her about the guys in the school. He was certainly right. No one had a body like him, so it was understandable for her to be so intrigued as well as nervous around him.

"Time for a workout and stay focused," she told herself as she tied her hair back in a high ponytail. She placed her dance bag on one of the wooden benches before heading toward the door.

Greg turned when he heard her exit the locker room but immediately had to turn away to hide his smile. Her black tank top and spandex shorts clung to her body snugly, outlining her every curve.

Greg couldn't help but wonder if she had worn that on purpose or if that was what she always wore when dancing and exercising. He wasn't sure, but he did know that he wanted to snatch that ponytail of hers while it danced from side to side as she made her way toward him.

"Okay, Mr. Riley, what's first on the list?" she asked, looking at him with such eagerness in her eyes.

"First, you start calling me Greg, then second, you stretch so you don't pull any muscles and end up hurting yourself."

"Fine, let's stretch," she replied as she moved to the middle of the room where there was more floor space.

Greg watched as Emily lowered herself down onto the floor and began stretching every muscle she could. He was quite impressed with her flexibility. He studied her as she rose to her feet, situated them a bit further than shoulder width apart then bent down to grab her right leg. He turned away and moved over to one of the machines, keeping himself busy while she finished stretching.

"Okay, all set," she stated as she walked over to him.

He immediately explained what the machine they were standing in front of did and then set her on it with enough reps to get her body warmed up. As she pumped the weight with her legs, he watched her carefully for any signs of a struggle. He wanted to help her, not hurt her. After putting her on machine after machine, the clock finally struck five.

"Wow...I don't think I've ever worked out for this long before," Emily stated as Greg handed her a water bottle.

"Come on, don't you and your girlfriends dance for like ten hours a day?" Greg asked playfully.

"Well of course we do, but dancing and working out are two very different things. It's just like the fact that I could dance nonstop for three hours straight, but I can barely run for three minutes before I get a bad cramp and have to stop," Emily replied as she took a seat on the bench press.

"I know how you feel. I used to be like that when I was around twenty. I started working out more often, jogging more often, and before I knew it, I could run for miles without a break."

Emily looked enthralled by his tale.

"Really? Well then that sums that up, I need to get my ass up and running more often. Oh, sorry about that," Emily apologized, a guilty expression in her eyes from cursing in front of him. It almost slipped her mind that Mr. Riley was still a teacher.

Greg chuckled softly as he moved to kneel in front of her.

"Em, you don't need to act like I'm an adult. I haven't been your teacher since your sophomore year since that was the last year you had to take both dance and gym. I'm just here to help you out. That's why you can drop all the professionalism. I'm just another guy," Greg insisted as he rested his hand on her knee.

Emily's body immediately tensed when she felt his hand against her. She could see by the look on his face that the gesture was innocent, but she couldn't help but feel nervousness radiate throughout her body. She smiled her appreciation and patted his hand gently, subtly trying to move it away.

"Thanks, it's definitely a lot better talking to you like we're friends rather than you're an adult and I'm a child," she replied, rolling her eyes at the word *child*.

"Sounds good to me, even though I've never thought of you as a child because as I can see, you're definitely not," he stated, his eyes slowly traveling from her head to where his hand rested on her knee.

"I'm glad, and I'm especially glad that my dad doesn't look at me like a child anymore either. So, should we keep going or is it time to quit for the day?" Emily asked before taking a few gulps of her water.

Greg took a deep breath before removing his hand from her smooth, angelic skin then stood up to move away from her.

"I think that's it for the day. You've worked hard and we've been at it for a few hours. I don't want to push you too hard," Greg replied as he turned his back to her.

Emily's eyebrows furrowed in confusion as she watched him. He seemed antsy, even fidgety. Her nervousness vanished as concern took its place.

"Is there something wrong, Greg?" she asked as she approached him and rested her hand on his broad back.

Greg slowly closed his eyes and tilted his head back slightly, enjoying the warmth of her hand against his skin. He turned to face her and smiled.

"No problem at all, just thinking," he replied, his eyes traveling over her once again.

"I do too much of that myself. Well, I'm going to go change. I'll be right back."

He watched her ponytail swing once again as she made her way through the machines to the locker room.

Emily shut the door behind her before heading back over to her bag to grab her clothes. She spread them out on the bench before making her way over to the showers.

"There's no way I'm getting back in those clothes like this," she muttered as she wiped the sweat from her forehead.

⋯⋯◆⋯⋯

Greg closed his eyes as he listened to the water of one of the showers turn on full blast. He slowly reached out and placed his hand on the doorknob, his fingers itching to open the door...but he pulled himself back.

"No...not now," he whispered as he slowly backed away. He smiled as he listened to her move within the hot spray as the sound of water splashed against the tile floor. He could imagine it, but it simply was not the same as seeing the real package with his own eyes. He stepped back up to the door and rested his hand against it.

Emily turned the water off once she finished then stepped out of the shower stall and grabbed her towel. Once she dried off and redressed, she lifted her dance bag off the bench and draped the strap over her shoulder then headed back into the weight room.

"So, when is the next time I should come?" she asked as she approached Greg.

He turned to her, a smile on his lips.

"Come in on Saturday, nine a.m. sharp."

"Sounds good to me," she replied. Emily bit her bottom lip before walking up to Greg and wrapping her arms around his waist, her gratitude overwhelming her actions.

"I just want to thank you for helping me. There's no way my body would be able to keep up with all my dancing if you weren't helping me."

Greg's arms slowly came around her, one hand resting on her head.

"No need to thank me, Emily. I know how much dancing means to you, and I'm here to help you in any way I can," Greg replied, his hand slowly sliding through her auburn locks.

Emily felt her walls go back up as he stroked her hair. She pulled back slowly, extracting herself from his arms as she smiled up at him.

"I'll see you Saturday…Greg."

He watched as Emily made her way out of the weight room.

"I'll see you Saturday, Emily," Greg replied, knowing she could no longer hear him. He smirked as he turned and headed back to the bench press. He immediately started his own workout, his body feeling a bit tense from all the resisting it had endured.

"So how did it go?" Mark asked as he drove home. He had been waiting outside the school for Emily.

"It was awesome. My body is getting stronger already. Seriously, Dad, it was amazing," she replied.

"Well I'm glad, darlin'. Don't overdo any of this though. You need to keep strong for dance but please just be careful. You girls already dance every single day. I don't want your body to give out on you from doing too much physical work."

She smiled as she turned toward her father.

"I already promised I'm going to be careful, remember? Plus, Greg won't let anything happen to me."

Mark smiled in return and nodded in agreement. Mark had known Greg for years. There was no one Greg trusted more with his motorcycle than Mark.

"He'll make sure of that," Mark replied as they pulled into their driveway.

4

"IT's FINALLY ALMOST Friday," Jetta stated happily as she leaned back in her chair.

Emily nodded in agreement. "Thank God, I definitely need a nice, peaceful weekend."

"Amen to that," Jetta replied. She lowered her eyes to her lap as her hands began to fidget.

Emily quirked an eyebrow at her friend.

"What's the matter, babe?" she asked as she leaned toward her friend, her curiosity peaked.

Jetta sighed heavily with a shrug of her shoulders.

"I have something to tell you, but I really don't want us involved in this stupid drama junk, especially this early in the morning on a Thursday."

"Uh-oh, what's going on?" Emily asked as she studied Jetta.

"Well at lunch the other day, I heard some stuff floating around. Do you remember that Sally chick in the beginners' dance class? Well, apparently, she's been talking smack on the advanced class. She keeps saying stuff about how you guys can't dance and she can dance better. She even claims that the dance teacher favors you guys," Jetta explained.

Emily's face darkened quickly as she listened to her friend's words.

"Are you serious?" she asked, her voice dangerously soft.

"Yes, it's complete crap. But I heard that her and her little followers are staying after school today," Jetta stated.

A smirk slowly spread across Emily's lips.

"Well in that case, I believe you. Jasmine, Kim, and I have to stay after school for a special meeting," Emily stated. The two then turned their attention to their English teacher when he stood and began speaking. It was difficult for her to pay attention after what Jetta had told her. Emily only knew Sally from passing her every now and then around campus so it didn't quite make sense to her why this girl had anything negative to say.

She'll eat her words, Emily thought heatedly.

"She said *what*?" Jasmine exclaimed once Emily reiterated Jetta's story to her.

"That's exactly what I said," Emily replied, eyebrows raised in expectancy.

"Are you thinking what I'm thinking?"

"Oh, you mean the fact that we have to stay after school because we have to go to the library?" Emily replied innocently.

"Oh yeah, we have to study for that test we have coming up," Jasmine replied with a smirk.

"Wait, I thought we were going to study at my house for that test!" Kim chimed in.

Jasmine tossed her a sideways glance.

"Kim…shut up."

All the girls couldn't help but laugh as it dawned on Kim that their discussion was far from being about studying.

⸺⸺◆⸺⸺

Emily, Jasmine, Kim, and Jetta made their way down the stairwell that lead to the cafeteria. The final bell had rung ten minutes ago and they had found out from different people around campus that Sally and her friends were congregating at one of the lunch tables.

"Now this will not get physical, all right? We have to at least attempt to be the voices of reason," Emily stated with confidence.

"Yeah, and I'm Michael Jordan," Jasmine retorted, sarcasm dripping from her voice. Kim and Jetta laughed as Emily smiled, leading them from a hallway to the cafeteria.

"I'll tell you now, if Shannon comes near me with that weave that looks like an electrocuted rat, I'm gonna rip it out of her ugly head," Kim stated with annoyance. Shannon, one of Sally's little followers, had aimed her bad-mouthing at Kim, claiming she didn't have any rhythm or any hips to create it.

Jetta didn't dance, but she went to every performance to support her friends, and she was always in the loop when it came to drama and the latest news about the dancer community at Kinley High.

"Kim, do not start with the antagonizing!" Emily admonished as Jasmine and Jetta tried to catch their breath from laughing so hard.

"Wow, did you girls ever notice that they can walk with more enthusiasm than they can dance?"

All four girls immediately glared in Sally's direction.

"Yeah? Well you're ugly," Jasmine retorted nonchalantly, throwing her friends into fits of laughter.

Sally's mouth dropped open as the four girls approached her.

"So that's how you want this to go?" Shannon chimed in, moving closer to interject.

"You guys are the ones talking trash on us for no reason. We get the spotlight on stage and around school because we work hard and we are good. Some people just don't have the capabilities of body movement like others," Emily stated reasonably.

"Yeah, like Kim," Shannon retorted.

"You know what, bitch…" Kim shouted as she lunged for the other girl.

Jasmine and Jetta held her back as Emily stepped up closer in Sally's face.

"You guys need to learn to watch your words and keep your nose out of our business. Tell your friend with the infected dead cat sitting on her head to back off, or we will make you all back off."

Shannon shrieked with insult as she turned to her friends with outrage.

"I love when white girls think they can dance. You know what? We'll back off when I get a shot at Aden. Oh! What's the matter? Afraid that he'll want me over your fat ass?"

Before Emily could stop herself, she lunged at Sally, knocking her to the ground.

"So much for talking this out with reason," Jetta stated as she watched Jasmine and Kim jump into the mayhem. Jetta tried as best as she could to break up the mass of girls but none of them were having it.

"Whoa! Whoa, cool it!"

Jetta sighed with relief when she saw Mr. Riley run through the doorway.

"Here comes the cavalry," she muttered.

Emily squealed when she felt herself being lifted off Sally. She took one more swing, missing completely since Greg had her hoisted in the air.

"Emily, what the hell's gotten into you?" Greg asked as he shoved her onto one of the tables.

"Stay right here," he demanded before hurrying over and grabbing Jasmine and Kim next. Ten minutes later, Jasmine, Emily, Jetta, and Kim were seated at one table while Sally, Shannon, Mary, and Denise were on the other side of the room at another table.

"We're screwed," Kim stated as she tried to put her unruly hair back under control.

"Greg and I are friends. Hopefully I'll get a chance to talk to him before he talks to the principal," Emily replied.

"Greg? Damn, you guys got that close that fast?" Jasmine asked before tossing a death glare in Sally's direction.

"He asked me to call him Greg. He's training me because my leg strength sucks for some of our dances and my arms could use some toning when Miss Gwen wants us to hold our whole body weight up on one arm. He's really sweet, and he's so smart when it comes to getting my body into perfect shape," she replied as she rubbed her throbbing cheek.

"Well, use your wiles, Em. Miss Gwen will kill all of you, and even me, if we all get suspended," Jetta stated.

Emily couldn't help but laugh.

"My wiles are out in the open enough when me and him workout together. I will admit that I flirt a little, but who can blame me? He's tall, built like a brick wall, funny, sweet…but that's not the point. The point is that I'm not going to flirt with him to get us out of this mess. I'll just talk to him straight and pray he can help us."

"Emily, get over here."

She turned and saw Greg standing in the doorway, beckoning her over with his finger, a very unhappy look adorning his face. She took a deep breath before making her way over to him.

Greg pulled her into the hallway, out of everyone's sight.

"What the hell were you thinking?" Greg whispered harshly. He studied her reddened face and tousled hair. He could see no severe injury other than the small bruise on her cheek.

"We only came down here to confront them and find out why they keep talking such crap about us. I came here with a level head and tried to talk this out with reason…but she made a comment about Aden, and I lost it." She ran her fingers through her hair as she stared at the floor.

Greg sighed and lifted her chin to look into her eyes.

"Promise me you won't fight in school again?" Greg asked with his eyebrows raised in question.

"I promise."

"Good, now I have to go talk to Principal Mathers and straighten this out."

"Is there any way you could help us? Greg, I never meant for this to happen," she pleaded.

"Don't worry about anything, Emily. I'll take care of it," he replied, a smile touching his lips. She sighed with relief as she returned his smile with her own.

"Thank you, Greg. This means the world to us."

"You can thank me later," he murmured as he leaned down toward her. He placed a soft, quick kiss on her cheek before walking away.

Emily stared after him with confusion as thoughts began to race through her mind. What did he mean when he said that she could thank him later? And had he really just kissed her on the cheek? She lifted her hand to the spot where he kissed her and flinched. She realized he had kissed right where her bruise was. Well, that helped calm her nerves. It reminded her of all the times her dad had kissed her injuries. She felt relief at the realization that he had probably felt that father-like protection overtake him. Emily took a moment to gain control of her senses. When she made her way back into the cafeteria, she saw Greg sending Sally and her friends off with another teacher. She was pleased to see them heading in the direction of the principal's office.

"Now, ladies, I'm sorry you had to suffer the indignity of their attack. No one seems to be hurt, so you are free to go home. I'm sure you all need the rest," Greg stated to all of them.

They all glanced over at Emily, smiles spreading over their faces.

"You're a cool ass nigga," Jasmine stated happily before covering her mouth. She almost forgot she was speaking to a teacher.

Greg tossed his head back with laughter, allowing the rest of the girls to follow suit before they burst from holding it in.

"Go on home, now," he stated before turning to Emily. He approached her as Kim, Jasmine, and Jetta gathered their belongings.

"I'll see you Saturday, right?"

It took her a moment to realize what he was referring to.

"Oh, my workout…yes, absolutely," she replied.

"I'm sure I'll see you tomorrow, and I'll see you around nine on Saturday," he stated with a wink before briskly heading off to have his chat with the principal.

"What was that all about?" Kim asked, wiggling her eyebrows.

"Would you stop it! You should be thankful that he just saved our butts from getting suspended," Emily replied as she grabbed her back pack.

"There's my girl, how come you're late?" Mark asked his daughter as she walked through the front door.

Emily smiled when she saw her father leaning in the doorway between the kitchen and living room.

"Hi, Daddy. Me, Kim, Jetta, and Jasmine stayed after to do some studying," she replied as she tossed her bag near the coffee table then flopped on to the couch.

Mark took three strides to the couch and leaned over, hovering above her.

"Really? Since when does studying involve a fist fight in the cafeteria?" he asked with his eyebrows raised.

Emily's eyes widened with surprise then shut tight with embarrassment as she groaned and pulled the nearest pillow over her face.

"Greg called you, didn't he…" she stated, her voice muffled from the offending fabric.

"Yes, he did, and I'm glad. Why would you lie to me about something like that?" he asked before swiftly hopping over the couch and settling down beside her.

Emily sighed heavily as she pulled the pillow away then moved to a sitting position.

"Dad, I swear I was gonna tell you. I was worried. I didn't want you to be mad at me or disappointed in me. I'm sorry, Dad."

Mark sighed as he pulled her to his side, her head resting against his shoulder.

"I'm not mad at you, and I'm not disappointed in you. Greg told me everything. That girl attacked you and you were simply defending yourself…poor innocent daughter of mine…"

Mark's voice dripped with sarcasm on his last sentence.

She bit her bottom lip as she glanced up at him.

"He told you the truth?"

"Oh yeah, every single thing he saw."

"She made a comment about Aden. I couldn't help it. By the time I knew what happened, I was already on top of her."

Mark chuckled. "Sorry I gave you my temper, sweetheart. Please make me a promise? No more fighting so Greg has to cover for you ."

Emily smiled as she reached up and kissed her father's cheek.

"I promise, and I will thank Greg tomorrow when I see him, and if I don't, then I'll thank him Saturday."

"Working out again? What time do I have to get up?" he asked with a playful grimace.

"He wants me there for nine, so it's not too early for you," she replied with a giggle.

"Yeah, knowing you, you'd drag my ass outta bed at five in the morning," he mumbled as Emily hopped off the couch. She grabbed her bag then headed toward the stairs.

"I wouldn't do that to you, Daddy. You can't handle anything like that anymore, not at your age," she stated with a satisfied smile.

"Oh, that's it!" Mark shouted as he leaped over the couch.

Emily squealed and bolted up the stairs, knowing that she was in for a merciless tickling if she didn't outrun him.

————◆————

Emily sank lower into the tub, her eyes drifting closed as the heat from the water surrounded her. She couldn't help but smile as her day ran through her mind. She still couldn't believe she had gotten into a fight. Never in her life had she fought anyone.

"Felt pretty damn good though," she stated softly to herself as she scooped up a handful of bubbles. She had truly not meant to fight anyone, but the moment Sally made a comment about Aden, she saw red. She was positive she could have held her temper if it had not been for Sally bringing Aden into the argument.

"Come in," Emily called out softly when a knock sounded at the door. Her eyes widened when the door cracked open and Aden popped his head in, his hand covering his eyes.

"May I enter, milady?"

She giggled as she pulled her knees up to her chest.

"Of course you may, good sir."

He stepped inside then closed the door behind him before taking a seat on the floor beside the tub.

"You can open your eyes now, baby. I'm covered in bubbles," she stated as she leaned against the side of the tub toward him.

He chuckled softly as he opened his eyes.

"You should wear bubbles more often, my love. You look simply ravishing," he stated playfully, making Emily giggle.

"I'll keep that in mind. So how was practice?"

"Great, but I would've liked to see you beat the crap out of Sally instead," he replied with a smirk.

"Does everyone know now?" Emily exclaimed with a laugh.

"No, your Dad told me."

"Good, now I'll have to tell him to keep his mouth shut so he doesn't go and tell the whole world."

"I'm sure he'll tell all his guys down at the motorcycle shop."

"Lord, that's the last thing I need, a bunch of my Dad's friends playing the parts of instigators," she laughed.

Aden smiled as he studied her face. Strands of her damp hair were sticking to her neck while the rest of her locks lay over her shoulders and back. He couldn't help but want to pull her into his arms and keep her there forever. Aden had never felt such a strong attachment to anyone before. He knew he loved Emily more than anything. All he ever wanted to do was keep her happy.

"How does your face feel?" he asked as he reached out to gently run his fingertips over the slight bruise marring her cheek.

Her eyes drifted closed at the feel of his touch.

"It's not that bad. A little bit of a sting, but nothing I can't handle."

Aden smiled at her brave words.

"I'd say I'm proud of you, but I don't condone you fighting with her. I understand it, but I don't agree with it," he stated with a wink.

"I know, I promise I had no intention of fighting. Sometimes people can't keep full control over their actions. I know there's no excuse for fighting but…the moment she said your name…I couldn't control myself," she replied as she glanced down at the bubbles, avoiding eye contact with him.

"Wait, why did she mention my name?" Aden asked with confusion.

"My Dad didn't tell you?"

"No…care to clue me in?"

"Sally was running her mouth when she decided to try and be slick, so she made a comment about her having a chance with you. I couldn't help myself." She stared down, ashamed she had let her temper get the better of her.

Aden lifted Emily's chin to study her eyes.

"No one in this world has a chance with me. I'm already yours. I would never give up what we have without a fight," he replied, his eyes shining with sincerity.

Emily leaned forward as Aden leaned down to accept her offered kiss. Emily felt the butterflies fluttering in her stomach as his lips pressed against hers. Kissing Aden was one thing she would never become tired of doing. His lips were so soft, yet they commanded her lips' attention and compliance. She knew she had nothing to worry about when it came to Aden's love and loyalty. She was simply afraid that someone would take him away from her. If she was so in love with him, then why shouldn't she think that another girl might do the same?

"Stop worrying," Aden whispered against her lips.

Emily giggled before kissing him once more.

"How do you know what I'm always thinking?" she asked, her voice soft.

"I can feel when you're worried, afraid, sad, and especially happy. I can always feel when you're happy, and I love when I can see it. Your eyes sparkle, your cheeks dimple when you smile, and your giggle is music to my ears," he whispered as he ran his fingers down her cheek to her neck.

"Mmmm, keep going," she stated sweetly, thoroughly enjoying his endearing words.

Aden laughed deeply as he leaned forward and placed a soft kiss on her forehead.

"I'll continue the list of your virtues later. I'll let you finish your bath. I'll be downstairs, talking to you father."

Emily nodded with resignation then kissed him once more before he walked out the door.

"I need to start behaving," she stated with a groan as she sank back down into the water.

You can thank me later.

Emily laughed softly as Greg's words rang in her mind. She needed to learn to loosen up and realize when someone was trying to joke with her instead of letting her mind wonder if it could have been something else.

"He was just kidding," she mumbled as she poked at the bubbles on her arm. She sighed when she thought about the way Greg had kissed her cheek. It had been a smooth and quick gesture that had been surprisingly more comforting than she had originally thought. Greg was her father's best friend and had known Emily since she was little. She knew if her father had been there after the fight, he would have kissed the bruise on her face the same way. However, he was her teacher after all, so not thinking about everything that had happened was probably the best course of action for her mind to take. She sighed heavily when she heard Aden and her father laugh from the living room bellow.

You probably shouldn't mention the kiss on the cheek to them. Knowing them, they would take it the wrong way, she thought before pulling the plug at the head of the tub. She watched as the bubbles slowly ran down the drain. "And take all my thoughts with you…"

"Remember now, boy, I like you a lot because I know you're a good kid and you make my girl happy…but she's still my girl."

"Mark, I'd never try to take her away from you. I love her to death, but she's always gonna be your daughter before she's my girlfriend."

Mark patted Aden's shoulder proudly.

"Those are the words I like to hear," Mark retorted.

"Talking about me again, I see?" Emily asked as she descended the stairs. She laughed when both men looked at her with guilty smiles.

"Dinner's almost ready," Mark stated as he stood from the couch. "Aden, are you staying?"

"I'd love to," he replied as he stood and moved to Emily's side.

"You look comfy," Mark said as he looked at Emily's black pajama pants and tank top.

"I am," she replied smugly.

"Go on and set the table you two," he insisted with a chuckle. He watched them hold hands to the kitchen and sighed when he saw Emily's facial expression. He saw the way her eyes shined at Aden with such innocent love. She always glanced at him and saw her world. Mark was terrified of seeing that all snuffed out. He trusted Aden, but just as he always kept in mind, Aden was still a guy.

"Daddy, I think the chicken is done!" He heard her call out.

Mark smiled as he made his way to the kitchen.

"Thank you, baby girl," he said as he kissed the top of her head. Once they all took their seats and food was passed around, the talking began.

"So, how did you convince Greg to cover for you and your friends?" Mark asked as he shook some salt onto his dinner.

"I begged," she replied with a giggle. "I tried to explain to him that it was an accident. He could tell that I never intended on fighting anyone."

"He knows you that well?" Aden inquired.

"No, but anyone could've told by the look on my face," she replied before turning her attention back to her food. An awkward silence fell over them.

Aden knew he should be thankful for what Mr. Riley had done. The last thing he wanted was for Emily to have a suspension on her school record for fighting, but he couldn't help the bit of jealousy he was starting to feel. Ever since her first workout with Mr. Riley, he was all she seemed to talk about.

Oh knock it off, he's just trying to help her become a better dancer. He's helping her, Aden thought as he reached under the table to rest his hand on Emily's knee.

She immediately felt tension radiating from Aden's direction so she quickly changed the subject.

"So, how are things going at the shop, Dad?"

"Busy, it's great. We got in about five more bikes today and expect a few more tomorrow. You can have the keys to the truck tomorrow if you want to drive to the school," Mark offered.

"Daddy, I don't have my license yet," she replied with a laugh.

"You've known how to drive since you were like six. Plus you've got that driving permit thing," Mark dismissed with a wave of his hand.

Emily laughed as she took the salt and moved it away from her father's plate.

"I can drive next year but until then, you're my taxi driver. And stop staring at the salt. You've had enough."

"Who are you telling not to have any more salt? You're the one with the igloo on your food," Mark replied with mock stress as he reached for the salt shaker.

"Well I drink more water than you and I'm young," she replied with a wink.

"One more old joke out of that mouth, and I'll tape it shut, li'l lady," Mark threatened, sending both Aden and Emily into fits of laughter.

"I'm sorry, Daddy. I'm just kidding. Trust me, you're not old," Emily stated, soothing her father's pride.

"So do you count Greg as old?" Aden asked with raised eyebrows.

"No, he's probably only in his thirties," she replied with a shrug and a smile. The image of Greg working hard on one of the bench press machines wafted through her mind. She could see his muscles rippling so clearly that she felt as though she were standing beside him.

"What's that look for?" Aden asked, eyeing her cautiously.

Emily swallowed as she cleared the image from her mind then smiled at him.

"Nothing, I just find it funny that my lovely father thinks he's old when he's always getting winks from girls in their twenties," she replied swiftly.

"I don't instigate them, little girl. They do what they're gonna do," Mark quickly defended.

"I know, Daddy. I was just kidding. I didn't mean anything by it," Emily quickly apologized when she saw the distress on her father's face. At times, Emily would forget her father's sensitivity when it came to women. Ever since Emily's mother passed away after giving birth to her, Mark had dedicated his life to Emily. His daughter was the most important female in his life, and he wanted Emily to always know it.

"It's all right, sweetheart. Don't worry about it. You're my one and only girl," Mark stated with a smile.

Emily smiled back as she felt her heart swell, filling with her father's love. It was as though her heart and life depended on receiving the approval, compliments, and love of her father. For such a fiery and strong young woman, she felt very dependent on Mark's strength. She was an only child with only one parent. She was Daddy's little girl and knew she could depend on his strength and pride always. Mark was her hero from the day she was born. When she had made her first finger painting in kindergarten, Mark was the one who hung it on the refrigerator. When Emily had learned to read her first book, Mark was the one who lay beside her to listen, so proud of her success. When she graduated from junior high school, Mark had been sitting in the front row to cheer when her name was called. All of Emily's success mattered to her greatly, but it made everything seem worthwhile when her father would tell her how proud he was of her.

"Remember not to overdo anything with this whole working out thing," Aden advised.

Emily sighed as she turned to him. She was beginning to get agitated with everyone's worries, but she knew they were just saying these things because they were worried about her.

"Sweetheart, I'm not going to get hurt. Greg watches everything I do very carefully. He would stop me if he knew I needed to," she stated, reassuring Aden once more.

He smiled and leaned in to place a soft kiss on her forehead.

"He better not be watching you too carefully," he murmured, lowering his head to press his forehead to hers.

Emily smiled softly, confident that all Aden's worries were in his head.

"I love you," she stated with a soft laugh. "No one is allowed to watch me like that except you."

"Okay, heel you two," Mark chimed in as he lifted his glass of water. "Don't make me pour cold water over both of you."

The two laughed heartily at Mark's threat. Emily seemed so happy with Aden as well as the rest of her life. He knew that dance was her passion and no matter how still she was standing, she'd still be dancing in her mind. Mark couldn't help but worry that something would take it all away from her. Mark was never one to worry about things that might happen, but when it came to his daughter's happiness, it was always on his mind. They finished with dinner and started carrying dishes into the kitchen.

"Daddy, are you coming to the pep rally tomorrow to see us dance?" she asked, almost bouncing up and down with excitement.

Mark chuckled as he pulled her into his arms. "I wouldn't miss it for the world."

Emily squealed happily as she hugged him tighter.

"You'll love it, we are completely prepared. I can't wait for you to see us."

"I can't wait either," he replied with a smile. "Now go on and help Aden load the dish washer, I'll grab the rest of the silverware."

Emily reached up to kiss her father's cheek before skipping off to do what she was told.

"Need some help in here, you big, strong man?" Emily asked playfully as she batted her eyelashes dramatically.

Aden laughed before leaning down to kiss her lips softly.

"Sure, Cinderella."

"Hey! I'm not Cinderella, I'm Belle. Get it right!" she stated sternly, her eyes fluttering.

"Does that make me the Beast?" He wiggled his eyebrows.

"Maybe," she giggled as he moved closer to her. Emily's head barely reached Aden's chin as he towered over her.

"It's impossible for me to be the Beast...you're love would've already broken even the strongest spell," he whispered as he trailed his fingertips down her cheek.

Emily's heart skipped a beat at his words. Aden was well aware that Emily's favorite movie of all time was *Beauty and the Beast*. He loved using lines from the movie to charm her or concepts such as spells and roses to take her breath away.

"God in heaven, I love you," Emily whispered on an exhale as she stared up into his eyes. Aden smiled as he slipped his arms around her waist.

"And I love you, my princess," he replied as he leaned down for her lips.

Emily forgot where she was or what she had been doing. All she knew was Aden's touch and his love as it radiated through her body like an electric charge. His lips seemed so soft against her own, his breath mingling with hers as he possessed her mouth. She clutched the front of his shirt for balance as she felt her knees weakening.

Aden slid his hand into her hair, tangling it around his fingers. Her hair felt like silk as he held it tightly in his fist. Aden could never understand how she could affect him to the point of no rational thought. The girl intoxicated him with her spirit, and the only way to sober him was by staying away from her. But he just couldn't. He had to feel her slim body against his, her sweet lips pressed against his, and her small feminine hands on his body.

"I can't get enough of you," Aden whispered as he loosened his grip on her hair and massaged away any pain he may have caused her.

Emily couldn't speak or even open her eyes. Her entire body was alive and tingling from what he had done to her. She was so distracted that she almost missed his words.

"Right back at you, sweetheart," she whispered, her words almost inaudible.

"I hear a lot of breathing, is it safe to come in?" Mark called from the dining room.

"It's safe," Aden replied with a sly smile, knowing Emily couldn't speak.

She swallowed hard as she scrambled to gather her wits.

Mark walked in and chuckled when he saw his daughter's disheveled state.

"Go on you two, I'll finish the dishes," Mark offered.

Emily and Aden took that opportunity to hurry from the kitchen and head up the stairs toward Emily's room.

"Y'all better behave up there!" Mark called after them as he listened to their thudding footsteps above.

Greg hissed through his teeth as he continued to lift the heavy weights over and over. Regardless of how often he lifted weights at Kinley High, he always went home to continue. His entire basement was filled with workout equipment, giving him his own gym as well as privacy. Once he finally decided to rack the bar on the bench press, he sat up and wiped his face and chest off with a small towel.

"Get outta my head," he mumbled as Emily's smiling face flashed through his mind's eye. Ever since their first day of training earlier that week, Greg could not get his mind off her. Her beautifully slim body dressed in tight spandex bending over every which way was the only thing on his mind. Greg growled in frustration as he stood and made his way up the stairs then into the kitchen.

"Control yourself...you can't touch her...not yet," he whispered as he poured himself a glass of water. His eyes fluttered closed as he downed the cold liquid, his entire body beginning to calm. He placed the cup into the sink once he was finished then headed up the stairs toward his bedroom to jump in the shower. He tried to ignore the sweet sound of her voice as it wafted through his mind. It was almost like he could feel her body as he helped position her on one of the machines in the gym.

"Saturday will be here soon enough," he stated as he turned the shower on full blast, needing to wash away the stress his body and mind were feeling from a sweet, little redheaded girl.

5

EMILY, JASMINE, AND Kim all laughed as they sprawled out on the dance floor. The pep rally was scheduled to start in a half hour so the girls were up in the dance room stretching and going over the two dance routines they had in line to perform for the school.

"So, anybody nervous?" Kim asked before the three girls exchanged looks between one another. They all laughed as they continued to stretch.

"If we're afraid to perform in front of the people that go to this school, then we need to get out of the dance profession already," Emily stated before pulling herself to her feet. She moved over to the large glass windows that looked down from the dance room into the large gymnasium.

"This is a hell of a way to start off our senior year, guys," Jasmine stated as she stood and made her way over to Emily's side. "Kim is talking to Sebastian…"

"Who is my favorite character in the *Little Mermaid*," Emily chimed in, finishing Jasmine's sentence. The two girls practically fell over one another as their laughter took over.

"You guys!" Kim shouted as she fell out on to the floor. Once Emily and Jasmine pulled themselves together, Jasmine continued.

"Like I was saying, Kim is flirting away with Sebastian, Ruud and I are doing just fine, and the ring is coming," she stated as she pointed to her empty ring finger on her left hand. Her words were an inside joke between the three girls. Jasmine and her boyfriend Ruud had been best friends for as long as they could remember, but they only recently embarked on a romantic relationship. So the girls always joked about how Ruud was going to pop the question sooner rather than later and that the wedding ring was on its way.

"And Aden and I are doing simply wonderfully," Emily finished for her friend.

"*And* you're even landing a teacher, now that's talent," Jasmine retorted, before snapping her fingers. "Hey, girl, hey!"

"I am not landing anybody except Aden. Greg is just training me, Kim stop laughing!" Emily shouted, her own laughter bubbling up inside her.

"I'm sorry, Em. But you and Mr. Riley do seem to be very friendly with each other," Kim replied as she made her way over to the other two.

Emily sighed as she ran her fingers through her hair, giving both girls an admonishing glare.

"Listen, you two, Greg and I are just friends. He's helping me, that's all. I love Aden and he's all I need," Emily stated firmly.

"We know that, girl. What fun would it be if we didn't pick on ya when the opportunity presents itself?" Jasmine asked as she draped her arm over Emily's shoulders. Kim moved around to the other side of Emily and did the same.

"We'd get bored. I think all three of us would need to find new hobbies if we didn't have each other," Kim said as the three exchanged smiles.

"Awww, are we all gonna kiss? This is a beautiful moment," Jasmine stated melodramatically, sending Emily and Kim, as well as herself, into fits of laughter.

Mark sat anxiously in the gymnasium as the students began to pile onto the bleachers. He had to call in one of his friends to hold down the shop so he could attend the pep rally. He would've called in anyone it took in order for him to see Emily's performance. He had promised her he would be there, and he would've done anything to keep that promise.

"What's an old man like you doing here?"

Mark turned his head, a smirk spreading across his face as he laid his eyes on Greg Riley.

"Came here to watch my beautiful daughter dance her heart out," Mark replied as he stood to accept Greg's handshake and hug.

"Well I'm sure you won't be disappointed," Greg replied with a laugh. "Her first time in the weight room was a great day, so I have no doubts that she'll be getting better and better as a dancer."

"Thanks for helping her, man. Dance means everything to her, so I'm sure she's gonna love you forever for helping her," Mark replied with a soft laugh.

Greg laughed along with him as his eyes slowly and subtly trailed off Mark and up to the windows of the dance room. A smirk spread over his lips as he caught sight of Emily with her two friends. They were dipping and twirling, disappearing and reappearing, so he knew they were practicing more before they performed.

"She doesn't need to thank me at all. I enjoy helping her," Greg stated as he turned his attention back to his long-time friend. "Listen, I have to go stand over near the other faculty unfortunately, but I'll catch you after the rally." Greg patted his friends shoulder before heading down the stairs of the bleachers and making his way over to the group of teachers who were beginning to converge near the rear left corner of the gymnasium.

I enjoy helping her, Mark. God…every inch of my body enjoys helping her, Greg thought as he leaned up against the wall, his large arms folded over his muscular chest. The students were almost finished filing into the gym which only helped to heighten Greg's impatience as he waited to see her. He could almost see her long red locks being tossed about as she gyrated her body to the music.

"God, that little woman's going to be the death of me," Greg muttered as he rested his head back against the wall.

"What was that, Greg?" Anna Johnston asked as she turned her attentions on him. Anna was one of the tenth grade math teachers who was young enough to blend in with the students. She seemed to be interested in Greg since she went out of her way to say hello or to make small talk. Unfortunately for her, she was simply not what Greg was looking for. Once he had met Emily, he had no need to look at anyone else. He had met her when she first started going to Kinley High, but he had only seen her a few times in passing. This was the first year he had truly had time to be alone with Emily so he could get to know her. She was so sweet, kind, loving, and strong. She was everything he could ever want in a woman. All he had to do was make her fall in love with him.

That shouldn't be that hard, Greg thought to himself with a soft chuckle.

"Nothing," Greg stated as his eyes trained on the gymnasium door. "Nothing at all."

<hr />

All of the dancers gathered in the hallway right outside the doors to the gymnasium.

"I'm so excited, my dad is here, so he'll get to watch all of us dance," Emily stated excitedly.

"Sweet, your Dad is so kickass. He's got a motorcycle shop, tattoos all over the place, and he always comes to see us dance," Kim stated as she stretched her arms above her head.

Emily smiled at her friend's words. She loved her dad so deeply and knew she could never ask for a better father than him. Everyone in the hallway went silent as the principal's voice came over the speakers.

"God, do we have to listen to this every year?" Jasmine mumbled.

Emily and Kim tried to muffle their laughter along with multiple other dancers. Principal Mathers was going on about school spirit and how every student in the school is cared about by the entire faculty.

"Yeah, just like Mr. Riley 'cares' about Emily," Jasmine whispered.

Emily's jaw dropped and she immediately took Jasmine's face in her hands and pulled her toward her.

"I'm gonna beat you," Emily whispered loudly as Jasmine laughed and grabbed Emily's face in return.

"You know you love me," Jasmine whispered back.

"Stop fooling around, you two!" Ms. Gwen whispered harshly. The girls immediately released each other and stood there innocently, their eyes aimlessly looking around the hallway.

"And now, to get everyone just a little bit more motivated to work together as a team, to stir up some of that Wildcat spirit, here is the advanced dance class along with Ms. Gwen Martins!" Principal Mathers announced. The gym doors burst open as the dancers made their way out onto the gymnasium floor. All of the students were screaming and clapping, hooting and hollering. The dancers always performed at pep rallies as well as a show called a.m. Artists in Motion. This collaboration of dancers, singers, and poets took place every March in the auditorium. So essentially, the stage in that auditorium was Emily, Jasmine, and Kim's home. Practically every student that went to Kinley High knew the dancers, which made the shows much more exciting.

Emily searched the crowd, trying to spot her father but was unfortunately having trouble since most of the students were standing and waving their arms.

"There!" Kim pointed when she noticed Emily's distress. A smile spread across her face when she followed the direction of Kim's hand. Her father was still sitting down, a smile on his face as he watched her. She thought it hilarious that he never stood at these events. He claimed it was because of his height.

"If I stand up, there's no way any of those kids could see you guys," her dad had joked. She couldn't help but agree of course, considering her father's height of six foot six. Emily waved to her father then glared at Jasmine when she mentioned that someone else was looking at her. Emily looked to her right and smiled when she saw Greg. He gave her a smile and a wink, sending Emily's heart into overdrive. Now she had to impress her father as well as Greg. Why would he want to help train someone who he didn't think was worth it?

"Let's kill it!" Jasmine called out to the dancers as they all got into their appropriate places. The music blasted through the speakers, causing shivers up Emily's spine and vibrations through her body, sending her mind into such peaceful focus. Dancing was in her soul, every nerve ending in her body would awaken at the sound of music. When the beat dropped, the friends on the floor became dancers. They hit every move with excellent precision and put their hearts into every step. Their faces were expressive. Their bodies were fast and flexible as the music wove around them.

Mark watched his daughter with proud and focused eyes as she danced. He couldn't believe what talent she had. The intensity in her eyes sparkled as she tossed her head back, her long auburn hair pooling down her back. Her moves were sharp and beautifully executed.

"That's my girl," he whispered as he watched her, his eyes never leaving her in fear he may miss something.

From the opposite side of the gym, Greg watched intensely as Emily's body moved with the beat. Her perfect hips swayed from side to side, her body rolling and bending in delicious ways.

"God…" he whispered. He clenched his hands into fists, his fingers itching to run through her long locks. He kept his eyes trained on her until they finally hit their last move, the music quickly fading away. The entire gymnasium erupted with cheers as the dancers held their last positions, trying to subtly catch their breath.

Greg smirked as he watched Emily's chest rise and fall rapidly with her heavy breathing. Her sweet lips were slightly parted and he forced himself to break his gaze when he saw her pink tongue dart out to wet her lips. The dancers then turned to face the other side of the gym before the second song began. Once their performances were finished, they waved and called out to the crowd to rev them up a bit more before heading out of the gym and back up to the dance room.

Everyone sprawled out on the dance floor, gossiping and chatting about who they noticed in the crowd, and if they had messed up at all during the performances.

"So did you see your lover boy?" Jasmine asked as she pulled herself up to a sitting position.

"I'd reply…if I could breathe. I hate…that I have to wear…a million bra's…just to keep my chest from bouncing all over the place when I dance. It makes it…so hard to breathe," Emily stated breathlessly. The girls laughed and talked as their bodies slowly calmed and cooled.

"Crap, I have to go see my dad before he leaves," Emily suddenly stated as she hurriedly got to her feet. She made her way back down the stairs then into the gym and smiled when she saw her father making his way toward her through the stream of students.

"You were incredible!" Mark exclaimed before sweeping his daughter up in his arms.

Emily squealed with excitement at his words.

"You really think so? God, it was so much fun. I'm so glad you were here to watch me," she stated as she looked into her father's eyes.

I see those eyes every time I look in the mirror, Mark thought as he studied her.

"Yes, I really think so, and I'm so glad you had fun. You need to stick with this, Emily. You and Jasmine and Kim have such talent and chemistry when you girls are on that dance floor. Don't let anything ever stop you from dancing, ya hear?" Mark admonished, a smile on his face.

Emily nodded and immediately wrapped her arms around his neck.

"I love you, Daddy," she said softly into his shoulder.

"I love you too, darlin'" he replied.

They exchanged hugs and kisses before Emily reluctantly watched him walk out of the gymnasium to head back to work. She then turned and headed back into the hallway then up the stairs to the dance room. Everyone was now scattered around the room talking while others were changing their clothes. Emily made her way back over to Jasmine and Kim.

"I really don't want to go to class. We should just sit up here the entire time," Kim stated as the girls all changed back into their regular clothes and grabbed their belongings.

"I wish," Jasmine and Emily stated simultaneously. That sent the girls into fits of laughter as they headed toward the door. They all said good-bye to Miss Gwen before heading to their next class which they happened to have together.

"So did you see the way Mr. Riley was watching you? Damn, you sure are his eye candy," Jasmine stated jokingly. "I'm just kidding, you know that."

"Joking, my butt," Emily replied laugh.

"Who knows, maybe he likes you," Jasmine said with a smirk as she looked innocently over at Emily.

"Oh, shut up, he doesn't like me. We're just friends. I mean, come on, he's our gym teacher. He's helping me train. He probably looks at me the same way my dad does, but if we were in some parallel universe and he did like me, it would never happen," Emily stated as they made their way into the class room. The teacher called everyone to attention as the students took their seats, but Emily's mind could not leave Mr. Riley. She wanted to know why he had covered for her with the principal instead of turning her in when they had been caught fighting. She sighed as even more important questions continued to run through her mind. Was it just an innocent, fatherly kiss he had placed on her cheek in the cafeteria after the fight or was it something else? Why had he looked at her with adoring eyes and watched her every move today at the pep rally? She knew that there was only one person who could answer those questions and that was Greg. She had too many questions with no answers, so she mentally decided she would go see him after school to confront him about her feelings. But the longer she sat in her math class staring down at her notebook thinking, her nerves began to get the better of her.

I'll just wait until our next workout, then I'll tell him how I feel, she thought to herself as she doodled on her notebook. Once math concluded, Emily, Kim, and Jasmine headed down to the cafeteria for lunch. They made their way through everyone then stood in the nearest food line. Emily stood with them while they got their food then followed them back to the table.

"What, you're not eating?" Jasmine asked as they took their seats.

"I'm gonna get a salad, I just want to wait a little to see if the crowd lightens up. I hate trying to walk through everyone," Emily replied as she glanced around.

"I'm so glad we have dance last period," Kim stated as she pulled apart her grinder, picking off the lettuce as she always did.

"Why don't you just put less lettuce on it?" Emily asked with a giggle as she watched her friend.

"Because I either put too much on or not enough," she replied before squealing when Jasmine flicked a piece of the lettuce into her hair. Emily and Jasmine both shook with laughter as Kim groaned, pulling the offending food out of her long ebony locks.

"Betta wash that when you get home," Jasmine advised, her eyes shining with amusement.

"Jasmine…Jasmine," Kim exclaimed as she glared at her friend before bursting out laughing. "Eat your damn hamburger."

"I'll be right back, I'm gonna go get my salad now before everyone eats it all," Emily said on an exhale, trying to catch her breath from laughing so hard. She made her way through the sea of students toward the salad bar, trying to hold in her temper. If there was one thing that annoyed her more than anything, it was when people would stand in the middle of the walking areas or they would be walking slower than snails. By the time she made it to the salad bar, she must have said the phrase *excuse me* over a dozen times.

"It does get annoying, doesn't it?"

Emily looked up and smiled when she saw Greg heading toward her.

"Extremely, now I can finally breathe. So, a man your size can be full after eating just a salad?" she asked, grateful for the open space around the salad bar and register.

"Absolutely, especially after having a grinder, some fries, and a little bag of chips," he replied before giving her a playful wink.

Emily laughed as she grabbed a plate to start making her salad.

"Wow, sounds like you could fit me in that stomach of yours," she replied.

Greg stared down at her, watching her delicate hands as she filled her plate with lettuce, tomatoes, and cucumbers. He wet his lips, suddenly feeling as though his entire mouth went dry.

"I'm sure I could," he muttered as he grabbed a plate then followed her.

"So how has dance been going?" he asked as he piled things onto his plate.

"Things are going good. I'm sure I'll start feeling more improvement with my stamina because of our workouts," she replied as she poured Italian dressing over her food.

"I'm glad. This Saturday, I'd like to work a bit more on your legs. We worked your arms pretty good last week so we'll let them rest for a bit longer," Greg suggested. The two made their way over to the register as they continued their conversation.

"You're the workout genius, so whatever you say works for me," she replied with a soft giggle. She greeted the smiling lunch lady at the register as she placed her food down to pull her money from her pocket.

"Don't worry about it. Today's on me," Greg stated. "Kelly, just put everything on my account."

Emily stared up at him with surprise before picking up her food when Greg ushered her along.

"Thank you, Greg. You didn't have to buy me lunch," she insisted as they stood aside out of everyone's way.

Greg smiled down at her, giving a casual shrug of his shoulders.

"Well, that's what gentlemen do for ladies. We treat them like princesses," he replied before leaning down so only she could hear. "Maybe Aden could use a few tips. If I was him, you'd never have time to look at any other man but me." He subtly tucked a strand of her hair behind her ear before pushing off the wall and walking away.

Emily could only stand there, watching him walk away, trying to close her mouth since it was hanging open. She couldn't believe what he had just said. If he was Aden? If he was her boyfriend? Did she hear him right? She momentarily considered getting her hearing checked at the doctor's just to make sure she was not hearing things. Once she pulled herself together, she hurried back through the students, being a bit less polite. She hurried over to her friends and immediately leaned in close.

"You will not believe what just happened," she stated which made Kim and Jasmine immediately lean in with curiosity.

"I ran into Mr. Riley and we started talking about our workout this Saturday. Then he paid for my lunch. Yeah, sweet, I know, but then we moved over near the stairs to get out of everyone's way. I thanked him for buying my lunch, and he was saying that he's a gentleman and I'm a lady and he said that if *he* was Aden that he would treat me like a princess, and that I wouldn't have to look at any other guy if he was my man."

Jasmine and Kim stared at her, their mouths both open.

"I know! That was my first response," Emily stated as she looked back and forth between them.

"So…Mr. Muscles wants to be your man?" Jasmine inquired, eyebrows raised as she tried holding in her nervous laughter.

"I sure hope not. I'm sure he was just being nice, trying to compliment me or make me feel special. I'm sure he didn't mean any harm by it," Emily stated as she pulled her salad in front of her.

"Isn't that weird though? He's like fifty, isn't he?" Kim exclaimed softly.

"No, he's thirty–six, I think my Dad said, and it's a little weird…kind of uncomfortable, but I told you I'm going to talk to him this Saturday and then everything will be fine. Everything will be back to normal," Emily stated.

"You sound like you're trying to convince yourself of that," Jasmine stated.

Emily laughed as she picked up her fork to start eating.

"I am, don't burst my bubble."

The girls finished eating and took a few more minutes to talk before they gathered their backpacks and headed toward their next class.

"Dance…thank God," Emily stated before she bolted into a run with Jasmine and Kim by her sides.

"Hi, Ma," they greeted Ms. Gwen simultaneously once they made it up the stairs then into the dance room.

"We're back already," Kim joked.

"Hey," Gwen greeted, her word drawn out as she looked at them from her small couch. "You guys don't know how hard it is. The other classes don't feel it. They come in here for a grade and think they can dance halfassed." The girls immediately set their bags aside then sat down around her.

"Well that's why you have us," Kim replied as she pulled her hair back into a ponytail.

"Some kids just take the class because they think it's easy but don't forget that there are others who will come in here to dance. We live it…hell, we wouldn't even be friends if it wasn't for you, Ma," Jasmine stated as she unzipped her dance bag to pull her dance sneakers out.

"Oh, you guys…" she groaned as she pushed herself up off her couch to head toward her computer. The three girls laughed at her words. Gwen Martins was the type of woman to hold her emotions inside, especially when she was at school. The advanced class was as close as family. Everyone would take turns hosting sleepovers at their homes, but Emily's held most of them. With the amount of friends that created the advanced class, Emily's house held plenty of space for everyone. But no matter what would happen in or out of the dance room, Gwen would never talk about her personal problems, especially with new students who thought they knew what it meant to dance. If there was one thing that annoyed Gwen Martins, it was a student coming to take her class who had already danced with a professional studio. The more disciplined the dancer, the harder it was to pull the emotions out of them and put it into their moves. Emily, Jasmine, and Kim all started dancing when they made it to Kinley High. Gwen taught them the technical aspects of dance while pulling their passion from their hearts and splashing it into their dancing, their faces, and their eyes.

Emily smiled as she pulled her dance sneakers from her dance bag as well. She heard Jasmine call Gwen 'Ma' once again, which always brought her happiness and comfort. Now that they were seniors, they were going on their fourth year of dancing with Gwen Martins, and over all those years, the girls had bonded with her. They all called her 'Ma' because it was the only way to describe her. She was like their second mother. Their bond ran much deeper than dancing in class at Kinley High School.

The next hour and fifteen minutes flew by as the class continued planning for the upcoming Artists In Motion performance in March. That gave them six months to choreograph and perfect their dances.

"I'll call you guys tomorrow after my training session with Greg," Emily informed them as they made their way toward their usual meeting spot, the tree on the corner of the front lawn of the school.

"Sounds good. Let us know how that talk goes and, seriously, Emily, you have to tell him the truth. Let him know it's weird and that he needs to back off a little bit. I mean it's kinda hot to have a teacher that looks like him be interested in you but, damn, tell him to chill out," Jasmine stated, her voice stern.

"I'll take care of everything," Emily reassured as she pulled Jasmine into a tight hug. She then hugged Kim before making her way to her bus. Once she took her usual backseat, she ran her fingers through her hair with a heavy sigh.

"You look like you have a lot on that mind of yours," Jetta stated as she smiled over at her best friend.

"Yeah, did you hear about what happened at lunch?" she asked as she got comfortable.

"No, what happened?" Jetta asked, sitting up straighter in her seat as worry began to build. Jetta was in complete shock once Emily told her everything that Greg had said.

"What? You seriously need to talk to him tomorrow, Emily. You still need to tell him that this entire situation is uncomfortable," Jetta stated, her face expressing nothing but seriousness.

"I promise I'll handle everything. Greg is a really great guy. He's close friends with my dad. I'm sure he's just being friendly and I'm taking things the wrong way. But I will talk to him," Emily promised. She sighed softly as she glanced out the window, watching the trees and buildings pass by. She bit her bottom lip softly before closing her eyes, knowing full well that tomorrow was going to be a trying day.

6

"CALL ME WHEN you're ready to come home," Mark stated as he hugged his daughter tightly.

"I will, Dad. I love you," she replied before kissing his cheek.

"I love you too, darlin'," he retorted as he watched her slide down from inside his truck.

Emily smiled and waved as she watched her dad drive away.

"Now keep calm and get a good workout in," Emily mumbled to herself as she headed into the building. She made her way down the stairs then took a deep breath before heading into the weight room.

"Good morning, young lady," Greg greeted as he finished rearranging the dumbbells.

"Good morning," she replied as she pulled her dance bag a bit more securely over her shoulder.

"You look like you're ready to go," he commented as his eyes traveled over her body, appreciating her tight black spandex pants and tank top.

"Absolutely, I just have to stretch then I'll be good to go," Emily stated as she walked over to one of the benches and set her bag down, making sure it was out of their way.

Greg watched her walk, her hips swaying and tempting him, calling him over to her. Before he could stop himself he walked up to her and reached out to grab her ponytail, twisting it around his fingers.

Emily immediately froze at the contact and turned to look up at him.

"Mr. Riley?" Emily inquired, bringing the formality back between them.

Greg smiled down at her.

"Sorry, it's always swinging when you walk and looks nice and soft. Guess I just let my hand get carried away," he stated, brushing it off as if his action was completely innocent. "And what did I tell you about calling me Mr. Riley?"

Emily bit her bottom lip, her skepticism beginning to build. She laughed nervously and maneuvered away from him toward the middle of the room.

"Sorry, Greg," she replied as she lowered herself onto the floor to begin her stretching. She made sure to thoroughly stretch her entire body before she stood and turned to face him.

"Let's get started on your legs," Greg suggested, leading her across the room. He helped situate her onto one of the leg press machines before setting the correct amount of weight. Emily was on her back with her feet planted firmly on a metal platform. She began lifting the weight with her legs, doing the amount of sets that Greg instructed. After putting her on multiple machines and through a dozen exercises, he finally set her up on the leg curl. She sat down in the chair and situated her legs properly with padding beneath her knees and the tops of her feet hooked to another piece of padding.

"Now just use your thighs to lift your legs until they're completely horizontal then continue using the strength in your legs to lower it back down. Don't just let it drop," Greg instructed.

"Sounds good," Emily replied as she set the weight to eighty pounds. She took deep breaths as she pumped her legs, feeling the incredible improvement of strength in them. She felt a bit winded, but she knew she could keep going. She was so proud of how strong her legs were slowly becoming. All she had to do was continue her training with Greg and her body would be as strong as possible for dance.

"Ow!" Emily suddenly cried out when a terrible pain gripped her left thigh. She immediately lowered the weight and pressed her hands against the pain.

Greg carefully scooped her up off the machine into his arms then carried her over to the bench where her dance bag rested.

"Now just try to relax. Take deep breaths," Greg instructed as he knelt down in front of her. He gripped her knee with one hand as he slowly slid the pad of his thumb over the top of her left thigh.

Emily bit her bottom lip as the pain vibrated through her.

"Does this hurt?" Greg asked as he carefully kneaded part of her thigh.

"A little," she replied.

"How about here?" he asked when he moved a bit to the right.

"No," she replied as she looked down at him.

"I'm pretty sure you didn't pull any muscles. It was just a bad cramp that decided to take over. Now that can happen at any time if you don't thoroughly stretch. You can also massage your own thigh to make sure that the muscles are loose and ready to be strained with a workout. Just carefully move from your knee up as high as you need to and move slowly, like this," Greg explained as his hands slowly began to move over her thigh.

She watched carefully, not wanting to experience that kind of pain again. He used his thumbs, knuckles, and palms to vanquish the pain. She committed his hand's movements to memory for future reference.

"So should I do this before I dance?" she asked as she looked from his hands up into his eyes.

Greg glanced up, his eyes catching her sparkling emerald orbs.

"Absolutely," he replied, a smirk slowly spreading over his lips.

A nervousness suddenly sprouted inside of her when she remembered the talk she was supposed to have with him. It was so hard for her to bring something like that up to him since he seemed so sincere about helping her. Maybe the entire thing truly was in her own mind. Greg was simply a man, a good-looking man, who Emily was in close contact with almost every day of the week. Of course her mind would run away with her at times.

He seemed intent on what he was doing, his full attention occupied by his hands. He slowly massaged the outer parts of her thighs before moving a bit higher. His fingers wrapped around the inside of her thigh and rubbed in gentle circles.

"As long as you remember to take care of your body then you'll be just fine every time you're active," Greg instructed as his hands worked their magic. Greg glanced up into her eyes and smiled when he saw her nervousness. He wanted to assure her everything would be all right but he refused to give her worries any notice. He tried with all his power to keep control over his body. The feel of his hands on her thigh was slowly driving him to the brink of insanity. He wanted to touch her everywhere, and he wanted to have free range to do as he pleased.

Just be subtle… he thought as he watched his hands move. Greg subtly slid his hands a bit higher and practically moaned when his fingers brushed between her thighs.

Emily's eyes widened before suddenly sliding his hands off her thighs and immediately standing and heading toward the middle of the room.

"I think it's fine now. The pain is gone," she said in a rush of words. She wrapped her arms around herself and hurried over to her dance bag.

"Well just keep that in mind. As long as you keep doing that before you work out and dance then you'll be just fine," Greg stated as he stood. He watched her fidget with her bag, trying to unzip one of the zippers.

"Everything all right?" Greg asked as he moved up behind her.

Emily whirled around, her heart nearly jumping out of her chest.

"Yeah, I'm fine," she replied with a nervous smile.

Greg smiled in return as he reached out to run his finger slowly down her cheek.

"Well you did a great job today. You're becoming more flexible, your legs are stronger. Slowly but surely, your entire body is improving," Greg stated as he moved a bit closer to her. He was staring down into her eyes with such an intense stare that Emily tried to take a subtle step away from him.

"Thank you, I've been trying hard. Well, I have to get going. I'll make sure to let my body rest and I'll…massage my legs like you showed me," she stated softly as she clasped her hands in front of her.

Greg reached out and grabbed her arm to pull her back when she moved to walk away from him. He leaned down and gently pressed his forehead to hers as he closed his eyes to concentrate on the feel of her skin. He knew he should back away. He knew that touching her was very dangerous at this point, but he simply couldn't stop himself. He had to feel her, if only for a moment.

"Have a great day, sweetheart," he whispered as he gently slid his hand down her arm, his smoke-gray eyes shining down at her.

Emily opened her mouth to finally speak about the way he was making her feel but instead she thanked him, grabbed her dance bag, and took off out of the school.

Greg chuckled deeply as he stared at the empty door Emily had just quit.

"So close, Emily...so very close," Greg stated, his voice rumbling from his chest. He immediately walked over to the bench press and decided it was time to get Emily off his mind. He was going to have to see her every day in school for the next week and not touch her. That was truly going to be a challenge.

Emily hurried out of the school then stood outside as she listened to her father's cell phone ringing in her ear.

"Come on, answer," she stated nervously as she looked over her shoulder.

"Hey, baby girl, I have bad news. I'm stuck at the shop. Mike can't come in. His wife isn't feeling well since she's getting closer to having their baby, so I'm here all day. Is there anyone that can come get you?" Mark asked. He felt terrible that he couldn't go pick up his daughter, but there was no way he was going to tell Mike to leave his pregnant wife and come into work instead.

Emily sighed heavily as she ran her free hand through her hair.

"Um…I'll have to call someone to see if they can come get me. Maybe I can—" Emily began to say. Her cell phone was suddenly taken from her hand, and she immediately turned to see who it was.

"Hey, Mark. What's going on?" Greg stated into the phone as he kept his eyes trained on Emily. "So the little lady needs a ride home? I'll take her home, no problem."

Emily swallowed hard and averted her eyes from his to the ground. She was feeling incredibly nervous about being alone with him. Granted what he had done to her was most likely an accident, but it didn't make her feel any less violated.

Emily, he was just massaging your leg, he didn't mean to touch you. He probably doesn't even know he did it. If you just bring it up to him, he'll probably apologize until the cows come home, her mind continued to tell her.

Greg finally hung up with her father then handed her cell phone back to her.

"He says he loves you and he'll see you at home in time for dinner. Looks like I'm your taxi for this afternoon," he stated teasingly as he lead her over to his truck.

"Well thank you, I could have called one of my friends. I'm sure you're busy," Emily stated, her reluctance obvious.

Greg turned to her, looking down at her with confusion.

"Is there something wrong? Have I done something to upset you?" he asked, his hands on his hips.

"Um…could we talk about this in your truck? People don't know how to mind their own business," Emily replied as she glanced around at the few students and maintenance men who were meandering around on campus.

Greg nodded as he placed his hand on her back and continued to lead her to his truck. He opened up her door for her and helped her up into it since his truck was so high off the ground, much like her father's. Once she was in securely, he closed her door and walked around to the driver's side.

"So what's wrong, darlin'?" Greg asked as he pulled his door closed then pulled his seatbelt across his chest.

"Well…when you were massaging my leg…your hand went a little too high. Your fingers kind of brushed against me…" she stated with a bit of courage.

Greg's eyes widened when he heard her words and immediately began his performance.

"Damn it to hell, Em. Why didn't you smack the hell outta me? I'm so sorry, Emily. I never meant for that to happen. Honestly, I was just trying to help. You seemed like you were in so much pain, I just wanted to make that pain go away," Greg stated as he rubbed his face with his hands.

Emily sighed with relief when she saw the regret in his eyes.

"It's okay, it just made me feel uncomfortable. I was pretty sure it was an accident," Emily stated as she reached over to pat Greg on the shoulder.

He slowly looked down at her hand then let his eyes travel over her arm then up to her eyes.

"It was a complete accident. I never meant to do that," Greg repeated once more.

"Well everything is forgiven," she replied with a smile, completely melting Greg's heart.

God, your just too trusting, little lady, Greg thought as he started up the truck.

"Thank you, Emily. And never keep anything from me. If you ever need to talk to me or tell me something, never hesitate. I'm always here to listen." Greg reached over to take her hand in his then lifted it to place a soft kiss on her knuckles.

Emily smiled and took her hand back once he released it.

"Thank you, Greg. That means a lot to me."

The drive to Emily's house was driven in silence. She felt as though everything was going to be all right, but she was still nervous sitting beside him in his truck. She was still a bit worried as to why he wanted to touch her so often. He had touched her ponytail in the gym, touched her body to help her workout, and then he had touched her between her legs when he was attempting to help her massage her thigh. How many times could he touch her before it was no longer innocent?

"What's that look for?" Greg asked as he turned onto her street.

Emily turned to him and smiled, realizing that she must have had a thoughtful look on her face.

"Nothing, just thinking is all. There's always something to think about with either school or dance or my family," she replied as she set her hands in her lap then turned to look out the window.

"I hear ya. I'm always doing something, always busy, never a moment's peace," he replied as he pulled into her driveway. "Well here we are."

Emily pulled her dance bag up onto her shoulder then turned to Greg and smiled.

"Thank you for the training today, and thank you for the ride home," she stated as she moved to open the door.

Greg reached over and pulled her back then smiled into her eyes before placing a soft kiss on her cheek.

"You're very welcome, Emily. I'll see you Monday at school," he stated softly, his eyes dropping to her mouth. His eyes seemed trained on her as he held her arm, his eyes studying her face, her lips.

Her heart began beating faster, pounding against her chest hard enough to where she thought it would burst from her chest.

"Right…see you Monday," she replied before shoving the door open and sliding out of the truck. Emily walked over the front lawn toward the door and chanced a glance over her shoulder.

Greg was sitting in her driveway still, one hand on the wheel, the other draped over the top of the passenger seat.

She gave him a friendly wave to assure him she would make it inside safely then turned and hurried up the porch steps. She sighed heavily when she realized she didn't bring her key with her so she knelt down and grabbed the key from under the mat.

Greg smirked as he watched her grab the extra key.

"Never show anybody where your spare key is, Emily. That's just not safe," he stated with a soft laugh as he finally shoved his truck into reverse and headed back to the school.

Emily hurried inside and closed the door behind her, making sure to lock it before heading up the stairs to her room. She grabbed her cell phone from her dance bag and immediately dialed Jasmine's number.

"Hello?" Jasmine answered.

"You will *not* believe what the hell happened today! Dear God in heaven, I'm not kidding you. I thought everything was going to go smoothly today. I planned on talking to him and getting everything off my chest but that didn't exactly happen. I was waiting until the end of our workout to talk, but something happened," Emily rambled on.

"Whoa, slow down, girl. What happened?" Jasmine asked, giving her complete attention and focus to her best friend. She could hear the nervousness in her voice and immediately sat up on her bed to listen carefully.

"I was working out with him and everything was going great, but then I ended up getting a really bad cramp. I mean, it hurt like a bitch. Greg picked me up off the machine and put me on the bench. He started massaging it and let me know that I didn't pull any muscles," Emily began as she sat down on her bed then flopped onto her back, her long red locks spreading over the sheets.

"Well, thank God you didn't pull anything. We gotta dance!" Jasmine replied with a laugh, bringing a smile to Emily's face.

"That's for damn sure. He showed me how I can massage my legs so I won't pull any muscles, and if I get a cramp like that, he showed me how to make the pain go away. All of that was wonderful, stuff I definitely wanted to learn…but then that's when something happened," Emily stated, her voice softening with her last words.

Jasmine's smile melted from her face when she heard those words.

"Emily, tell me what happened," Jasmine encouraged, not wanting to force it out of her. She felt such worry and panic rising in her chest, practically making her dizzy.

"Well…when he was massaging my thigh, his hands moved a bit too high. Next thing I knew, his fingers started rubbing against me, touching me. I immediately pushed his hands away and walked over to my dance bag. I didn't know what to do. I didn't know if it was an accident or not. I was kind of freaking out," Emily stated, finally spitting out the words.

Jasmine was now sitting on her bed with her mouth hanging open. She wasn't quite sure what to say.

"He did what? Did you say anything to him? Did he apologize? Did he even mean to do it?" Jasmine asked, her mind a jumble of emotions and questions.

"I did ask him about it when he gave me a ride home," Emily quickly stated, trying to keep her friend from wanting to kill Greg.

"He gave you a ride home?" she demanded.

"I had no choice. My dad couldn't come get me! He got stuck at work. Greg grabbed my phone out of my hand and started talking to him before I could do anything. Then he told my dad he'd give me a ride home and that was the end of that. So when I got in the truck with him I told him that he touched me and he immediately started apologizing. He asked me why I didn't smack him or something. I really don't think he meant to do it. But…" Emily paused as she bit her bottom lip.

"But what?" Jasmine prompted.

"But before I got out of the truck, he kissed my cheek. The whole day, he was touching me, but it seemed like he didn't mean anything by it. He played with my ponytail earlier, he pressed his forehead against mine at one point, he kissed my hand, and then before I got out of the truck, he kissed my cheek," Emily stated in a rush of words as she ran her free hand over her face.

"Okay, that's it. This is too much, Emily. You have to talk to him before next Saturday. I mean, you see him all the time during school, so just talk to him at lunch or something. Then when you guys workout nothing will be awkward," Jasmine firmly suggested.

"You're right, I'll talk to him whenever I get the chance. I'll talk to him Monday if I see him long enough," Emily agreed. The two girls talked for a bit longer before Emily decided she needed a dip in the pool.

"I'll talk to you later, honey. I'm going to jump in the pool for a bit, take some time to think," she stated as she pulled herself to a sitting position. They exchanged their love then good-byes before Emily closed her phone and tossed it down on to the bed.

"Why does shit like this always seem to happen in my life?" she muttered to herself as she slid off her bed then headed over to her dresser to change into her bathing suit. If there was one true fact for the day, it was that Emily had plenty of problems to drown out of her mind.

7

EMILY PEERED OVER her shoulder as she made her way around the school from class to class. She had told Jetta in homeroom what had happened between her and Greg on Saturday then hurried away when the bell rang. Emily was pretty sure she was going to be strangled, so she was trying to keep the air in her lungs for as long as possible.

"Looking for me?" Jetta asked as she stood at the bottom of the stairs of the main building.

Emily sighed heavily as she approached her.

"Okay, you can kill me. I told him and he apologized. He didn't mean to do it, I mean why would he?" Emily asked as she approached her friend.

Jetta sighed heavily as she ran her hand through her long hair.

"Emily, Mr. Riley has no right touching you like that! Accident or not, you need to tell someone. How many times can he accidentally touch you before you finally realize he's doing it on purpose?" Jetta asked incredulously.

Emily sighed when she realized that her best friend had a good point.

"You're right," she agreed as she followed her friend into the building.

Jetta turned and pulled her friend into her arms, hugging her tightly.

"Emily, I'm tough on you because I love you. I don't want this dude taking advantage of you. It's not right. He's friends with your dad, so it's easy to think that he wouldn't do anything to hurt you. But he had no right touching you the way he did. You need to tell someone," Jetta insisted before pulling her friend back to look into her eyes.

"Well before I go running off to destroy this man's career, let me talk to him first. I didn't get the chance to tell him that touching me all together is making me feel uncomfortable. I just told him about when he touched me…there," she stated as she looped her arm with Jetta's and lead her down the hall toward their class.

"Fine, talk to him. But I'm guaranteeing you that it won't do you a bit of good. He'll tell you you're right, and he'll apologize some more, but he won't change. He'll keep touching you because you keep letting him," Jetta stated as they walked.

"I'm not letting him! Do you have any idea how afraid I was when he did that? Why do you think I jumped off the bench and ran to my dance bag?" Emily asked with disbelief as tears welled in her eyes.

Jetta sighed heavily as she pulled her friend closer.

"I didn't mean it that way, Emily. I wasn't insinuating that you enjoyed it. I know you're afraid, and that's why I want you to tell someone instead of trying to handle it on your own. I just want you to be safe. I don't want anything to happen," she explained as she stared into Emily's emerald eyes.

Emily could see how sincere Jetta was and it warmed her to know that she could always rely on this girl.

"Thank you, honey. I promise, I'll talk to him today if I see him, and I'll get everything straightened out," Emily promised.

Jetta agreed and gave her another hug before they made their way into the classroom.

Greg smirked as he walked out of the dark classroom directly across the hallway from the room Emily and her friend just walked into.

"I think some friends need to keep their noses out of other people's business," Greg muttered as he stared through the small window of glass on the door. Emily was now smiling and laughing about something Jetta was saying, and he felt his heart skip a beat.

"God, she's beautiful," he whispered as he reached out to let his fingertips graze the cool wood of the door.

Well if she wants to talk, then I don't see why now can't be a good time, he thought . He turned the knob and pushed the door open which halted the teacher in mid-sentence.

"Mr. Riley, is there something I can do for you?" Ms. Johnston asked as she tossed her curly blond hair over her shoulder.

Greg smiled while on the inside he wanted to roll his eyes. Did the woman ever give up?

"Actually, I need to snatch Emily from your class for a few minutes, if that's okay," he replied, his eyes training on the redhead.

Emily turned the moment he walked in and never took her eyes off him. Why would he want to talk to her? What could he possibly need to discuss with her?

"Absolutely, take as long as you need," Ms. Johnston replied, her eyes trailing over Greg's body.

Emily glanced over at Jetta before rising from her chair and following Greg out the door. He made sure to close the door behind them then lead her into the darkened room across the hall.

"What is it you need to see me about?" Emily asked nervously as she picked at her fingernails. It was another nervous habit she tended to exhibit.

Greg turned to her before taking a seat on one of the empty desks, his arms folded over his chest.

"Well, I couldn't help but overhear your conversation you were having with your friend. I think you're the one that needs to talk to me about something," Greg stated, his gray eyes studying her every move.

Emily laughed nervously when she realized he had been listening to their conversation.

"So, um, how much of that conversation did you hear?" Emily asked, bringing a fake smile to her lips to try and ease the tension she felt.

Greg did not smile nor frown as he stared at her.

"Enough," he replied simply.

Emily sighed heavily as she moved over to take a seat on one of the desks across from him.

"Greg, I love training with you. We have a good time together and it's really helping me, but I'm uncomfortable with the way this friendship seems to be going. I feel uncomfortable with the way you touch me sometimes. I'm not trying to say you do anything on purpose, and I'm not trying to insinuate anything. I'm just letting you know how I feel. If we could keep things a bit more student and teacher between us, then I think that would be the best thing to do," Emily finally stated. Her body was shaking a bit from the intense look Greg was giving her at that moment.

If she thinks I'm going to stop touching her, then she's beautifully insane, Greg thought as a friendly smile spread over his lips.

"Emily, you know I've never meant to make you feel uncomfortable. I'm close with your Dad, which makes me feel automatically close to you. I mean, you look just like him, Em. I feel almost like a second father to you, that's all.

I never meant for my touches to be taken in the direction you're thinking," Greg stated as he stood from the desk. He walked up to her and tucked a strand of hair behind her ear.

"I'm harmless, Emily. That I can assure you," Greg stated with a soft laugh.

Emily felt a bit of weight being lifted off her chest as she studied the easygoing demeanor Greg was sporting.

"Well, I'm glad that we have this all situated. Now, no more awkwardness and no more uncomfortable feelings," Emily said confidently.

"You have my word," Greg replied. "Well I better get you back to class before your teacher has my head."

Emily laughed softly and shook her head.

"I think she has a bit of a crush on you. She's always looking at you and flipping that blond hair of hers when she sees you," Emily stated with a laugh. She laughed even harder when she saw Greg roll his eyes with disdain.

"Lord, that's the last thing I need is a blond coming after me. I'm much more partial to redheads," he stated with a wink. "See how well we get along? If I dated that woman, I'd probably want to strangle her."

Emily tried to catch her breath as she continued to laugh. This was more like it. This was the interaction she wanted with Greg. She felt completely comfortable which was such a fresh change.

"All right, we can badmouth her later but for now you have to go back to class," Greg insisted as he lead her towards the door. "I'm sure I'll see you during the week and I'll see you on Saturday bright and early."

"Sounds good, and Greg?" she stated as she turned toward him. "Thank you for talking with me. This made me feel a lot better. I didn't want anything bad to happen between us, so I'm just happy that we had this chance to talk and figure everything out."

Greg smiled down at her before ruffling her hair.

"No problem, kid," he replied as she squealed.

"Now you messed up my hair!" she stated with a laugh as she slid her hair from her hair tie then pulled it back to retie it.

"Well I apologize for that," he stated with a laugh as he watched her slender fingers slide through her silky locks.

Come on now, keep your mind out of the gutter. Don't touch her...not yet, Greg's mind admonished. He took a deep breath to steady himself and calm his rising need to feel her skin against his. He pulled open the door and led Emily back across the hallway to her classroom.

"I'll see you later," Emily whispered before walking into the room back toward her seat.

Greg watched her intently as she sat down beside her friend who then looked up at him with a slight glare to her features. Greg couldn't help but chuckle when he saw the look Jetta gave him.

Oh don't worry, I'll be taking good care of your best friend, Jetta. I'll be taking really good care of her.

Emily made her way down to the cafeteria for lunch and immediately started looking around for a specific individual.

"Does a pretty girl like you plan on eating alone?"

Emily smiled and turned to find Aden towering over her as always.

"Would a gentleman like yourself care to join me?" she asked playfully as she slid her arms around his waist.

He chuckled as he leaned down and placed a soft kiss on her lips.

"I would love to," he replied as he took one of her hands in his then led her over to one of the tables.

"What would you like to eat?" he asked as they set their backpacks down.

"Probably a salad and maybe a pretzel," she replied as she reached into her bag for her wallet.

"If you're reaching into that bag for what I think you are, then I'm going to throw it right back in," Aden stated as he slid his wallet from his back pocket.

Emily glared playfully up at him before shaking her head.

"You don't have to pay for my lunch, baby," Emily insisted as she tried to continue reaching for her wallet.

Aden laughed as he reached over to grab her bag then tossed it under the table.

"Now let's go get food before we starve to death," he said with a smile as he took her hand and lead her over to the salad bar.

Emily said excuse me over a dozen times as usual as she and Aden made their way through the crowd of people.

"I can't wait to get out of this school," Emily muttered.

"Think of it this way, you're the only one with manners around here," Aden suggested with a sweet smile.

Emily laughed at his words, feeling as though her worries and stresses no longer mattered since Aden was near. Once they purchased their lunches, they made their way back to the table.

"So how is everything going with football?" Emily asked as she set her water bottle aside and pulled her salad toward her.

"Going great. Mr. Riley has been around a lot lately helping all of us out in the weight room. He helps pinpoint who needs help with what part of their body. It's going good," Aden replied as he picked up one of his fries to dip in his ketchup.

"I'm glad, sounds like Greg is making himself useful for everybody," Emily replied before taking a forkful of salad into her mouth.

"Are you sure you should be calling him Greg? Maybe you should just call him Mr. Riley," Aden suggested as he glanced over at her.

"Aden, he's really close to my dad and I work out with him every Saturday. He just didn't want the whole professionalism stuff between us," she replied before continuing to eat her lunch.

"Well just so you know, I think I would be more comfortable with you calling him by his last name," he stated before continuing with his food as well.

Emily studied his face and watched the way he refused to make eye contact with her. He was worried about her. Emily had not told him about what happened between her and Greg at their last training session, but it seemed as though Aden was getting nervous anyway.

"Everything is fine, Aden. Don't worry about me and Greg. He is helping me. My body has never felt so incredible and that's all thanks to him. Nothing is wrong with me calling him Greg and people won't look at me weird for it," she insisted.

Aden sighed softly as he turned toward his girlfriend.

"I know, I'm sorry. I just hate that Mr. Riley seems to see more of you than I do," he replied as he scooted closer to her.

Emily smiled up into his eyes as she moved closer as well, letting Aden wrap his arm around her shoulders.

"I'm sorry. I've been working really hard on everything for school and dance and all of the workouts with Greg. We just need to try and set aside time to be together, just the two of us," she stated with a coy smile.

Aden laughed softly as he kissed her forehead.

"Sounds good to me," he replied. The two finished their lunch with a few interruptions from some of Aden's fellow football players before gathering their belongings. They made their way out of the cafeteria and started heading toward the English building, hand in hand.

"Well, I have to head to the tech building for math, but I wanted to walk my lady to her own building," Aden stated as he gently spun her toward him. He studied her face, memorizing her eyes, freckles, and the sweet angles of her cheekbones.

"You're beautiful, Emily. I always hate this part of the day. I hate being away from you," Aden whispered as he leaned down to press his forehead to hers.

Emily laughed softly on an exhale as her eyes fluttered closed.

"Trust me, I hate being away from you too. I promise we'll be able to spend more time together," she stated as her hands slid up over his shoulders then linked around his neck.

"Good, that's what I like to hear," he replied before placing a soft kiss on her lips. They both sighed with frustration when the bell rang loudly in their ears.

"Get to class, little lady. I don't want to make you late," he stated as he slid his arms fully around her, completely engulfing her with his body.

Emily giggled as she held him tightly in return, loving the way he could make her feel so dainty and small.

"I'll meet you at the tree, as usual," she promised. They kissed once more before Emily headed into the building.

Greg glared heatedly as he watched Emily walk into the building after kissing Aden. It made him sick to think about that boy touching her. Emily did not belong to Aden and he was going to make sure Aden knew that.

"Hey there, son," Greg called out as he made his way toward him.

"Hey what's up, Mr. Riley?" Aden greeted as he headed in his direction then shook hands as they usually did.

"I was heading to the gym when I saw you and Emily together. Now you're an incredible football player. I don't think this will just be a high school activity. You're heading toward college football, and if you keep working as hard as you are, you're heading toward a professional career, but if you let distractions like Emily get in your way, you won't even make it in college football," Greg stated as he towered over the boy.

Aden gave him a confused look before laughing softly.

"Trust me Mr. Riley, you have it backward. I think about Emily when I play. That's what makes me such a good player. She's definitely not a distraction," Aden insisted as the two began walking toward the other side of the campus.

"Aden, listen to me. Women are nothing but poison when it comes to a man's career. If you want to succeed in football…you'll get rid of her," Greg suggested, staring down into the younger man's eyes.

Aden watched him, incredibly baffled as Greg walked away from him.

"What the hell was that all about?" Aden muttered to himself as he watched the large man disappear into the gym. He turned and glanced at the building Emily had gone into then sighed heavily.

"This is getting too weird," he mumbled before hurrying toward his next class.

———◆———

Emily and Aden met at the tree once the final bell of the day rang, but she could immediately tell that something was amiss.

"What's wrong?" she asked as she wrapped her arms around his waist. He smiled down at her and held her tightly in his embrace.

"Nothing, just a stressful last class is all," he replied. "You go get on that bus before it leaves without you."

Emily continued to look up at him, confusion registering on her face.

"Well if anything is wrong and you want to talk about it, just let me know. I love you," she stated before reaching up on her tiptoes to kiss him.

Aden held her tightly as he accepted her kiss then deepened it. Her hands clutched the back of his shirt as their tongues intertwined in a dance of love. Greg's words rang in Aden's ears as he held her, which frustrated him even more. He didn't believe Greg's words by a long shot, but why in the world would Greg want Aden to break up with Emily? Well regardless of the reason, Aden would never let Emily go. The girl he was holding in his arms was his reason for breathing. He would do anything to keep her by his side.

"I love you too," Aden whispered once their lips parted. He smiled down into her eyes as he released her, urging her to catch her bus.

"I'll call you later, I promise," Aden called out to her.

She stepped up into the bus before pausing and looking back over her shoulder. She gave him one more breathtaking smile before climbing the last two steps.

Aden sighed heavily as the bus doors closed then began to drive away. He couldn't help but smile when he saw her head pop up into the window in time to wave good-bye to him.

"Poison to my career?" he asked himself as he watched the bus drive away. "I don't think so."

8

EMILY STARED UP at her bedroom ceiling as she lay on her bed, pondering her day. Once she had gotten home from school, she had spent time with her dad in the living room. They had talked about school, dance, her workouts, and then Greg. Mark told her all about the meeting between him and Greg at her pep rally, which immediately put Emily on edge. Mark told her about how Greg talked so highly of her and thought she was a beautiful girl.

"Great," Emily muttered as she stretched out fully on her bed. The last thing Emily wanted was to be the topic of conversation between Greg and her father. Mark gave her a big speech about how incredible Greg was when it came to exercising and lifting weights. He assured her that Greg would take care of her, and he trusted Greg to help her strengthen her body.

"See, if my dad trusts him then so should I," Emily whispered as she twirled a lock of her hair around her fingers. Mark had known Greg for over a decade, and they were close enough to be brothers. Emily sighed suddenly and rubbed her hands over her face.

"No more dwelling on all of this," she insisted as she pulled herself to a sitting position then slid off her bed toward her bathroom. She started up her shower, letting the thick steam fill the room as she stood at the sink. She studied her reflection in the mirror, feeling a slight sadness as she inspected her freckles. Now that summer was fading and the weather was jumping into autumn, her freckles were beginning to fade. The warm summer sun always exploded her freckles over her nose and cheeks and also brought out the red in her hair.

"Well I'll see you next summer, freckles," Emily stated before laughing softly. She turned and stripped off her clothes before climbing into the shower. She smiled when she thought of Aden. He had called her immediately when he got home from school. He said he needed to hear her voice; he needed to talk to her even though it was about nothing in particular. Emily could feel that something was wrong, but Aden had insisted he was just stressed out because of football and school. She knew that if there was something Aden had to talk to her about, then he would, so she refused to push the subject. They had conversed for over an hour on the phone about school, football, and then working out.

Emily couldn't help but cringe when Aden brought up that subject. She knew for a fact that her workouts with Greg were still bothering him, but there was simply nothing Emily could do. She tried to ensure him that there was nothing to worry about but, confusingly, Aden had insisted that their workouts were not the problem. Emily sighed heavily as she conditioned her hair, not knowing what there was that she could do to help Aden feel more comfortable.

"Who knows, maybe Greg could talk to him," Emily mumbled to herself. Once she finished her shower, she made her way back into her bedroom with a towel wrapped around her body.

"Come in," Emily called out when she heard a knock on her door.

Mark popped his head in and smiled at his little girl.

"Hey, sweetheart, feel like going to the Low Down?" he asked, eyebrows raised in question. The Low Down was Mark's favorite bar and restaurant that happened to be owned by one of his friends, Steve Wills.

Emily immediately smiled at his words.

"I'll get dressed right now," she replied as she hurried over to her dresser.

"Take your time, darlin'. I'll be downstairs whenever you're ready," Mark replied before backing out and closing her bedroom door.

Emily quickly dried off with the towel before dressing in a pair of tight light-blue jeans and a black tank top with her favorite jean jacket. Two years ago, Emily had asked Mark for a jean jacket for her birthday, but it was not just any jean jacket. The one she had wanted was a very thin denim material, the kind she could wear just to keep her covered instead of keeping the cold out. It had taken Mark trips to three different malls, but all he had found were big, bulky jackets. Luckily his next stop had been at the local Macy's and, lo' and behold, the exact jacket he'd been searching for was on the first rack of clothes when he walked through the door. Emily had been wearing the jacket ever since. She hurried to brush out her hair then tied it up into a high ponytail to keep it out of her face.

"Looks good to me," she complimented as she took one more glance in the mirror. She grabbed her purse and made sure to turn off all the lights in her room before heading downstairs.

"I'm all set," she called down to him as she made her way down the staircase.

Mark looked over his shoulder from the couch and smiled when he saw her.

"Yeah, well, you need to stop looking so pretty. You're lucky I let you go out in public," he stated with a soft laugh as he stood from the couch and headed toward the door.

Emily giggled and felt a blush creeping up in her cheeks.

"Daddy, I'm only pretty for you and Aden, my two main men," she stated proudly as she followed him out the door.

Mark chuckled at her words as he pulled the door shut behind them and locked it.

"Well like Aden said, you're my little girl before you're his girlfriend," Mark replied smugly.

Emily couldn't help but laugh as she skipped her way down the porch steps toward his truck with Mark right behind her. He opened up the passenger side door and lifted her up into the seat before walking around and getting into the driver's seat.

"We need to go here more often. No one has better food than Steve's place," Emily stated as she rolled down her window, letting the cool wind flow over her skin. She could feel summer fading, but the chill of autumn was still nowhere to be felt.

"You're very right, lil' girl. I was talking to Steve the other day, and he was complaining that we haven't shown our faces in a while. Plus, I'm not in the mood to make dinner, so we'll go make Steve happy and pay him a visit," Mark replied as he glanced over at her. He took his time studying her, watching the way the wind made her fiery ponytail dance. She looked so comfortable, so calm, and peaceful, and he couldn't help but feel proud of their likeness. They had the same color eyes, color hair, and the same nose, but she could thank her mother for her cheekbones and her brilliant smile. He trained his eyes back on the road as they sped down toward town.

"I love you," Mark stated as he glanced over at her once more.

Emily turned and smiled at his words. She unbuckled her seatbelt and slid to the middle of the seat to rest beside him.

"I love you too, Daddy," she replied softly before buckling the middle belt around her. She rested her head on his shoulder and smiled when he lifted his arm to wrap it around her, pulling her closer to his side.

She loved the feeling of his arm around her. She felt so secure and safe when he was near.

"What is it, darlin'?" he asked as he glanced down at her.

"Nothing, just thinking," she replied before leaning up to kiss his cheek softly. She smiled as she looked down and studied his tattooed arm.

"When can I get a tattoo?" she asked as she smiled up at him, wiggling her eyebrows. Mark looked down at her before laughing.

"How about for your eighteenth birthday?" he suggested as they pulled into the restaurant parking lot.

"Deal," she agreed. Mark parked the truck before getting out and walking around to the other side to help Emily down. Emily slid her hand into Mark's as they made their way into the Low Down. They both looked around at the people sitting at tables, sitting at the bar, and milling about.

"Hey, Mark!"

Their heads raised at the sound of Mark's name being bellowed then smiled when they saw Steve behind the bar. He held Emily's hand as he led her through the crowd and over to the bar.

"How are ya, man?" Mark asked as he pulled out a stool for his daughter to sit on.

"Doin' pretty good. Business is pickin' up and look who we have here," Steve stated as he finally laid eyes on Emily. "You just keep gettin' more gorgeous as days go by."

Emily giggled as her cheeks blushed furiously.

"Watch it, Steve," Mark stated as he glared at his friend jokingly.

Steve laughed as he poured his friend a Scotch.

"Relax, boy. I like 'em a bit older. No offense, sweetheart," Steve replied as he gave the redhead a wink.

"None taken," she replied with a wink of her own as she looked up at him. Even while sitting on a high stool at the bar, Steve was still much taller than Emily. He was not quite as tall as her father, but he was not far off. His deep southern accent, shaved head, and trimmed goatee made him the true Texan he was. Her favorite attribute of this man was his eyes. They were deep crystal-blue and they could never hide the truth from either Emily or Mark.

"Could I have a bottle of water, please?" Emily asked politely as she folded her arms on the bar.

"Of course, what'll ya have to eat?" Steve asked as he reached under the bar and pulled a bottle of water from a mini refrigerator.

"I'll have the crispy chicken salad as usual, thank you," Emily replied as she popped open the water bottle and took a few sips. She glanced around the bar, watching everyone enjoying themselves as Mark and Steve ensued with a conversation. Emily loved the Low Down and was very thankful that Mark and Steve were friends, otherwise she wouldn't be able to sit at the bar with them. Emily's eyes suddenly widened with surprise when she saw Greg make his way through the front door. She watched as he looked around aimlessly then started heading toward the bar.

"Greg!" she called out, her automatic reaction. When his eyes laid on her, she wondered whether she should have opened her mouth.

Greg's head immediately turned at the sound of her calling out his name.

"Well, well, well, what's a pretty little girl like you doing here?" he asked as he made his way toward her. Greg then noticed her father sitting beside her and couldn't help but smirk. He couldn't believe his luck.

"Greg, how are ya?" Mark asked as he shook his hand.

"Not bad, not bad," he replied as he pulled out a stool. "I'm actually glad I ran into you. There's something I have to discuss with you."

"Sure. Em, why don't you go fill the jukebox with some music," Mark stated as he turned to his daughter. He pulled out a few quarters from his pocket and handed them over.

"Thanks, Dad," she said excitedly before kissing him on the cheek. Both men watched as she hopped off the stool then headed over toward the jukebox.

"So what's going on?" Mark asked as he took a sip of his drink.

Greg sighed heavily as Steve handed him a beer.

"Look, your daughter is absolutely incredible. She's sweet, funny, she has so many friends who care about her and look up to her...but I'm not too sure about this Aden kid," Greg stated, a sincere expression adorning his face.

Mark stared at him quizzically as he pondered his words.

"Aden? Trust me, if there is any guy that Emily should be with in that school, it's definitely Aden. He's a good kid. He respects her and he really does care about her. Granted, he's still a guy, but he hasn't done anything wrong yet and he hasn't done anything to hurt Emily," Mark replied before downing the rest of his Scotch.

Greg took a few gulps of his beer before turning to look straight into Mark's eyes.

"If Aden is such a good kid then why are they doing what they're doing?" Greg asked as he leaned in so only the two of them could hear the conversation.

Mark's eyes immediately narrowed at his words.

"What are you talking about?" Mark demanded as he turned toward his friend. Greg sighed before downing the rest of his beer and setting the bottle aside.

"Mark...Emily and Aden are sleeping together," Greg stated as he leaned against the bar. Mark's eyes widened.

"They're *what*?" Mark bellowed as he stood from his stool.

"Hold on!" Greg whispered harshly as he pulled his friend back down on to the stool. "Now don't go screaming at her. I was heading toward the weight room at the school when I heard them talking near one of the locker rooms. Granted, it sounded like Emily was the one doing the instigating, but she's a normal teenager. She's curious and is full of raging hormones. Just go easy on her, man. I wanted to tell you this because I don't think Aden is good enough for Emily, and she shouldn't be giving herself to someone like him," Greg stated sternly. Mark took slow deep breaths as his hands clenched into fists.

"How could she do this after everything we talked about. Damn it, I wanted her to wait!" Mark growled. "Steve, pour me another Scotch!"

Greg tried with all of his self control to hold in his laughter. He had planned on going to their house and doing this there but by running into them at the restaurant, they saved him a trip. His entire plan was slowly taking its shape.

"Maybe you should talk to her about this, Mark," Greg insisted as he watched Mark down another drink.

"I'll talk to her. I just can't believe this. She was so adamant about waiting until she was married. What the hell happened to that?" Mark asked angrily before sighing heavily. "Thanks for letting me know, Greg. Luckily, Emily has you to help keep her in line when I'm not around. Now I just have to figure out how to talk to her about this." Mark was not looking forward to talking to his daughter, once again, about sex, especially now that he knew she was participating in it.

Emily watched from the jukebox as Greg and her father conversed.

Why in God's name does Dad look like he's about to kill someone? Emily thought as she lingered where she was standing. When her father was wearing that kind of expression, she always felt sorry for whoever had made him that angry. It wasn't often that he looked like that, so she knew it had to be something big, maybe about work, but she could only guess.

"What could Greg possibly be telling him that would make him so mad?" she muttered before making her way over when she saw Steve set her food on the bar.

"Dad, is everything all right?" she asked as she took a seat back up on her stool. Mark sighed as he turned to look at her, his expression almost a look of sorrow.

"Everything is fine," Mark replied before looking back over at Greg. Emily felt an extreme awkwardness radiating around the two of them and was not interested in being a part of it.

"Well, I'm going to go pick a table to eat at so you guys can finish talking," Emily stated softly. She kissed Mark's cheek once more before heading away to find a small table for herself.

"Wait! I want you at the bar. I want you near me. Greg and I are gonna be right over here then I'll be right back to eat with you," Mark insisted as he stood from his stool.

"Um, all right," Emily replied with a bit of confusion as she walked back over to the bar then took her seat. Mark took a moment to stare down at her with such a heavy expression before heading to the other end of the bar out of Emily's hearing range.

"Just stay calm and try and think about things from her point of view," Greg stated as he patted his friend on the shoulder. Mark sighed and shook the man's hand.

"Thanks again, man. I'll talk to her soon, hopefully," Mark said as he glanced back at his baby girl. He wanted to grab her and shake some sense into, her but he knew that would get him nowhere. He had to sit down and talk to her, but he knew he would still procrastinate as long as possible. They made their way back over to their seats once Mark decided he could not have a liquid dinner and needed actual food in his stomach.

"Well I hope the two of you have a wonderful night, and Emily, I will see you tomorrow morning bright and early," Greg stated as he leaned down to pull her into a gentle embrace.

"Sounds good to me," she replied as she hugged him back. Greg inhaled deeply, savoring her scent of lilacs before he finally released her.

"Good night," Greg stated charmingly with a wink before turning and heading out of the bar.

Emily stared at the door with a soft sigh as she let the past forty-five minutes run through her mind. She was dying to know what in the world Greg had to talk to her father about, but she knew she had no business asking. So she decided to enjoy the evening with him and forget there ever was a conversation between him and Greg.

"So what are you gonna order, Daddy?" Emily asked as Mark finally sat back down on his stool. He turned to her and studied her intensely, seeing his baby girl through her emerald eyes.

"Steve, I'll have the steak dinner. You know how I like it," Mark called over to him before turning back to his daughter, "My usual." He mustered a smile despite the disturbing images Greg had planted in his mind.

Emily stared at him and studied his every movement. She knew something was wrong, but she simply couldn't put her finger on it. For the rest of the night, they ate in almost complete silence. She was highly agitated how such a wonderful night could end up going so badly, so awkwardly. The drive home was almost physically painful as Mark clutched the steering wheel in a death grip. He prayed Greg's words were false and this entire situation was a misunderstanding, but Mark knew how Emily felt about Aden, he knew she couldn't resist him.

Please don't let her grow up on me too fast, God, Mark thought to himself as they pulled into their driveway. The two went inside for the night, but Mark could feel his entire body continuously tensing as he watched her head up the stairs to her bedroom then listened to her footsteps once she was above him. It was driving him insane not knowing the truth about Emily and Aden, but he just wasn't ready to ask. Hours later, when Emily was fast asleep, Mark found himself in her bedroom doorway, watching her sleep. Her long red hair was spread out over the pillows and her blankets pulled up close to her chin. Her doll, which only her closest friends knew about, was cuddled up in front of her as always, which caused his heart to clench. He remembered the day he gave her that doll when she turned two years old. Sleeping with it had become a habit no matter how old she got.

"I know you can't stay my li'l girl forever…but I thought I'd get longer than this," he whispered before slowly and silently closing her bedroom door.

9

EMILY MADE HER way through the hallways of the school, her dance bag slung over her shoulder as always. Her hair was tied back in a ponytail and she was clad in her normal attire consisting of white spandex pants and a tank top. She felt calm and confident about her training session with Greg today. Her talk with him had helped her let go of all her worries and paranoia so they could vanquish any discomfort and concentrate on working out her body.

"As long as he's the teacher and I'm the student then everything is fine," she whispered to herself. She headed into the gym and smiled when Greg turned to her from the center of the weight room.

"Well good morning," he greeted as he made his way over to her.

"Good morning to you," she replied as Greg took her bag from her shoulder. Emily immediately started stretching as

Greg carried her bag over to the bench and set it down. Emily hopped up and down a few times while shaking her hands, letting out any excess tension and stress. She twisted from one side to the other to be sure her back and sides were ready then cracked her neck just to be sure.

Greg made certain once more that her back was to him before he quickly and securely locked the weight room doors then slipped the key into the pocket of his jeans. He turned away from the door and let his eyes travel over her body. Her tight little pants were clinging to her every curve, leaving just enough to his imagination.

"All set?" Greg asked as he made his way over to her

"All set," Emily replied as she rolled her shoulders. She was afraid of having a repeat of last Saturday when her thigh felt as though it was being torn apart. She could not imagine what it would feel like to have that kind of pain in her shoulder or even her neck.

"Let's work on your form a bit before we start on the machines," Greg suggested as he made his way over to her. She turned and smiled up at him.

"Sounds good, what should we fix? I do feel a bit off sometimes when I'm on the bench press," she stated as she stretched her arms up over her head.

"Well the key with the bench press is to always keep your body parallel," he indicated as he walked around to stand behind her. He slowly rested his hands on her shoulder before pulling back on them, straightening them out.

"If your shoulders are not flat on the bench then you'll be putting stress on your shoulder blades and putting more weight on one arm than the other," Greg instructed as he slid his hands down her arms. He took her wrists in his hands then raised her arms to be perpendicular with her body. He took a step closer to her so his body was pressing gently against her back.

Emily listened intently to his words and watched the way he lifted her arms. The last thing she wanted was to hurt herself using one of the machines by not using it properly.

"Now, make sure your arms are at the same length before pulling them back toward me. Put them in the position as if you were holding the bar," Greg said softly, his voice almost a caress as he lowered his head closer to her. Her head perked up a bit as she watched Greg's hands slide slowly up her arms, over her shoulders, then slowly down her sides. His large hands encircled her hips as he turned her a bit to the right.

"Always make sure the rest of your body is aligned with your arms and shoulders," Greg whispered, his lips mere inches from her ear. Her heartbeat suddenly picked up tenfold as her breathing quickened.

"Okay, I think I can do it now," she stated, failing to keep the panic out of her voice. She was just about to pull away from him when suddenly he spun her around to face him and grabbed hold of her wrists, holding them tightly against his chest.

"Greg, what are you doing?" Emily asked as she began taking steps back as he took steps forward.

"I was just thinking about that day a few weeks ago when I helped you and your friends out of trouble. You still owe me for that," he stated in a matter-of-fact tone as he smiled down at her.

Emily stared intently into his eyes as her fear began to race through her veins in a rush of heat.

"I owe you? What could I possibly give you? I mean I'm only seventeen, I don't have a job yet since my dad wants me to concentrate on school so I can't give you money," Emily rambled on nervously.

Greg chuckled as he continued to back her up through the room.

"Oh, it's not money that I want, Emily," he stated, his voice deep and hoarse as his eyes bore holes through her ivory skin.

Emily squeaked with surprise when her back hit the wall. She looked from left to right with growing terror as Greg released her wrists then placed one hand on each side of her head, boxing her in.

"Well…what do you want then?" she asked as she raised her hands and pressed them to her chest. Her entire body was beginning to shake as she looked up into his eyes. She didn't have to look up anymore considering Greg lowered himself to her eye level.

Greg smirked as his eyes slowly slid down her body then back up to her eyes, those fearful emerald eyes.

"Just a kiss…all I want is one kiss," he whispered as he leaned in a bit closer.

Emily tried to move backward, wanting the wall to swallow her so she could get away from him. She could not rid the shock from her face nor her mind as she stared at this man.

"You want what?" she exclaimed as she tried to pull away.

"No, no, no," Greg stated playfully as he held firm, denying her freedom.

Emily turned back toward him, her body physically shaking as she stared into his eyes.

"Greg, I have a boyfriend that I love very much. You're supposed to be my teacher! We can't do this!" she whispered harshly as she pressed her back flat against the wall to back away from him.

Greg chuckled deep from his throat as he licked his lips slowly.

"Oh, we can, sweetheart. It's just a little kiss. Just give me this one joy," Greg asked softly as he stared her down.

Emily laughed on an exhale as she tilted her head back to look at the ceiling. She could not believe this was happening. She could not believe that she was trapped in the weight room with Greg in her face asking her, practically begging her, for a kiss.

"Why don't you go ask Ms. Johnston for a kiss. She definitely wants you, for sure," Emily stated as she glanced around her, trying to find an escape route.

Greg's expression darkened at her words.

"I wouldn't touch her with a ten foot pole. I don't want some big-breasted blonde with no brain. I don't care if she's a teacher. She's dumber than a bag of rocks," Greg insisted angrily before he calmed himself. "But not you, Emily. You're so smart, sweet, talented, and you drive so hard to reach your goals. You're beautiful and you care about your body. You do have to learn how to not tempt people though." He slid his hand over to grab the end of her ponytail and slowly twirl the end of it around his finger.

"So soft," he whispered, his words almost a moan as her silky red locks caressed his skin.

Emily flinched at his touch and continued to take deep breaths, trying to keep herself from screaming. She wanted to handle this calmly but also knew in her subconscious that even if she screamed, no one would hear her. After all, it was a Saturday morning, which meant both students and faculty would be hard to find.

"Greg, please just let me go. We should end this. I don't think we can continue our training if you can't be professional with me. Now please let me leave," Emily demanded, desperately trying to gather a little bit of courage.

Greg laughed, his smile and eyes adoring her.

"That's why I want you so much, Emily. That's why I can't stay away from you. You always make me laugh and smile. You always brighten my day. Now, I'll let you go. You can go home and take a nice bubble bath as you always do, but first I want my kiss," Greg stated, his voice taking on a more demanding tone.

Emily's eyes widened at his words. How did he know she took bubble baths all the time? Had be been watching her? But this was not the time to wonder such thoughts as she watched the muscles in his arms begin to flex, his hands pressing harder against the wall. She felt her terror rise anew as she thought about what he could do to her. This man could bench press over four hundred pounds, and she had seen it with her own eyes. If he wanted to hurt her, he could easily snap her in half.

Stay calm, just give him what he wants, so he'll let you go and you can get the hell out of here, Emily thought to herself as she looked into Greg's eyes.

"If I give you what you're asking for, do you promise to let me go?" she asked quietly as she lowered her head to stare at the ground.

Greg smiled as his hand released her hair then moved to take her chin and raise her head. Their eyes came together and locked in an electrified moment mixed with Emily's fear and Greg's need.

"I will let you go," he agreed as he held eye contact with her.

Emily sighed heavily on a shaky exhale as she did a full body shiver of dread. She could not believe what she was being forced to do, but she knew she had to in order to get away from him. Once she was away from him, she planned on telling her father everything that's happened, starting from day one. Emily took a deep breath before quickly leaning forward and pecking Greg on the lips then pushing her back flat against the wall once more.

"There, now let me go," Emily stated confidently as she glanced over Greg's shoulder at the two connecting doors that lead out of the weight room.

"I don't think so, Emily. I didn't ask you to kiss me the way you kiss your father," he stated as he pulled his hands away from the wall then stepped closer to her. "I want you to kiss me the way you kiss Aden."

Emily's eyes widened at his words as she felt her heartbeat increase. It felt as though it would burst from her chest as her fear and nervousness continued to grow.

"Greg…Mr. Riley, is this really necessary?" Emily asked desperately as she looked up into his eyes.

Greg chuckled as he continued to hold her chin in his hand.

"It's very necessary, Emily," he insisted.

Emily wanted to jump out of her body as Greg lowered his lips closer.

"I won't hurt you," Greg whispered before carefully pressing his lips to hers.

Emily squeezed her eyes closed when she felt their lips touch. She tried to keep calm and let this pass. She kept in mind that she would be home with her father in no time and she would be able to tell him everything Greg had said to her, and about this kiss that he forced her to endure.

Greg felt his entire body tingle at the feel of her sweet, soft lips against his. He pressed her further against the wall to touch his body to hers as his free hand reached behind her head to pull the scrunchie from her hair, allowing her long red tresses to cascade over her shoulders. His hand delved into those locks as he continued to kiss her. He never wanted to release her from his arms, but he knew he had to keep his word and let her go. He slid both of his hands into her hair, relishing the feeling and committing it to memory.

Emily practically held her breath the entire time and had no choice but to allow him access to what he demanded. Her arms had been pressed against her chest but now that Greg was pressing against her body, her arms were trapped between them. She tried to subtly pull back to end the kiss, but he would not release her.

Greg felt her resistance but he couldn't bring himself to let her go. He just wanted to hold her. He wanted to prove to her that he was better than Aden and was more of a man than he could ever be. His entire body was on fire from touching her, from feeling her in his arms, from feeling her slim body pressed against his full of need.

"Wow…" Greg whispered once he broke the kiss, still holding her firmly.

Emily immediately closed her mouth and looked away from him, not wanting to see the smug look she was sure was on his face. When she glanced up at him, she felt her entire body begin to shake. His eyes had darkened to a deep gray like the sky of an oncoming storm.

His eyes were heavy with lust as he studied her face, feeling the arousal flood his body as he slowly ran the pad of his thumb over her swollen lips.

"You're even more beautiful after you've been kissed," he stated with a smile, the words rolling off his tongue like a caress.

"I have to go," Emily insisted as she ducked under his arm. Greg watched as she hurried over to her dance bag then tossed it over her shoulder before making a beeline for the door. She felt tears threatening to flood her eyes, but she held them at bay, knowing she had to keep strong. She tried desperately to keep her breathing under control and slow her heart rate, but the fear coursing through her veins was enough to make her feel faint. She grabbed the doorknob and tried to pull it open, but the knob refused to turn. She tried once more, yanking on the knob a few times before turning slowly to Greg.

"Why won't the door open?" Emily demanded, her voice almost squeaking from the constricted state of her throat.

Greg slowly moved closer toward her as he reached into his pocket.

"I can't let you go, Emily. I know I promised, but I just can't let you go back to Aden. He's *not* what you need! You need a man, you need me!" Greg stated firmly, his voice rising slightly with his words as he held the key to the door in his hand.

Emily stared at his hand, realizing she needed that key to get out.

"Greg, this has gotten out of hand. Let me out," she demanded, her voice soft and coaxing.

Greg shoved the key back into his pocket before striding toward her with intent.

"No!" she cried out as she turned to continue yanking on the doorknob.

Greg grabbed her upper arms and pulled her away as he shoved her dance bag out of her grasp.

"Someone please help me!" Emily screamed as she tried to fight. She slammed her hands against his chest and tried to kick with all her strength.

"Stop!" Greg shouted as he tossed her over his shoulder. Greg held her firmly as she squirmed, knowing that she wanted him just as badly as he wanted her. It was simply hard for her to admit it.

"Greg, put me down! I'm not playing with you, I swear if you don't let me go—" Emily squealed as she hit him repeatedly on his back. Greg carried her to the far side of the weight room, furthest from the door before gently setting her on her feet. She shoved him away before backing up until she was pressed into the corner of the wall.

"I want you," Greg stated as his eyes studied her entire body. He slowly moved toward her regardless of her soft pleas.

"You're my teacher!" she shouted as she desperately looked around for a route of escape. Her body was dripping fear from every pore as her heart threatened to leap from her chest. This man was towering over her, refusing to let her leave as he slowly made his way closer. She felt like a caged bird being stalked by a cat.

"I love when you wear white. You should wear white more often. It makes you look so angelic," Greg stated with a sweet smile as he closed in on her. Emily knew it was now or never. She ran to the right side of Greg, knowing it was unlikely that she would make it to the door, but she knew she had to try.

"No, no, no, it's not time to leave," Greg stated with a laugh when he easily caught her with his large arm. He turned her around to face him as he pulled her tightly against his body, rendering her arms and legs useless.

"Don't do this," Emily begged as she trembled against him. Greg swept her legs out from under her and carefully lowered her to the floor.

"So perfect," he whispered as he grabbed her wrists and held them above her head with one hand. Emily tried to twist out of his grasp and cried out when his grip tightened harshly.

"Are you going to stop fighting?" Greg asked as he slowly increased the pressure on her wrists. Tears welled in her eyes as the pain exploded down her arms. It felt as though her wrists were going to snap in half. She refused to simply lay there and allow this man to touch her, but the pain in her wrists was the most excruciating pain she had ever felt.

"Yes…I'll stop," she whimpered with resignation. Greg immediately loosened his grip then slid up to gently run soft kisses up her arms and over her hands.

"I'm sorry if I hurt you," he whispered as his lips slowly trailed back down her arms then over to her neck.

Emily turned her head away, not wanting to look at this man. She couldn't believe that everything she had thought about Greg had been a lie. She felt as though she and Greg had been growing closer, when the entire time, he had simply been trying to get her guard down so he could attack her.

"Please let me go," Emily begged as she felt his lips caressing the skin of her neck. He ignored her words as his free hand slid over her stomach, slowly sliding down each leg to touch every inch of her body.

"It's okay, Emily. Just let me touch you," Greg murmured in her ear. She refused to open her eyes as she felt his hands roaming all over her. Her stomach was beginning to churn as she was forced to endure his touch. This man was her father's best friend and now here he was, disgracing his best friend's daughter. Emily cried out when Greg started pulling at her pants, yanking them down her legs. She bucked her entire body, trying with all her strength to knock him away from her.

Greg released her so he could pull off her sneakers then toss her spandex pants aside, leaving only her panties to cover her lower body.

Emily desperately tried to crawl away from him when she realized he had released her ,but her attempts were thwarted by Greg grabbing her ankle and pulling her right back to him.

"Emily, I know you want this. You've been flirting with me since day one of your freshman year. It's okay to admit that you want me," Greg stated huskily as he pinned her shoulders to the floor. Emily reached up to shove against his chest to keep him from settling on top of her.

"Stop!" she screamed as she reached up to slap Greg hard across the face. Greg snagged her wrists and immediately slammed them against the floor above her head once again.

"Knock it off," Greg growled down at her as he slid his hand across her stomach then up over her chest. He maneuvered his body so he was straddling her hips, rendering her entire body useless under his weight. He slid his shirt up over his head then tossed it aside before reaching down to run his fingers through her hair.

"This is gonna feel so good, sweetheart," Greg commented before sliding down her body to lay against her, chest to chest.

"No one will ever hurt you, Emily…not while I'm with you," Greg promised as he ran his lips over hers then slowly down her neck once more.

Everything seemed to happen so quickly. Despite her struggles, Greg rid her of her clothing and stole her innocence in a swift movement of his blind lusts. She squeezed her eyes closed, cried out for help, cried out for her father as he desecrated her body. She had tried to scream for help again, but Greg swiftly clasped his hand over her mouth. The pain was explosive, the discomfort paramount, but the disgust and embarrassment was all encompassing. Her body trembled and shook as tears streamed from her eyes and her breath caught in her throat. Before she knew it, he finished with her. As if he was adding insult to injury, Greg rested his forehead against hers and stayed inside her as he caught his breath. He removed his hand from her mouth before releasing her from his body and his grasp.

Emily whimpered and continued crying as she quickly rolled away from him then struggled to gather her clothes which were strewn about.

He smiled over at her as he dressed then caught her and pulled her into his embrace before she could run.

"You were wonderful, Emily," Greg whispered in her ear before forcing one last kiss on her lips.

"I have to go home," Emily whispered, her voice quivering and barely audible as she avoided eye contact with him.

She watched as Greg picked up her dance bag and handed it to her before releasing her. He walked over to the door and pulled the key from his pocket before unlocking the door and holding it open for her. She held her sobs in as she made her way toward the door but suddenly shrieked when Greg grabbed her throat with a decent amount of strength, staring deep into her eyes.

"Now remember that this is our little secret, Emily. No one would understand our desires, baby. So we have to keep them to ourselves. Do you understand?" he asked, growling out his last words as he tightened his hold on her throat. Emily stared fearfully into his eyes before nodding at his words.

"Yes," she coughed out as she held his wrist, trying to make him loosen his grip.

Greg chuckled and kissed her lips once more before releasing her and giving her a soft shove out the door.

Emily immediately took off up the stairs as her heart pounded in her chest. Her lungs seemed to malfunction as she ran. She couldn't breathe. She couldn't speak. Her head was spinning in every direction. She burst through the doors and felt the warm sun on her skin as tears slid down her cheeks. She hurried to the front of the school then looked around frantically, not knowing what to do as her entire body shook and her breathing became out of control. She almost cried out when she saw her father's truck pulling in and ran across the parking lot to meet him. She pulled open the passenger's side door the moment he stopped then jumped in.

"Hey, baby girl, what's the matter?" Mark asked, his smile immediately falling from his face when he saw the redness of Emily's face and her demeanor.

"Nothing, I just don't feel good. I just want to go home," Emily stated softly as she shoved her dance bag down toward her feet then curled up in a ball on the front seat.

Mark saw the way she was clutching her stomach and immediately assumed it was menstrual cramps considering that's what he had always seen her do.

"Okay, baby, that's where we're going," Mark replied as he took off out of the parking lot. He reached over and rested his hand on her arm but became confused when she flinched at his touch then immediately grabbed onto his hand.

"Are you sure you're all right, Emily?" Mark asked as he headed toward their home. Emily held back her sobs as she clutched her father's warm, protective hand.

"I'm fine, Daddy," Emily whispered as she turned her head to look out the window with tears streaming down her cheeks, "I'm fine."

10

"Wʜᴀᴛ ᴅᴏ ʏᴏᴜ want for dinner tonight, darlin'?" Mark asked once he unlocked the front door and pushed it open. Emily immediately walked inside and headed for the stairs.

"I'm not hungry…maybe soup later," she replied softly, trying to act as normal as possible.

"Emily, wait," Mark called out before striding over to the stairs. Emily slowly turned to face him, their eyes level with one another since she was standing on the third step.

"Tell me what's wrong," Mark coaxed, his voice soft and full of concern as he reached out for her. Emily leaned away from his touch then sighed and moved forward to lay her head on his shoulder.

"I just don't feel good, Dad. My stomach really hurts, my cramps started hurting me earlier. I just want to take a bath and lay down," she insisted as tears streamed down her face. Mark rubbed her back lovingly as he sighed.

"I'm sorry, baby girl. Go on, go take a nice bubble bath and rest. I'll make something and bring it on up," Mark replied before kissing her forehead softly. Emily nodded at his words, kissed his cheek, then turned and hurried up the stairs to her room. Once inside, the floodgates opened. She immediately tossed her dance bag down before her knees hit the floor. Her entire body was shivering violently as tears streamed down her cheeks. She could not believe what just happened to her. She had been saving herself for when she got married; she had been saving herself for Aden. Greg had just taken her most precious possession and ripped it away from her. She was no longer innocent, and there was no way for her to regain what had been taken from her. Emily snapped her head up when she realized that Greg's disgusting scent and touch was still lingering on her body. She pushed herself up to her feet then hurried into the bathroom. She started the water and plugged the drain before moving over to the sink to stare into the mirror. She had a slight bruise on her neck from when Greg had grabbed her, her wrists were bruised from Greg's vice grip, and her abdomen was truly aching with more pain than she had ever felt with any cramps. Sobs completely consumed her body as she stripped her clothes off. Once she tossed the offending fabric to the other side of the bathroom, she paused before climbing into the tub. With her foot resting on the ledge of the porcelain, she finally noticed the red stain on her inner thighs, the evidence of the loss of her virginity. She whimpered painfully before stepping into the tub then sliding down until the water reached her neck. She tried to control herself and keep calm, but the tears simply would not stop. Her cries echoed off the tiles of the bathroom walls as her body ached and shivered.

"Why…" she whispered as she wrapped her arms tightly around her chest. Her eyes were squeezed shut as tears leaked from their corners. She never wanted to open her eyes again. She never wanted to see Aden again or anyone else. How was she going to be able to face everyone after what Greg had done to her? How was she going to be able to hug and kiss Aden when she could barely handle her father's hugs? Emily opened her eyes and immediately reached out for her wash cloth. She poured on her lilac-scented liquid soap before beginning to scrub every inch of her body until it was raw. She never wanted to relive Greg's touch or smell his scent ever again. She wanted to let everything go and simply forget.

Tell your father, her mind insisted as she scrubbed viciously at her neck then down to her legs. She shook her head adamantly. She couldn't tell her father. He would be disgusted and never look at her the same again. She didn't want that. She refused to let Greg ruin their relationship.

"Get off…get off," she whimpered as she continued to wash herself, needing to feel free of his vile touch. She could still feel the way he touched her stomach, her chest, her legs, then further between. She choked on a sob as she hung her head, letting her damp hair cling to her shoulders and face. She had to remember to breathe. She did not necessarily want to, but she knew she had to.

"I can't...I can't do this," she whispered as her heart clenched. She could hear his voice, she could hear him whispering in her ear about how amazing her body felt.

"No!" she cried out as she clamped her hands over her ears. Her face cloth sunk, absorbing the water, and releasing more suds to surround her. Emily let her tears continue to fall as she leaned backward against the side of the tub. She pulled her knees up to her chest then buried her head between her knees, her arms wrapped around them.

"Make it go away..." she whispered as her tears fell, "Somebody make everything go away."

————◆◆◆————

Mark finished stirring the bowl of chicken noodle soup, blowing on it slightly to help it cool. He sighed heavily as he listened to the sound of the water running upstairs in her bathroom. He knew something was wrong and it hurt him that she felt as though she could not confide in him. Emily had always told him everything, and he had always been honest with her. He hoped that maybe she was regretting what she had done with Aden and that was why she felt she needed to be alone. Maybe Greg had talked to her about it himself, and now she was regretting her actions. He hated the idea of his daughter having sex, so hopefully now she had learned her lesson.

"Hope he wasn't too hard on her, but hopefully she'll stop what she's been doing. I gotta talk to her about it," Mark mumbled to himself before lifting her bowl off the counter then carrying it up to her bedroom.

"Baby girl?" Mark called softly through the door.

"Who is it?" Emily asked with alarm as she hurried around her room, gathering her clothes.

"Emily, it's me," Mark stated with complete confusion. Why was she asking who it was when the two of them were the only two people who lived in the house?

"Wait, I'm getting dressed," she replied as she hurriedly pulled on her sweatpants and high-collared, long-sleeved shirt. The last thing she wanted was for anyone to see her without her clothes on, and she knew she had to hide her bruises from him, otherwise he would make her talk. Emily sat gingerly on to her bed as Mark slowly pushed open her bedroom door. She tried her best to hide the pain that showed in her face as it radiated between her legs. There was no way she was going to let her father know what happened to her.

"Ready for some soup?" Mark asked with a smile, trying to lighten the mood as he carried in the soup bowl then set it down on the night stand.

"I'm not hungry," Emily stated softly as she wrapped her arms around her stomach. Her entire body was shaking as she tried desperately to wipe away the thoughts of Greg's hands on her. All she wanted to do was burrow into a hole in the middle of her field in her backyard and never be found.

Mark sighed heavily as he studied his daughter. There had to be more than what she was telling him. He knew her time of the month could be very painful for her, but he was positive that it had never been this bad. He gently took a seat on her bed beside her then leaned forward to place his hand on her shoulder.

"Em, please tell me what's wrong," Mark pleaded, the desperation showing in his eyes. She attempted to hide her tears as they threatened to fall but she failed.

"I can't, Daddy. I don't want to talk about it, please!" she begged as she turned to him, revealing her bloodshot eyes. Mark's heart almost shattered at the sight of such pain.

"Emily, I'm worried about you. I know I'm your father, and it may be hard to talk to me about certain things, but you know you can always talk to me. Is it about Aden?" he asked, knowing he had to push at least a little further.

"No…it's not Aden. Please, I just want to be alone for a little while…please," Emily requested as she laid down on her bed, curling into a small ball. Mark sighed as he patted her thigh.

"Okay…I'll leave your soup here in case you get hungry." He stood from the bed and turned to leave but first leaned down to place a soft kiss on her forehead before heading out of her room. The moment she heard the door click shut, her tears began once again. They poured from her eyes as her chest clenched tightly with agony. She felt her stomach heave, she felt dizzy and lightheaded. She never imagined that something as horrible as this could happen to her. All she wanted was to finish high school and move on with her life as a dancer. She wanted to go to college and have a career her father would be proud of. Now everything seemed so far away. Everything seemed as though it was not within her reach. She wanted to tell someone, anyone about what had happened, but the thought of talking about it made her sick. She didn't want anyone to know her shame. She didn't want anyone to know what Greg had done to her.

Mark made his way to his bedroom and sat down heavily on the soft mattress. He stared at the floor with his elbows on his knees, his hands folded together. He just couldn't see why she wouldn't talk about Aden with him. At first, he had thought she was just feeling guilty about sleeping with Aden without telling him, but now he was beginning to think otherwise. Why would she be crying? Why would she be in so much pain? It would make sense for her to feel some guilt, considering she had told him everything throughout her life and never kept secrets from him, but not enough guilt for her entire demeanor to change.

"Maybe Greg was wrong. Maybe her and Aden haven't slept together," he mumbled as his hands fidgeted in his lap. But then again, if she was truly in trouble and she needed help, he trusted that she would come to him.

She'll be fine, he thought as he stood from the bed then headed toward his bathroom for a shower, wanting to wash away the day. *She's a big girl now. I guess I gotta realize that I can't solve all her problems for her.*

—•—•—◆❖◆—•—•—

Emily stared at the ground as it rushed by her eyes. Her legs were bringing her toward the dance room for class, but the rest of her body felt detached. She felt as though she wasn't the one walking, as if it was someone else doing it for her.

"Emily!"

She turned at the sound of her name being called and quickly looked away when she saw Jasmine heading toward her. She didn't want her to see the bruise on her neck so she tried to pull her collar up higher to ensure it was covered.

"Hey," she replied when Jasmine caught up to her.

"Ready to kick it out?" she asked excitedly as she glanced up at the windows of the dance room then back at her friend.

"Yeah, always," Emily replied, her voice distant.

"Whoa, what's wrong? Somethin' ain't right with you," Jasmine pointed out as she stepped in front of her to stop their movement. She studied her friend's face and tried to look into her eyes, but Emily avoided eye contact.

"Nothing is wrong...I just don't feel well. Dancing will help. Come on, we're gonna be late," Emily replied as she grabbed her hand then headed toward the stairs.

Jasmine stared at her, trying to pinpoint what it was about her that seemed different. Her skin was paler than usual; she had dark circles under her eyes indicating her lack of sleep. She tried to think what Emily had done over the weekend. Maybe Emily and Aden had a fight and she was really upset about it? That couldn't be it because Jasmine knew she would be the first person Emily would go to for support and someone to talk to. She had worked out in the gym on Saturday then gone home, but did she do anything else that day? Maybe on Sunday? She had no idea and could tell Emily did not want to talk about it. Jasmine pulled ahead of her and pulled open the heavy metal door and allowed Emily to pass through.

"Well you better know that I'm here for you to talk to, Emily."

Emily froze at the bottom of the second pair of stairs which lead to the door of the dance studio.

"I know...I can't talk about it. Not yet...I just...I can't," she whispered before continuing up the stairs. When they walked through the door, they were met with joyful voices and the laughter of their fellow dancers as everyone fooled around before the class began.

"Hey, there, pretty lady."

"Hey, Emily,"

"What's up, girl?"

Emily gave everyone a slight wave in greeting before walking across the dance floor over to the changing area. She set her backpack down with a heavy thud as she tried to gain control of her trembling hands and body. She had only been around her father ever since Saturday, and she was extremely afraid of being in school around everyone. She was afraid someone could look into her eyes and see her secret, could see the depravity she suffered. Deep breaths ran in and out of her lungs as she squeezed her eyes closed.

"Em?"

Emily's head snapped up at the sound of Jasmine's voice.

"I'll be ready in a minute," she stammered as she unzipped her backpack then pulled out her dance shirt, spandex pants, and dance sneakers.

"Okay, well we'll wait for ya," Jasmine replied before walking away to give Emily some privacy. Once alone, she quickly changed her clothes then tightly tied her dance sneakers before walking out of the changing area and out onto the dance floor. She sat down and began stretching, keeping her mind occupied on the dances she was about to perform with the other girls.

Just think about dance…just concentrate on what you're doing, she thought to herself as she made it to her feet.

Jasmine moved beside her just as the music blasted through the speakers.

"Five, six, seven, eight!"

Emily's body began moving with the music, her mind being dissolved into the beats, the base, the voices. She hit the floor on two, she brought her leg over her head at six, she made it to her feet by eight. Her moves seemed fluid, seemed natural as the rhythm began to comfort her. Her misery began to flow away from her as she spun, and a small smile played on her lips as she truly felt the music to the depths of her soul. She had been dancing for almost four years, and it had always been her escape from the world around her. When she had problems with her math class, dance was always there to take her mind off it. When she had dreams of her mother and wondered what she had been like, dance was there to comfort her and lift her heart.

Now after what Greg had done to her, she felt relief as her mind began leaving her body behind. It was an answer to her prayers as the music consumed her, draining her mind of everything that had transpired that past Saturday. She twisted around to take four steps away from the mirrors along with the rest of the dancers, but out of the corner of her eye, she saw the dance studio door slowly pull open. Her eyes widened when she saw Greg slip into the room then close the door behind him. She tore her gaze away from him and continued to dance. Her chest heaved with her breathing as she spun, twisted, turned, jumped, slid, and snapped her body to the music. The world around her began to lose its form as it blurred into a spiral of colors and sounds. Her breathing was coming in short gasps as she continued on, demanding her body to finish what it started.

Greg leaned against the wall with his large arms crossed over his chest as he watched her body moving along the floor with such a delicious deviant sway. Her lithe movements were beautiful and graceful in their executions, but as he watched her, he realized that something was wrong. Her breathing was not steadied. Her movements were graceful but harsh on her body. She was snapping her head from one side to another. She was slamming her body to the floor with no regard for her safety. He held himself in place, not wanting to pull her off the dance floor and embarrass her in front of her dancer friends.

She'll know when she needs to stop...she won't overdue it much more, Greg thought as his eyes trailed over her.

Finally she could hear the song coming to an end. On the final count of eight, everyone slammed the last move, freezing in their last positions as the music faded and silence filled the room. Emily's gaze darted around the room, trying to see where Greg was. She had to know he was nowhere near her. She had to get out of the dance room. She had to run. She had to breathe!

"Hell, yeah, that was hot!" Jasmine exclaimed as she made her way over to Emily.

Emily panted heavily as she looked to her friend and tried to hear her words. They were mumbled, the world was spinning.

"I can't..." she whispered as she tried to breathe. She stumbled slightly and swayed before her head rolled back, her eyes slid shut, and her body crumbled to the dance floor.

"Emily!" Jasmine called out as she immediately knelt down beside her fallen friend. Greg dashed forward the moment her body hit the floor and examined her before moving her neck or head.

"Miss Gwen, call the nurse's office and let them know that I'm on my way with Emily. Let them know what happened," he instructed as he carefully lifted her into his arms.

"Is she okay? Can I go with her?" Jasmine pleaded both to Greg and Miss Gwen.

"Yes, go with her," Miss Gwen insisted. Jasmine and Greg hurried down the dance studio stairs then out the door. Jasmine held it open to allow Greg through then followed them down the concrete ramp.

"She's never done this before. Sometimes she overworks herself and goes home with bruises, but so do I and a lot of others. But she always slows down or takes a breath when she knows that she's going too fast too hard," Jasmine explained as they approached the nurses office.

"Has anything been bothering her? Has there been a dance, maybe, that she's been having trouble with?" Greg asked as he studied Emily's peaceful face. There was a fine sheen of sweat on her forehead from overexerting herself, but she was still beautiful. His heart was still pounding with worry and curiosity. He would find out why she hurt herself like this and would ensure it never happened again. Jasmine pulled open the office door then followed them inside.

"Hey, Mary, this girl is top priority," Greg stated sternly even before they made it to the secretary's desk.

"Absolutely, Greg, set her in the first room on the cot. Prop her head up on the pillow," Mary instructed as she stood from her desk and made her way to the other side. Mary was a short, petite woman with chestnut-brown hair she always kept pulled back in a bun on the back of her head. She was the kind of person the students loved to talk to, considering she could meet a student once then remember their name and face without a reminder. Every student that went to the nurse's office always felt welcome and comfortable with her whether they were there for an illness or to simply give Mary the office's mail. Emily and Jasmine happened to be two students that Mary had become very fond of.

"Mary, you have to get the nurse to see her now. She's never done this before. I need to make sure she's okay," Jasmine stated firmly, the fear and concern evident in her demeanor.

"Jas, don't worry. I'm sure she'll be just fine. Let Greg and Jodie take care of her, and you tell me exactly what happened so we can figure out why she passed out." Jodie was an older nurse, in her early fifties who had been working at the high school for longer than any of the others.

"Okay, I had a feeling something was wrong when I caught up with her outside the dance room," Jasmine began.

Greg gently laid her down on the cot then carefully tucked the pillow behind her head as instructed. He knelt down beside her and watched her chest for a moment to ensure she was breathing properly. She was, her chest was rising and falling at a steady pace.

"You scared the hell outta me, honey," Greg whispered as he leaned forward to run the backs of his fingers down her cheek. He tucked a strand of her hair behind her ear as he slid just a bit closer.

"Wake up, sweetheart. You're safe now that you're with me," Greg whispered, his lips mere inches from hers. He could feel her soft breath on his lips as she continued to sleep. He moaned softly as he pressed his lips to hers. Those sweet, soft lips always invited him to have a taste. He closed his eyes to soak in her luscious kiss and burn the feeling into his mind. He carefully pulled back from her when he heard the sound of footsteps moving toward the room.

"Hey, Greg, how's she doing?" Jodie asked as she approached the cot.

"Still not awake. I'll let you take over from here," he replied as he stood. "Take good care of her."

Jodie moved around the room grabbing her blood pressure cuff and stethoscope.

"You know I will."

Greg nodded before quitting the room and moving toward the office door. He saw that Jasmine was still reiterating the event to Mary, so he decided to head back to the dance studio to inform their dance teacher that Emily was being taken care of.

"So, she wouldn't tell you what was wrong?" Mary asked with confusion, knowing very well how close Jasmine and Emily were.

"No, I don't know why, but she'll talk to me when she's ready. I can't push her. That won't do any good," Jasmine replied.

"I understand. Well maybe this was just an accident, and she just danced a little too hard. Maybe what's going on that had her upset didn't have anything to do with what happened."

"Maybe...I don't know, but she trusts me. She'll let me help her eventually," Jasmine stated, more hopefully rather than confidently.

"No!"

Mary and Jasmine jumped up from their seats and hurried toward the room Emily had been resting in. A sickening chill shot down Jasmine's spine as she listened to Emily's screams. When she got to the door, her eyes widened and her jaw hit the floor. Emily was writhing on the bed, screaming at the top of her lungs.

"Please stop! Get away from me!" Emily screamed. She couldn't see. All she could do was feel. He was there, he had been touching her. He was touching her now. She needed to get away. She had to escape, or she would become his victim again.

"Emily, it's all right!" Jodie stated loudly, trying to make her voice heard. Emily forced her eyes open as she pushed up into a sitting position and shoved her body against the wall, moving as far away from everyone as possible. Her eyes darted fearfully and frantically around the room, trying to make sense of her surroundings.

"What's going on? Where am I?" she asked as tears welled in her eyes.

"Em, it's okay," Jasmine said comfortingly as she moved closer. "We're still at school, you passed out in dance class." She moved closer to the cot before taking a seat beside her best friend.

Emily was breathing heavily as her fear slowly began to fade. She slowly moved closer to Jasmine before letting her head drop down on to her lap.

"I'm safe," Emily whispered, her voice so soft that only Jasmine heard her words.

"Emily, I'm going to call your father and have him come get you, okay? I think it would be best if you went home and got some rest. You're body has had a trying day," Jodie stated before heading out of the room with Mary in tow.

"Call Mr. Connors and let him know what happened," Jodie instructed before heading down a small hallway to another room. She grabbed a small bottle of Tylenol before heading back to the room to give it to Emily. She knew after the scare she had, her head was most definitely pounding.

"Here you go, Em. This will help your head," Jodie stated kindly as she placed the pills in Emily's hand. Emily popped the Tylenol in her mouth before taking the small cup of water that Jodie had gotten for her from the sink. Emily laid her head back down on Jasmine's lap and closed herself off, not responding to any of the nurse's questions. Jodie realized she was not going to get anywhere trying to ask Emily what was wrong, so she headed out of the room to give them some privacy just in case she ended up telling Jasmine what had happened instead.

"Emily, what's going on?" Jasmine asked in a whispered voice, "What happened?"

Emily closed her eyes when she felt Jasmine's hand slowly stroke her hair in the most comforting way.

"Nothing, I just got a little carried away," she replied as she tried to hold back her tears.

"Are you sure it didn't have anything to do with what happened on the weekend?" Jasmine asked, pushing just a bit further.

"No…nothing happened this weekend. I just don't feel well. I…I don't want to talk about it," she stated loudly before her voice fell to a soft whisper.

"Okay, we won't talk about it. Emily, I want you to come to me when you feel you're ready to talk about what happened, okay? Nobody's closer than me and you, nobody. You know I have your back, you know I'll be the first one to listen to you and help you with anything," Jasmine ensured as she continued to stroke Emily's hair, wanting to comfort her as much as possible.

"I know…I know, Jas."

Jasmine nodded as she held her friend. Jasmine had never seen Emily so vulnerable, so afraid, and so distant. They had been friends since they met each other the first day of their freshman year. Emily had been the spunky, redheaded white girl who grabbed her heart and connected it with her own. They were sisters, closer than anyone else they knew. When they had discovered that they were both dancers, their friendship simply flourished. No matter what had happened in all the years, they had been friends, she had never seen Emily so helpless. She had seen Emily cry when she watched Lifetime movies where so many of these young girls had mothers that would fight for them in every way. She would cry for the loss of her own mother, the mother she never truly had the chance to know. She had been with Emily at her happiest moments, especially when Emily had won the Mattie F. Land Prize for Creative Writing when they were in their junior year of high school.

Emily was a strong girl, tough, independent, sweet, and caring to the point where she trusted people just a bit too easily. Maybe this whole thing had to do with Aden? Maybe they had a fight or maybe he had broken up with her? Jasmine couldn't see that happening, but there were just so many possibilities as to what could be wrong to upset her to this magnitude.

"Have you talked to Aden?" she asked, her curiosity mounting. Emily fought back her tears valiantly as she thought of Aden's beautiful face.

"No...I'm sure he's worried," she replied, her voice soft and meek.

"Maybe you two should talk, honey. It could help you so much to get your feelings out and get things off your chest," Jasmine suggested. Emily shook her head.

"No, that wouldn't be good. There's nothing to talk about. None of this has anything to do with him. Honestly, it doesn't," she stated firmly, her voice almost desperate.

"Okay, we'll stop talking about it. New subject, how did it go on Saturday? Did Greg work you to the point where you wanted to fall over?" she asked with a laugh, trying to lighten the mood. Emily squeezed her eyes tightly closed as she gripped the sheet on the cot.

"It went...fine," she replied after a moment of silence. Jasmine stared down at her friend strangely after hearing her words. Why did she almost spit the word *fine* out? Why did her entire body tense up at her question? What in God's name had happened to her best friend?

——•—◆●◆—•——

Mark hurried past the library and up the stairs of the nurse's office. His heart had practically leaped out of his chest when Mary had called him and said that Emily had blacked out in dance class. He was thankful that Greg had been there to quickly take her to the nurse's office.

"Hey, Mary, where's Emily?" Mark asked urgently once he pushed through the office door.

"Mark, she's in the first room with Jasmine. She's okay, but something is wrong," Mary stated, her concern evident in her eyes. Mark paused, his heart beating faster as his nerves began to fidget inside him.

"What do you mean?" he asked. "Did she hurt herself?"

"No no, not physically. When Greg brought her in here, she was still out cold, but after laying her down and giving her time to rest, we thought she would be okay. Jodie checked her blood pressure, which was high for a young girl her age, but her respiration was fine. Jasmine was out here with me, telling me what happened, and Emily just started screaming. She woke up in a complete panic and tried to push the nurse away from her. After that, she curled up on Jasmine's lap and hasn't moved since."

Mark stood there, flabbergasted as to why Emily flew off the handle.

"Is everything okay at home?" Mary asked gingerly, expecting Mark to reply to that indignantly which he did not disappoint.

"What? Of course everything is fine! What the hell kinda question is that?" Mark replied, his voice rising with every word.

"Mark, I didn't mean anything by that, but I mean... something is wrong, and I want to make sure she's all right," Mary explained. Her words seemed to calm the storm that had begun to stir in Mark's eyes.

"I'm sorry, didn't mean to jump on ya like that," he apologized. "She's been acting strange the past couple of days. She wants to be alone, she hasn't danced in her room like she usually does. I could always here that damn CD player thumping through the ceiling when I'd be in the living room. She didn't hang out with her friends at all this weekend. I was thinking that maybe her and her boyfriend had a fight, but she won't talk to me about it. She started to cry last time so I just let it go."

"Maybe she just needs time. If something is bothering her, then she'll want to talk about it, but only when she's ready," Mary suggested. Mark sighed heavily as he scrubbed his face with his hands.

"I'm taking her home," he stated as he walked past her and headed toward the room he knew his daughter was in.

"Baby girl," Mark stated softly when he entered the room. Emily's head snapped up at the sound of his voice then slid off the bed and into his arms.

"I'm sorry, Daddy," she whispered as she held him tightly. Mark stroked her hair as he embraced her just as strongly.

"There's nothing to be sorry over, sweetheart. Let's go home."

"Text me later, okay?" Jasmine asked as she stood from the cot.

"I will," Emily replied before turning and leaving with her father. Mary handed Mark Emily's backpack that another dancer had brought to the office for her.

"Are you okay? Did you get hurt, sweetheart?" Mark asked as he led her over to his truck in the parking lot. Emily snuggled her face against his side as she shook her head.

"No, I'm fine. I just danced too hard. I'm sorry you had to come get me."

"No more apologizing, girl. Ya have nothing to be sorry about."

He opened up the passenger side door then lifted her up inside before placing her backpack at her feet. The drive home seemed to creep by as Emily watched the clock ticking on the dashboard. She was thankful to get away from the school. She knew Greg had brought her to the nurse's office. She could smell him on her clothes and could feel his touch on her skin. She needed to get home and submerge herself in the shower so she could get clean.

"I'm here when you wanna talk to me, Emily. I can help you," Mark said softly, his voice comforting as the low rumbling of the truck lulled her.

"I know, Dad. This had nothing to do with anything. I…I just made a mistake. I danced too hard…that's all," she

WHAT YOU'VE DONE TO ME | 167

stated a bit defensively. She looked to him quickly to ensure she hadn't angered him.

"I'm sorry," she apologized once again. Mark sighed when he saw her look at him like a deer in the headlights just for answering him in a frustrated tone.

"You gotta stop apologizing, honey," Mark stated as they turned onto their road. "We've had our fair share of arguments, but you've never been afraid of me before, and I don't want ya to start now."

Emily nodded in understanding before turning to gaze out the window. She watched the trees make their way by as they moved closer to their home.

"I just need to rest. Maybe a nap will help," she replied, her voice soft.

"Rest…that's a good idea," Mark concurred. She felt her heart beat faster once Mark pulled the truck into the driveway and slowed until he halted in front of the garage. Emily hopped down from the truck and followed her father up the stairs to the front door.

"I'll let you know when lunch is ready," Mark replied as they stepped inside. Emily started up the stairs before slowly coming to a stop. She turned, ran back down the steps, and landed right in her father's arms.

"I love you so much," she whispered as she held onto him tightly. Mark scooped her small body up into his arms and held her tightly while rocking her gently from side to side.

"I love ya too, my girl. I love ya more than anything in this world." She exhaled slowly and thoughtfully as she absorbed the love and support she felt from her father's arms.

"You're beautiful, my girl. You always deserve the best," he stated softly as he made his way up the stairs toward her room. Emily felt tears threatening to well in her eyes as she listened to her father's words. Once he reached the top of the stairs, she kissed him on his cheek before slipping out of his arms then walking into her room.

"I'm not so sure about that," she stated as she held onto her door. Before she could close herself into the room, Mark did not miss the small tears that slowly trickled down his daughter's cheeks. He'd heard her words and felt his confusion grow. When had her self-esteem plummeted to the point where she no longer thought she was attractive or deserved the best things in life? What was forcing her to cry every day and lock herself away in her room? He was desperate to find out but knew he couldn't force her to speak about it. He cast one last glance at her closed bedroom door before heading back down the staircase then into the kitchen to cook up a little lunch.

11

WEEKS BEGAN PASSING. Emily took quiz after quiz, test after test in her classes, but she felt as though she was simply circling A, B, C, or D. She couldn't concentrate on anything in her classes. She had forced herself to dance every class to the point where she was moments from passing out, but she didn't want to inconvenience her father like she had weeks ago so she would stop just in time.

"Emily, can I speak to you for a moment?" Mrs. Anderson called to her over the sound of the bell ringing, signifying the end of class.

Emily turned to her mid-stride toward the door then made her way over to her teacher's desk.

"Is everything okay, Emily?" Mrs. Anderson asked as she slid her small-framed glasses from her face. "Your grades on the past few quizzes haven't been as good as your others, and you haven't handed in any of your homework for the past few weeks. Is there anything you need to talk to me about?"

Emily shook her head as she averted her eyes toward the dry-erase board then toward the floor.

"I've just been really tired lately. I've been drowning in schoolwork. I just need to catch up is all," she replied as she fidgeted with her backpack.

Mrs. Anderson could obviously see Emily's skittish demeanor, which indicated there was something wrong that she was uncomfortable talking to her about. This surprised her, considering she had known Emily since the girl's freshman year of high school.

"Are you sure? I'm a really good listener," Mrs. Anderson stated with a smile and a wink, trying to strengthen her and comfort her.

Emily looked up into her teachers eyes and conjured the best smile she could.

"I'm fine, really. I just need to get back on track. I can do it," she replied before turning and leaving the classroom, needing to distance herself from her teacher's curious and concerned gaze.

"Hey, Em! Wait up!"

Emily halted at the sound of Jetta's voice. She hadn't spoken to her in a few days, and she knew her friend would try and make her talk. But talking was the last thing she wanted to do.

"Hi," she greeted in return.

"Everything okay? I haven't heard from you, and I didn't get any replies from my texts I sent you." Jetta studied her friend with confusion when she finally caught up with her.

Emily tucked her hair behind her ear as she situated her backpack on her shoulder nervously.

"Sorry, things have been hectic lately. I haven't had the chance to talk to anyone."

"No biggie. I know the feeling. I'm working on three essays and a science project that has to get done…"

Jetta's words faded in her ears when Emily spotted Greg standing at the end of the hallway. He was heading toward them. Emily looked around her, trying to find a place to hide, but Jetta hooked her arm and led her down the hallway, not knowing what her actions may cause.

"Hey, girls, how's your day going?" Greg asked as he stood before them, his eyes running over Emily from head to toe. She cringed and looked away.

"Pretty good, keeping busy for sure," Jetta replied.

"And how are you, Emily?" Greg asked, her name tasting delicious on his lips. He watched as her body began to quiver and her eyes refused to meet his. He wanted to reach out and pull her into his arms, but he knew he couldn't give in to his desires in the middle of the hallway.

"Fine," she replied. "I have to go to class."

Greg watched as she circled around him then took off down the hallway as the final bell rang.

"I wonder what's gotten into her?" Jetta asked herself. "Sorry, I'm not sure why she's been acting weird lately."

"Maybe her and her boy toy had a fight. Who knows with you high school kids," Greg replied with a chuckle before heading down the hallway after her. "I'll make sure she's all right."

Jetta stood there with confusion before shrugging and making her way to her next class.

Emily hurried through the hallways, searching for a safe haven. She glanced behind her and her alarm grew when she saw Greg was following her. She turned to her right and moved down the hallway to the nearest bathroom. She practically threw herself through the door just as Greg rounded the corner.

He chuckled as he watched the girls' bathroom door slowly settle closed.

"If you wanted a rendezvous in the bathroom, why didn't you just say so?" Greg muttered to himself, a smirk plastered on his lips. He glanced around at the empty hallways before moving closer to the bathroom door then pushing it open for entry.

Emily squeezed her eyes shut as she cowered on top of the toilet of one of the stalls. The door was latched and her knees were pulled up to her chest. She prayed it wasn't Greg, but as the sound of heavy footsteps moved closer to her stall, her heart began to beat feverishly with the sinking realization that it was.

"Em? Come on out so we can talk. You took off in such a hurry, we didn't get the chance to really chat," Greg spoke, his voice soft and his words almost gentle. He waited a moment for her response and became confused when he received none.

"Em, come on. I want to see you. Don't make me come in there and bring you out," he threatened, his voice deepening with each word.

Emily tried to slow her breathing as she carefully stood off the toilet. She unlatched the door before flinging it open and making a dash for the door.

"Whoa, whoa, what's the hurry?" Greg laughed as he snatched her by her waist and pulled her into his arms.

"No! Please let me go!" Emily pleaded as she struggled against his grip.

"Hey, now, calm down and let me hold you. I've missed having you in my arms."

Emily flung her elbow back and caught him in the ear, forcing him to release her. She ran to press her back to the wall since his large frame was blocking the door.

"What was that for?" Greg asked with agitation as he rubbed his ear.

"Let me go," Emily begged as she stared into his eyes.

"What is your problem?" Greg shouted as he approached her.

"My problem? After what you did to me? You're the one with the problem! You're sick!" Emily shouted back as she struggled to get by him.

Greg gripped her arms and shook her.

"You're the one who has the problem! I thought you were mature enough to handle what we shared. You're the one throwing away your life. Your grades are garbage, your dancing is falling apart. You're ruining your life!"

"Get off me or I swear I'll tell!" Emily threatened, her eyes burning into his.

Greg's grip tightened on her arms before he shoved her against the wall.

"You wanna tell somebody? Go ahead! Tell your Dad, I already told him that you and Aden are sleeping together so he won't believe a word you say, girl!" Greg replied viciously.

"I was a virgin until you..." she tried to say but ended her sentence when she felt her stomach heave.

"If you really want your Daddy knowing that we made love, you go right ahead and tell him, but I suggest you keep our relationship to yourself. I don't need that kind of agitation in my life. I can have you whenever the hell I want. Your Daddy won't help you. Your teachers would laugh you out of their classrooms. So get used to me being wherever you go. When I want you...you're mine!"

Emily whimpered as she tried to hold back her tears. No matter how much she wanted to spit in his face and tell him he was wrong, she couldn't. She knew he was right. Her teachers wouldn't believe her. Greg was everyone's favorite teacher and in the school's eyes, Greg Riley could do no wrong.

"And you know damn well that you've been flirting with me for months and your friends have seen it. Everything is against you, Emily. Everything!" he shouted before pushing her against the wall once more. His grip was biting into her arms and her back was throbbing from the harsh tile wall.

"You're hurting me!" she cried out as she struggled once again.

Greg felt his anger rising as he wrapped one hand around her throat as the other wrapped around her waist.

"I can hurt you if I feel like it or I can make you feel only pleasure, Emily. Now, what are you going to do?" he asked as he squeezed her throat a bit too hard.

She clawed at his hand as she struggled to breathe.

"Are you going to keep quiet?" he asked.

Emily nodded her head as best as she could as she felt her body start to tingle from lack of oxygen.

"Good girl," Greg stated with a laugh before releasing her throat.

Emily coughed and wheezed as she tried to catch her breath.

He lowered her back to her feet before reaching in his back pocket.

"Now, give this pass to your teacher so you don't get in trouble for being late," he stated as he wrote out the pass.

Emily regretfully took the piece of paper, knowing that she would get a detention for showing up so late with no pass.

Greg moved over to the stall Emily had been hiding in and grabbed her backpack for her.

"Now get to class," he ordered as she slipped her bag over her shoulder.

Emily squealed with fear when Greg suddenly grabbed her face. He studied her emerald eyes before pressing his lips to hers.

"Sweet as always," he whispered against her lips. He took one more kiss from her before backing out of her way.

Emily immediately hurried out the door as she wiped her mouth on her sleeve.

"That's my girl," Greg muttered as he watched the door close behind her. Greg made a cautious exit from the girls' restroom before heading back to the gym to work off some tension.

Emily handed the pass to her teacher once she made it to class and made sure she pulled her shirt collar up higher on her neck to hide the evidence of Greg's anger. All she could do was sit at her desk and wipe away the tears that refused to stop falling.

Emily hurried toward her bus when the end of the day finally arrived. She needed to be home, away from the school, away from Greg. She needed to be near her father so she could feel safe once again.

"Baby!"

Emily sniffled and took a deep breath before turning toward Aden. Her heart broke at the sight of the pain in his eyes. She loved him with all her heart, but she was afraid of her own emotions. How would she react to his touch after what happened? How would she react to his love and affection when the last thing she wanted was to be touched by anyone?

"Emily, what's going on? You haven't returned any of my calls. I haven't gotten any text messages back from you. Did I do something wrong?" Aden asked as he approached her, his annoyance and frustration evident.

"No, it's not you. I'm sorry," Emily whispered as she stared at the ground, her hands gripping her backpack strap with enough strength to turn her knuckles white.

Aden studied her and watched her entire body begin to quiver.

"Please tell me what's going on," he begged as he gently rested his hands on her arms.

"Ouch!" She exclaimed as his hands contacted the bruises on her arms.

"What? What's wrong?" Aden asked, alarmed as to how he hurt her with such a light touch.

"Nothing, I have to go. I love you." She cried as tears began to pour from her eyes before she turned and hurried toward her bus.

Aden stood there, staring at her with such hurt in his eyes that if Emily had looked back, she might have collapsed from the pain.

Why was she avoiding him? Why did she no longer have the light and spirit in her eyes that was true to who she was?

"I love you too," he whispered before turning and heading toward his truck.

Emily watched out the window of the bus as Aden headed toward the senior parking lot. Her heart sank as the realization set in that Aden's father had finally bought him his own truck. Usually, he would borrow one of his parents' vehicles to drive to her house, but they had never liked the idea of parking one of their vehicles at the school. High school students were just too unpredictable. They had been waiting months for this day, but she couldn't feel his touch right now. She couldn't see the look of love in his eyes after what had happened. She was no longer pure for him. She had been forced to endure the touch of a man she now feared more than anything. How was she supposed to love Aden and give herself fully to him when all she could do was cry and quiver in fear when anyone came near her? She wouldn't, couldn't admit that she now feared Aden's touch. Would he think he could touch her the way Greg did? Would he think he could have his turn? Emily shook her head to rid her mind of such thoughts. Aden would rather die than hurt her, and she had to remember that. She cast one last glance out the window before the bus lurched forward toward home.

"Baby girl, you have to eat something," Mark stated as he watched Emily at the dinner table. She was pushing her food around on her plate but none was making it into her mouth.

She looked up with a jerk of her head before lowering her eyes back down.

"I guess I'm just not hungry, Dad," she replied with a soft sigh.

Mark needed to know what was wrong. It pained him so much to see his daughter in such anguish. As Emily tilted her head to the side to rub the tension from her shoulder, Mark caught a glimpse of something purple and blue on her skin that peaked out from her turtleneck.

"Emily, what the hell is on your neck?" he asked with alarm when the realization hit him that it was a large bruise.

She immediately pulled her shirt back up to cover the hand print Greg had left behind.

"Nothing. I hit myself accidentally. It's nothing," she replied as she held back her tears. Why couldn't she just tell him? Why did she have to hold it inside? She knew her father would protect her from anything, but she feared what Greg would do if he found out she had told someone.

"Dad, can I be excused? I don't feel well."

Mark sighed heavily, not wanting to let her go. He wanted to sit her down and squeeze the answers out of her. But he knew he would be making things worse rather than helping.

"Go ahead, darlin'," he stated.

She slid her chair back before hurrying out of the dining room then up the stairs to her bedroom. Once she was safely behind the closed door, she broke down into tears. This was not how she wanted to spend the rest of her life. All she could do was cry and cower in fear.

"I hate him. If I could kill him, I would!" Emily exclaimed as she threw herself down onto her bed. She sniffled and inhaled heavily, trying to calm her racing heart. She closed her eyes, willing her tears to cease so she could have a moment of peace, but the moment they shut, Greg was there. She could see him touching her, holding her down, chasing her as she ran for the door only to find her freedom denied from her.

"No!" she shouted as she snapped her eyes open. She whimpered helplessly as she rolled onto her back and reclined against the pillows. She stared at the ceiling, asking herself over and over what she had to do to get him out of her mind and especially her life. No one could ever possibly know how painful and traumatizing it was for her to go to school and be assaulted every day by her rapist.

<hr />

Mark stared at the ceiling above his bed, his mind in tumultuous chaos. What was he supposed to do? He wanted to help Emily solve whatever problem was affecting her so greatly. It had been hours after she had gone to her room and he had checked on her not long ago to make sure she was all right. Luckily, she had been sleeping. Mark knew she had not gotten much sleep, so he was thankful that she was resting now.

One thing still concerned him that also involved Emily's strange behavior. Mark had spoken to Aden that evening after Emily buried herself in her room. Mark had asked him if him and Emily had been sleeping together. He wanted the truth, and he knew Aden couldn't lie to him. Aden had told him truthfully that they had fooled around and they've touched and kissed, but he respected Emily's wishes to remain a virgin until marriage. If that was the case, then why had Greg pulled him aside and fired him up with thoughts of Aden and Emily having sex? Maybe they were just Greg's assumptions and he had felt the need to let Mark know. She was still a virgin, and Aden was adamant about it.

"I want to make her happy," Aden had said strongly. "She wants to wait until marriage and since I know how much she really wants it, I wouldn't let it happen before I put a ring on her finger. And I still have a little while to go before I get that paid off."

How could he not believe Aden's words? The boy was sincere and had never lied to him in the past, so why would he start now? Aden had also asked Mark that night for Emily's hand in marriage. He had explained that it would not happen for a while, but he wanted to know that they had his blessing when the time came.

"Maybe Greg was just mistaken. They could have been talking about something, and he took it out of text," Mark mumbled as he rubbed his hands over his face.

"No!"

The moment Mark heard Emily's scream, he was off the bed and charging down the hall toward her bedroom.

———◆◈◆———

Emily could feel him. He was touching her. He was putting his lips and hands all over her body and she could not make him stop.

"So perfect…Just let me touch you."

She thrashed around on her bed, her mind being tormented by Greg's words and touch.

She could see him grabbing her and holding her down. She could hear his voice and his sickening words. She could feel what he was doing to her and she was powerless to stop it.

"No!"

Her eyes snapped open, yanking her unconscious mind from the nightmare it had been trapped in. She turned and saw her bedroom door swing open and a very large, dark figure stood in the doorway for a moment before hurrying toward her. It had to be Greg.

"No! Get away from me!" she screamed as she shoved her bed sheets away and launched herself off her bed.

"Emily, calm down," Mark cooed as he slowly moved closer to her, his hands up in a peaceful gesture.

"Please don't hurt me, don't touch me!" Emily screamed before bull rushing her father. She tried to run past him but her frantic state made her easy to capture.

What in God's name had gotten into her? Why was she running away from him? All he knew was whatever had frightened her, it was the source of her strange actions as of late. Mark pulled her against his chest and held her tightly, cooing soft words to soothe her fears, but she was having none of it.

"Let go! Stop! Please don't do this again!" she screamed as tears began to stream down her face.

"Emily, it's Dad!" Mark finally shouted over her screams.

Emily's screams halted and her struggles stopped at the sound of her father's voice. She looked up into his eyes, her entire body quivering with fear.

"D...Daddy?" she whimpered, choking back her sobs.

"It's me, angel. What are you so afraid of? Talk to me!" Mark begged as he held her tightly, looking down into her terrified emerald eyes.

Emily simply stared at him as her chest heaved up and down with her sporadic breathing. She could still see Greg grabbing at her, holding her down, trying to lick away her tears as she cried out for help. He was going to get her.

Maybe he was hiding in her closet or under her bed. She was not safe here. She was never going to be safe.

"Emily!" Mark exclaimed when her eyes rolled into the back of her head and her body went limp in his arms. That was the last straw. He scooped her up quickly in his arms and hurried out to his truck before speeding to the hospital as fast as he could.

12

"I'm fine, Daddy. Really, I'm fine," Emily insisted as she tried to climb out of the hospital bed.

Mark kept her in place easily.

"No, you're not Emily. You lost it the moment I walked into your room and I want to know why," Mark stated as Emily held the neck line of her hospital gown high, shielding her throat from his view. Her father had not mentioned anything about the bruises on her, so she assumed it had been too dark in her bedroom for him to notice. She surely didn't intend on showing him now nor later.

"Mr. Connors, may I speak with you for a moment?"

Mark turned his attention to the nurse who peeked into the room.

"I'll be right back," Mark stated softly before leaning down and placing a soft kiss on her forehead.

Emily sighed heavily as she watched her father leave the room. The nurse had checked her blood pressure and had put her on oxygen to ensure she was breathing properly. She had just sat there and let the woman do her job, but she did vocalize one of her thoughts to the woman. Emily's abdomen had been radiating pain for the past few days and it concerned her. Even if having the nurse take a look to make sure she was all right would reveal what had happened, Emily had to take that chance. What if something was wrong and if she waited something horrible would happen? She had to make sure her body was all right. So after she told the young woman about the pain, she offered Emily a gynecological examination so she could properly diagnose the problem. The exam had hurt a bit but the nurse tried her best to ensure Emily's comfort. Come to find out, the pain was being caused by small rips in the tissue of her vaginal wall.

"I'll have the doctor prescribe you with some cream to help heal the tissue. May I ask how this happened, Emily?"

Emily had refused to talk about it, but thanked her for her help. She sighed heavily when she thought about the look in the nurse's eyes. She knew what had happened despite her polite question. But maybe she just misread the woman's expression. She had been under so much stress and through such depression that the look in the woman's eyes could have been a figment of her imagination. No one was going to find out what happened as long as she did what Greg told her to do and that was keep her mouth shut.

"Is everything okay?" Mark asked once Emily's hospital room door was closed behind them.

"Well, there's nothing wrong with Emily that's life threatening. Her blood pressure is back to normal and her breathing is normal, so the faint was from this nightmare you spoke of and probably from her hyperventilation, but there is something wrong." The young woman tucked a strand of her long brunette locks behind her ear.

Mark gazed at her with confusion.

"What's wrong?" he asked with concern and impatience.

The young nurse hated delivering this kind of news, but Emily was seventeen years old and still a minor. She was a terrified girl who was trying to deal with what happened to her all on her own. She wanted to help her, and the only way Emily would get help was if someone knew.

"Mr. Connors, there is no easy way to say this. I can see how close the two of you are, so I believe you'll be able to help her and talk to her," she stated, dreading to deliver the news.

"What the hell happened to my daughter?" Mark asked, his eyes taking on a slight darkness as his thoughts began running haphazardly in his mind.

"Mr. Connors, I believe your daughter was sexually assaulted," she finally stated as she held her clipboard in her hands tightly.

He almost swallowed his tongue when she finally spoke. His stomach dropped to his feet and the thought of breathing seemed almost impossible to achieve. Sexually assaulted? Someone had forced his daughter to have sex? Someone put their hands on her while she probably begged them to stop, cried for mercy?

"Raped?" he whispered, spitting out the word as if it left a horrendous taste in his mouth.

"She complained of abdominal pain so I offered a gynecological exam, which she accepted. Her vaginal walls were torn up and the only way for that to have happened to someone of her age is rough penetration with no kind of lubrication or preparation. Unfortunately, I see it every day. She has bruising on her wrists, one ankle, her hips, and her inner thighs, but they are almost completely faded. It would take a trained eye to see them. That means that this attack happened approximately a few weeks ago. However, she has a handprint bruise on her neck which is much more fresh. I'd say that bruise is no more than a day or so old."

Mark raised his hands to slowly rub them over his face as the young woman's words began to bombard him. This could not be happening.

"Did she tell you this happened? Do you know it for a fact?" Mark asked, desperate to hear another opinion which would dispute that such a disgusting act was forced upon his daughter.

"I'm almost positive, Mr. Connors. She won't speak about it to me, but if you talk to her about it and tell her that you know what happened, she may talk to you then. Hopefully she'll decide to file a police report. No one should get away with rape," she stated.

Mark could see the passion in her eyes and that only made him more sick. He doubted the nurse would have such a look of certainty and empathy on her face unless she truly believed that this had happened to Emily. Everything began to make sense. Her lack of friends visiting, her withdrawn nature, and the way she cried every day. Someone had hurt his little girl, and he was hell-bent on finding out who. He turned away from the nurse and reentered the hospital room, needing to be near his daughter.

"Daddy, can we go home? Please?" Emily pleaded as she pulled her knees to her chest, her hands still holding firm to the neckline of her hospital gown.

Mark moved up to her bedside and looked down into her eyes. Those emerald gems stared back at him with such desperation and sadness that he had to choke back his tears as well as his fuming anger. His tears were for the innocence and childhood of his daughter that had just been destroyed, and his anger was for the man who had destroyed it by laying his hands on her.

"Daddy?"

Mark simply reached out toward her and rested his hands over hers, gently sliding her hands away from her neck.

Emily tensed at first, refusing to let go, but then decided against it. Her hands fell away and the hospital gown fell around her shoulders, exposing her neck.

Mark had to take a deep breath when his eyes settled on the large handprint bruise that marred her fair skin. He almost couldn't breathe. The bruise almost encompassed her entire neck which insinuated the man's size.

"Why didn't you tell me?" Mark whispered as he cupped her cheeks in his hand. "Who did this to you?"

Emily's eyes widened at his words. He knew. What was she supposed to say? Should she tell him everything? Should she hide the event and deny it? Would he think she was disgusting? The way her father was looking at her in that moment told her that he would never think of her in such a way.

"I…I can't…" Emily whispered as she reached out and clutched his hand tightly. "Daddy, please don't make me."

Mark's entire body began to shake as he slid her over then sat beside her before pulling her into his arms. The nurse was right. His mind was being overloaded and it was threatening to explode. His daughter had been raped.

"Please, baby girl, tell me. He'll never breathe again, I promise you."

"No! Please, Daddy, don't make me say anything. I can't…nothing happened. Everything is fine," Emily stated. She already couldn't sleep, couldn't eat, couldn't focus on anything in school or even on dance. Greg Riley haunted her dreams, turning them into nightmares every night. She felt as though no matter where she walked, he was right behind her. Unfortunately, when it came to her being in school, he always was. She wanted to tell her father everything. She wanted him to do something to keep her safe. But she knew if she told him that Greg was the one who hurt her, she would never be safe and neither would her father.

"Emily," Mark pleaded, "if you tell me who did this to you, I can keep you safe. He'll never come near you again, I swear, baby girl."

She stared into his emerald eyes which mirrored hers. Should she tell him? She took a deep breath as tears welled in her eyes, beginning to spill over onto her cheeks. She was dying inside. All she wanted to do was scream and reveal everything to him, but she was terrified. What would happen if Greg found out that she had told her father? Would he even believe her? Greg and Mark had been friends for years and both of them were friends with all of the local police officers. So it would be only her word against Greg's.

"Was it Aden? Did he do this to you?" Mark asked when the thought dawned on him.

"No! No, Daddy, it wasn't Aden. I...I haven't talked to him. I can't talk to him! I can't talk to anyone!" she whimpered as her grip on his hand tightened.

Mark tightened his hold on her when the realization hit him that Emily had not told anyone about what happened, not even her best friends. She had been suffering this all alone.

"I promise I'll protect you. Let me protect you. I swear he'll never touch you again..." Mark whispered harshly against the top of her head, begging her to confide in him.

Emily snuggled into his arms and sobbed as she felt his chest rise and fall against her head. His breathing worked to soothe her, calm her. She could feel his strength and power around her and knew he could protect her, but how could he possibly protect her twenty-four hours a day, seven days a week when she had to go to school, away from him and in the death grip of Greg Riley? She took slow deep breaths as she worked away her tears.

"Mr. Connors? I was wondering if I could speak with your daughter for a moment."

Emily and Mark both looked up at the young brunette nurse as she reentered the room.

"Is that okay?" Mark asked as he looked back down at his daughter.

Emily didn't want her father away from her, but the look on the nurse's face told Emily that she was going to tell her something that she would want to hear.

"It's okay."

Mark quit the room after kissing the top of her head, leaving them alone to speak with one another.

"Emily, my name is Jessica. I really wanted to talk to you about something," the young woman stated as she pulled a chair up to Emily's bedside.

"Okay," Emily nodded as she pulled her knees back to her chest.

Jessica reached into a low cabinet at the bedside and retrieved a fresh warm blanket before spreading it out over the bed and covering up Emily's body.

"I know what happened to you is something that no woman should ever suffer. You did not deserve it, and it was not your fault," Jessica stated as she studied the young girl in the hospital bed. Her fair skin was bruised black and blue, her eyes were distant, her entire body portrayed fear of anyone who came near her.

"Yes, it is…" Emily whispered before sniffling back her tears. "It was my fault. My friends even said I flirted with him without even knowing it. If they saw it, then so did he. Maybe if I had changed the way I acted, stopped being so friendly, then this wouldn't have happened."

"You cannot blame yourself. He had no right to touch you. He had no right to take something from you that you were not willing to give. You said no, you said stop, and that's enough. You are a beautiful young girl who is full of life and love. This is *not* a consequence of being a friendly, happy girl. You did not deserve this, Emily. You have people in your life that can protect you and support you through this. Holding this inside you is going to make it much worse. The thoughts of what happened will fester in your mind. You'll constantly be looking over your shoulder, fearing that he'll be right behind you even though he won't be."

Emily swallowed hard at Jessica's words before looking straight into her eyes.

"He is there when I turn around…every single time."

Jessica's brows furrowed at the young girls word's. She had just revealed that she knew her rapist and that she had some kind of contact with him on a daily basis. That cut down the options of who it was greatly. It had to be either a friend, a boyfriend, one of her friends' parents, or even some kind of authority figure like a teacher or coach.

"Tell your father who did this to you, and you will be safe. You can bring this bastard to justice and put him in prison for what he did. You'll be able to get on with your life and grow in every way. Please, tell your father," Jessica begged.

"Why do you care? Why do you care about what happened to me? Why should I tell anyone?" Emily cried out as her tears began again.

Jessica took a deep breath, wetting her lips.

"Because I was raped ten years ago by my gymnastics coach. I was fifteen years old. My life fell apart until I finally told my mother what happened. She and I fought through the legal system until finally he was put in prison. If I had to live with the knowledge that the man that raped me was running around free, able to attack me again or someone else at any time, I wouldn't be able to handle it. You will be able to go on. You will go to college. You will grow with your dancing and by the look of the promise ring on your left hand ring finger, there is a boy out there that loves you. The two of you can grow together once this man is locked up in jail for what he did to you," Jessica stated passionately.

Emily held the woman's gaze before looking down at the ring Aden had given her. She loved Aden with all of her heart, but she knew that if she did not tell him the truth, she might lose him. Aden would protect her, her father would protect her, and so would everyone else who loved her in her life.

"Do the memories still come to you? Do you still have nightmares?" Emily whispered as she leaned in close.

Jessica smiled and shook her head.

"I did for a year or so after it was all over, but this is the first time I've thought about it in a very long time. I've named my rapist for what he is, and he is sitting in jail for a long time. My family still supports me and comforts me to this day even if I don't need it anymore. I'm married now to a man who loves me with all his heart and would rather die than hurt me. So, no, Emily, those images and nightmares were banished by the courage that was given to me," Jessica stated confidently, happily.

Emily nodded at the young woman's words and sniffled as she tried to stop the tears. "Okay...I'll tell him," Emily stated on a soft whimper.

Jessica stood from her chair and gently hugged her, giving her the support and comfort that she knew her father and the rest of her friends and family would soon deliver her.

"Stay strong," Jessica whispered in her ear before leaving the room and allowing Mark back inside.

"Are you all right, darlin'?" Mark asked as he returned to her bedside and pulled her close to his side.

"Daddy...I have to tell you something," Emily blurted out as she looked up into his eyes. "It's...it's about what happened."

Mark held his breath at her words. He didn't want to interrupt her in fear that it would give her a slight moment to change her mind.

"Tell me, little one," Mark stated softly, tightening his hold on her to ensure she felt safe.

Emily took a long, deep breath before staring into her father's eyes.

"Gre..." she began before turning away from his gaze and shaking as sobs began to rack her body. She turned back to him, determined, as she inhaled deeply and shakily.

"Daddy...Greg Riley raped me!"

She dropped her head against her father and let the sobs and cries completely take over her body.

Mark held her tightly, frozen in his place as her words stabbed at his mind. Greg Riley was a dear friend of his. They had known each other for years, and Greg had even met Emily when she was a little girl. Then realization struck. Emily had been working out with Greg at the school every Saturday for about a month, but then, she suddenly stopped. That's when her strange behavior began to emerge.

"Oh my god," Mark whispered as he looked down at his daughter as she cried in his arms, holding him tightly.

"It's okay, baby girl. Everything's gonna be okay," he stated as his anger boiled to the point of complete disaster.

The moment he could ensure Emily's safety, he was going to pay Greg a very special visit.

—◦—◦—◆◉◆—◦—◦—

Emily sat at home, sipping the last of her soup her father had made her once they returned home from the hospital. She lifted the bowl in her hands and drank the last of it before gently pushing it toward Mark.

"Feel a little better?" he asked as he took her bowl and brought it into the kitchen.

"A little," she replied as she stood from the dining room table. She hurried into the kitchen and straight into her father's arms. She didn't want to be away from him after everything that had transpired that night. He immediately lifted her into his arms and held her head against his chest, tucking it under his chin.

"I got you, sweetheart. I got you," he cooed as he carried her up the stairs toward her bedroom. "You have to try and get some sleep, angel. Everything is going to be okay." It took about half an hour to get her to fall asleep, but once she did, she slept peacefully and soundly.

Something that she probably hasn't done in weeks, Mark thought to himself as he silently closed her bedroom door before making his way down the stairs. He whipped open his cell phone and called his friend Steve immediately.

The moment Mark explained the situation, Steve was on his way with his pistol by his side, just in case. Mark sat in the living room, staring at the floor as he thought. His daughter had been raped by one of his best friends. He could only repeat that to himself, not truly comprehending it. Maybe this was a misunderstanding. Emily was a young girl with raging hormones. Maybe something had happened between Emily and Greg while they were exercising and she had misinterpreted it.

"What the hell is your problem?" Mark growled to himself as he abruptly stood. He began pacing through the living room as his thoughts began to fester in his mind. Emily was smart. She would never claim something that horrendous had happened to her if it had not. She also had the bruises to prove it. Greg was three times her size and practically three times her weight. He had held Emily tight enough to mar the skin on her neck. The bruises the nurse claimed were on her inner thighs and hips were the ones that made him physically ill. What was he supposed to do? He wanted to kill him. He wanted to murder a man who was once his closest confidant. But he knew he couldn't. If Mark went to jail, then Emily would have no one. She would be alone. Mark turned toward the door abruptly when a loud knock sounded, but he soon calmed when he realized it was Steve.

"Hey," Steve greeted once he pulled open the door.

"No one comes into this house. Check on her every ten minutes or just sit outside the damn door. If anything goes wrong, I don't want him getting in this house."

"He'd be lucky if he'd get within ten yards. Just be careful, man. Don't do anything stupid. You're all she's got," Steve stated as he glanced up toward Emily's bedroom.

Mark sighed heavily as if to calm himself.

"To be honest, I don't know what the hell I'm gonna do," he replied before heading out the door toward his truck.

Greg could not sleep for the life of him. Emily's sweet face and lithe body kept wafting through his mind. He could practically reach out and touch her. He was worried about the way she passed out during dance, and he wanted to make sure she was all right. She and Mark lived maybe ten minutes from his house, so why not just stop by? Maybe he could even peek into her bedroom to see her in her night clothes. He'd always wondered what she wore when she slept. Maybe she didn't wear anything. Those thoughts were too much for him to resist. He quickly got out of bed and dressed before heading down the stairs toward the kitchen where he left his keys. Just as he reached for them, there was a rather loud knock on his front door.

"Who the hell..." he mumbled before pulling it open. "Mark? What the hell are you doing here at this hour? Come on in, looks like it's gonna storm."

Mark stood there for a moment, tempted beyond any rational thought to attack Greg where he stood. He resisted the urge then stepped inside.

"We need to talk," Mark stated, his back to him.

"Sure, go ahead and sit on the couch, I'll get us some beers," Greg replied before heading into the kitchen.

Mark stood near the door, motionless. He didn't know what to do. He had been so close to Greg for years. He never thought he would be capable of rape, and he could have never imagined that Emily would be his victim.

Greg walked back in the room, two beers in hand. He could tell something was wrong as he stared at his friend. Had something happened to Emily?

"Is everything okay? Did anything happen to Em?" he asked with concern. He had to make sure she was all right.

Mark's eyes shot up to Greg's, fire burning inside them at the mention of his daughter.

"That's what I'm here to talk about," Mark replied before accepting the beer and downing it in moments. "Have you noticed that she hasn't been herself lately?"

Greg paused for a moment. Either Mark was extremely upset and concerned about why Emily's behavior had changed, or he knew. He had terrified Emily into silence at school the other day, but perhaps she had told him.

"Yeah, she's been acting strange for weeks. She hasn't come to the gym for our workouts in a while. Maybe she and Aden broke up. I'm not sure," Greg replied as he headed toward the living room.

"We've been friends for so long. I deserve the truth out of you," Mark growled viciously, stopping Greg in his tracks. If he kept up this innocent charade, he was going to beat the truth out of him, then finish him off when the truth came out.

Greg turned to stare at him as his suspicions were confirmed. Emily had told him. All he could do was enjoy the rage he could see boiling inside Mark Connors, his best friend. He couldn't help but wonder if she had gone into detail about their coupling.

"Greg, you were one of my closest friends. I trusted you! Emily trusted you! You raped her, Greg! All I can do is wish she's just misunderstanding something or that she's confused. But how could she be? Tell me, Greg. Just tell me you didn't do this! Tell me you would never do this!" Mark shouted as his anger and desperation boiled over.

Greg simply stood there staring at him, not saying a word or moving a muscle. He didn't have the heart to deny it. What he and Emily shared was beautiful whether she and Mark saw it that way or not. He didn't regret it for a moment, and if given the chance, he would do it again and again.

Mark had to leave before he exploded. He knew he couldn't do anything yet. He had to be there for Emily. Mark turned and headed toward the door.

"Do you wanna hear what I did to your daughter?" Greg blurted out, freezing Mark's steps. "Do you wanna hear about how she squirmed to get free? How good she felt underneath me? How she cried out for you to help her?"

Mark's entire world went red as rage and pure hatred consumed him to his very soul. He didn't know whether to beat Greg or just kill him. He roared like a monstrous beast as he turned and charged toward his former friend. Greg and Mark went sprawling to the ground as Mark hammered Greg with fists, elbows, and forearms, roaring like a man possessed.

⁂

"What!" Steve exclaimed after Mark updated him over the phone. "You better hope they don't keep you in that cell all night. Can't say I'd have done anything different. What am I supposed to tell Em?"

Emily peeked over the banister, listening carefully to Steve's words. Her father was in jail? What had happened while she was asleep?

"Well, call when you know what the hell is going on," Steve stated before flipping his cell phone shut.

Emily hurried down the stairs, walked to the coffee table, and grabbed his keys before handing them to him.

"We're going now. What did he do?" she demanded.

Steve didn't know what to say.

"He went to Greg's and you don't need to go over there. Greg's there too. They locked them both up. You don't need to be anywhere near him," Steve stated firmly.

Emily feared Greg more than anything, but she needed to be near her father and make sure he was all right.

"I need to be there, Steve. Please take me. You'll be right there. No one will touch me," Emily reassured, desperation evident in her voice.

Steve sighed heavily, hating the idea but knowing if he didn't take her that she would find her own way there. At least this way, she'd be safe.

"Get in the truck," he stated before taking his keys.

"Thank you."

———◆❖◆———

Mark sat brooding in his cell. He had many friends in the police department but so did Greg. Mark attacked him but for a damn good reason. However, neither of them would speak as to why they were fighting, so they had no choice but to arrest them both. His main consolation was that Greg was in a cell as well so Emily's safety was guaranteed. He didn't know what to do to help her. She refused to tell anyone and refused to file a police report. How was he going to keep her safe if he was on the loose?

"Dad!"

Mark whipped around at the sound of Emily's voice.

"Damn it, Steve why the hell did you bring her here?" he demanded angrily.

"I made him bring me. God, are you okay?" she asked with concern when she saw the bruise on his face.

"I'm fine, baby girl. You need to go home," Mark said firmly as he reached through the bars to caress her cheek.

"Good luck with that," Steve muttered, his arms crossed over his chest.

Mark tossed a glare in his direction.

"She needs to be locked in the damn house."

"Daddy, I need to be here with you. I'm fine," she insisted.

Not a moment later, Greg entered the room, being led toward his own cell.

"Hey, Em. I don't know why your Dad attacked me. Something's wrong with him. He might be in that cell for a while," Greg stated, false sincerity dripping from his words.

"You son of a bitch, stay away from my daughter!" Mark shouted as he gripped the bars in a vice grip.

Steve stepped in front of her to protect her from his gaze.

"Em, he's insane. They both are!" Greg shouted. "I don't know what's going on."

Emily clung to the back of Steve's shirt, the sound of Greg's voice terrifying her, but she knew what she had to do. There was no way they would keep Greg for long, so she had only one option.

She stepped out from behind Steve and looked to the detective who was holding Greg's arm.

"Detective Michaels...I want to report a rape," Emily blurted out.

Greg's eyes widened at her words for a brief moment before he caught himself. He replaced it with a look of concern.

"Who was raped?" Detective Michaels asked, holding on to some hope that she would not say herself.

"I was," she replied with a shaky voice as she stared into his eyes, refusing to look anywhere in Greg's direction.

"Who would do such a sick thing?" Greg asked, his act making Emily nauseous.

"Do you know who raped you?" Detective Michaels asked with a sickened look on his face. He had known Emily since she was a little girl. To find out like this that she had been raped made his stomach heave.

Emily opened her mouth to respond, but then saw a dark shadow overtake Greg's eyes. She knew he could attack her with a simple movement if she named him as her rapist, but she had no other choice. If she refused to file a police report, then she was refusing to enable her own safety. No matter how terrified she was of Greg, she had to be strong and take her future into her own hands.

"Yes…I do," she stated as she lifted her chin with a new level of confidence. "It was Greg Riley."

Greg's eyes widened at her words. Emily had just fingered him in front of a police officer. His head started spinning as a rage he'd never known in his life boiled up in his veins and seeped from every pore.

"Damn it, Emily!" Greg roared as he lunged at her, grabbing her face in his hands. "Why are you doing this to us! Why? You know you wanted me! Don't deny what we have!"

Emily cried out at his rough handling and struggled only momentarily before Steve pried him off of her. She immediately clung to him as Detective Michaels struggled to pull Greg down the hall back to his cell.

"Are you okay?" Steve asked urgently as Mark shouted words to the same effect.

"I'm fine…I'm fine," she insisted as she backed away. She moved over to her father's cell and reached through the bars for his embrace.

"I'm sorry, baby girl. If I can help it, he'll never touch you again," Mark growled as he held her tightly.

"I love you…I had to tell them. I need them to know what happened, and I need to know that he's in prison."

"Mark, you're free to go," Detective Michaels stated as he approached the cell with his keys. "I'll take her statement, and we'll hold him as long as we can, but if we don't have any hard evidence, then our hold on him expires tonight. The fight was on both of your parts so, it's all we can do right now."

Mark held his temper in place. He knew Michaels was doing everything he could. He didn't deserve his wrath.

"You have to keep him in there until we're out of here… just do that for me?" Mark requested.

"You got it," Michaels stated. "Emily, are you ready to give me your statement? I'm gonna need to know everything. It's gonna be hard to talk about, so I wanna make sure you're ready."

Emily took a deep breath, her heart pounding faster as the images of that day began swirling around in her mind. She shook her head, desperately trying to control her emotions.

"I'm ready, I can do it," she stated as Mark walked out from his cell.

"Are you sure you want to do this?" Mark asked, concern spilling from his eyes. He wanted nothing more than for Greg to rot in jail, but his daughter's mental state and health was his first priority.

"I can do this, Daddy. I need him to pay for what he did to me. I can't just sit back and let him enjoy life after what he did. He needs to suffer the way he's made me suffer," she stated as tears welled in her eyes.

"Okay, let's get this over with," Mark said as he draped his arm over her shoulders and led her toward an interrogation room with Detective Michaels not far behind.

"Sorry about the room. They don't make things very pleasant or comfortable in a room like this," Michaels apologized.

"Don't worry about it. We'll just get this over with as fast as we can," Emily replied.

Detective Michaels sat down at the table with Mark and Emily for over two and a half hours as Emily wove her horrific tale of what Greg had done to her.

Emily stopped periodically to gather her courage before she gave herself the chance to back out, but she trailed on as confidently as possible. "I don't feel so good..." Emily stated once she finished. "I wanna go home."

"We'll go right now. Let me finish up with Detective Michaels and then we'll be ready to go," Mark stated as he stood from his seat. "Steve! Stay in here with her. I ain't takin any chances." He didn't budge from the doorway until Steve was seated right beside her.

"Are you okay?" Steve asked as he draped his arm over her shoulders.

She immediately leaned her head against him and let out a heavy sigh.

"I guess. It's my fault though. I'd seen the signs that something wasn't right, but I kept thinking that he couldn't do anything to hurt me. He'd been touching me a lot. He was always looking at me. He'd pull me out of class just to talk to me. When he asked for a kiss, I should've stuck to my word and said no. But he wasn't going to let me go until I did…so I did. What was I supposed to do?" she asked with desperation.

"You didn't do anything wrong. Never think that you did. He's the one with problems. That bastard is gonna rot in prison for what he did. As long as your father and I are around, he won't get anywhere near you," Steve promised.

Emily nodded, her mind beginning to drift. What if Greg would be acquitted? What if there was no evidence and the DA declined to prosecute? After all, why would they try a case they had no chance of winning? What if Greg got a hold of her in the meantime? She shook her head again, needing a physical movement to shake her thoughts.

"I wanna go home."

13

THE CLOCK STRUCK seven in the evening when Greg walked out of the police station a free man. He knew they wouldn't be able to hold him because they had no evidence to hold him on. He didn't know how to feel about what Emily had done to him. He was going to love her and want her forever, but at that point he felt like bruising that soft flesh that tasted so sweet. She made his body tingle with electrifying sensations, but she could also boil his blood like no other. There were times he wanted to kiss her senseless, but at that moment, he wanted to grab her by her flaming red hair and beat some sense into her.

"She'll change her mind…and if not, I'll have to have a little chat with her."

He flipped open his cell phone to call a cab since his ride there had been a police car, but once it arrived, he planned on settling this entire situation.

⬥

"I don't want you leaving this house without me or Steve with you. If Steve's not here, then call him and he'll get here, no matter what time it is," Mark stated as he moved around the kitchen, locking all the windows and the doors leading to the backyard.

"Okay…I promise," she stated as she rolled her grapes around on her plate. She had been hungry for a snack when they got home but not anymore.

"Daddy, when will this be all over?" she asked as she stared down at her plate.

Mark sighed heavily as he took the seat beside her.

"Hopefully sooner rather than later, Em. We have to give them time to catch him and put him where he belongs," Mark replied as he gently pulled her into his arms.

"They won't get him…there's no evidence. They took pictures of my bruises, but there's no evidence of him on me to prove he touched me. I took a bath when I got home after it happened, and I waited so long before telling anyone. I'm not stupid, I watch Lifetime movies all the time. I don't want to kid myself into thinking that they'll get him," Emily stated as her confidence began to falter.

"Don't think that way. Science works miracles these days. Something will point a finger at him. He'll rot in prison, baby girl. Just believe that, stay strong as long as you can," Mark encouraged.

Seeing his daughter in such pain was slicing away at his heart as the moments passed. Just like his daughter had said, she wasn't stupid. *Law and Order SVU* was her favorite show to watch on television. She knew how wonderful but how horribly flawed the justice system was. Without strong enough evidence, it was her word against the school's favorite trainer and everyone's friend, Greg Riley. All he could do was pray that everything was going to be all right and work its way toward a positive outcome. He was afraid that she may never feel safe as long as Greg was roaming free. It killed him to know that if the case made it into court, or even past the grand jury, Greg could be acquitted. He could walk away unscathed, free to rape whoever he wants or worse, he could come after Emily again. The way he spoke earlier at the police station had him thinking. He said that he loved her. Was he that delusional? He'd surely make for a good psychological defense and that's what Mark was afraid of. He didn't give a damn what was wrong with him. He admitted to Mark that he raped Emily and he was proud of it, even gloated about how he enjoyed every moment of it. He was going to pay no matter the cost.

"Let's get you into bed, sweetheart. Monday morning at school, you're gonna have Steve following you to every class. I don't want you alone until they either fire him or arrest him," Mark informed her before finishing the grapes she hadn't eaten.

"Poor Steve, he's stuck babysitting me. But I'll feel safer having him around. I wish you could be with me," she replied as they headed up the stairs toward her bedroom.

"I know, I wish I could be there too. I don't have anyone that can be at the shop alone yet. We've been busy lately, so if people drop off their bikes, only one repair guy will be there," Mark explained as he locked all the windows in her room.

"I know…it's okay. I'll be fine," she stated as she sat down on her bed. Her mind began drifting to Aden. She hadn't spoken to him in forever it seemed. She loved him with all her heart, but she feared that she wouldn't be able to let him touch her. Would he leave her if he knew what Greg had done? Would he be disgusted? She wouldn't be able to handle it if he walked out of her life after everything that happened to her.

"What are you thinking about, little one?" Mark asked as he sat down beside her. He could tell that she was thinking and her thoughts brought a sad look in her eyes. "Is it about Greg?"

"No…I'm thinking about Aden. I'm afraid to talk to him after what happened. What if he won't come near me? What if he's repulsed by me after I tell him?" she asked with such desperation.

"He loves you, baby girl. I know that boy pretty well. He's gonna wanna kill Greg the minute you tell him. He'll hold you and comfort you. He ain't gonna walk away," Mark stated confidently as he stroked her hair.

Emily pulled away from his touch as images of Greg playing with her hair flooded her mind forcefully. She whimpered as tears welled in her eyes.

"I'm sorry, Daddy. I don't mean to keep pulling away," she apologized as Mark pulled her into his arms.

"It's okay, Em. That's gonna happen for a while. God, I should've killed the bastard when I had the chance. I should've protected you...you didn't deserve this. I'm so sorry, angel," Mark stated, feeling as though he should be apologizing, not her.

"You couldn't have stopped him, Dad. He was your best friend, and you never knew what kind of monster he was. How would anyone else know?" she asked, easing a bit of Mark's guilt but not by much.

"I know...let's get you to bed. I'll be right down the hall if you need me. The house is locked up tight, so sleep sweet, darlin'. Nothing is getting in this house," Mark assured as he helped her get under the covers and tuck her in. "I know you're almost eighteen, but I still love tuckin' you in at night. Hope you don't mind obliging your old man."

Emily smiled for what seemed like the first time in a long time. It was genuine, sweet, and pure.

"I don't mind. I love you, Daddy," she replied as Mark leaned down to place a soft kiss on her forehead.

"I love you too, darlin'," he replied before flicking out the light then closing her door after his departure.

Emily sighed heavily as she stared at the ceiling above her bed. She wasn't going to be able to sleep for quite a while. She could feel it in her body and restless mind. All she wanted to do was talk to Aden. She reached over to her bedside table for her cell phone and took a deep breath before dialing his number. She practically held her breath as she listened to it ring. It was three o'clock in the morning so maybe he wouldn't answer.

"Hello? Baby? I've been calling you and texting you, and I haven't gotten anything back. So what's going on?"

Emily opened her mouth to speak but all of her words refused to come out.

"Hello?" he repeated.

Emily tried once more to speak, begging her mouth and voice box to function.

"Hi," she whispered finally, her body trembling over the upcoming conversation.

"There you are! Em, please tell me what's going on. Did I do something wrong? Is your ignoring me a hint that you don't want to be with me?" Aden asked desperately, his heart being torn from his chest as he waited for her response.

"I…I love you, Aden. I will always love you," she replied as she sniffled back her tears.

"God, you have no idea how relieved I am to hear you say that. Why are you crying, baby? Why have you been so distant? And what the hell is going on with dance and your grades?" Aden asked, all of his questions he'd held inside spilling out at once.

"I…I want to tell you, but I'm afraid…I don't want you to hate me…I don't want you to leave me," she cried softly, clutching her cell phone tightly in her hand.

"Emily, I love you more than anything in this world. There is nothing you could say to me that would make me leave you or not love you anymore," Aden promised, his concern growing.

She wanted Aden to know everything about her and she wanted to be honest with him, but she was terrified. He could look at her with disgust and be mortified by what happened. But maybe he wouldn't.

"I need to talk to you…I can't say it over the phone. I…I just can't, Aden," she stated, her heart racing.

"Are you home?" Aden asked. He was already throwing on a T-shirt and his shoes by the time she confirmed her whereabouts. "I'll be there soon."

Emily carefully slipped her phone closed and placed it beside her on her bed sheets. He was on his way over. Maybe she should have told him over the phone so she wouldn't have to see his face when she told him the truth. She could imagine the horror on his face when he realized she was no longer a virgin and the person that had taken it from her was Greg Riley. And even worse, that it had been taken by force.

"I have to be strong…I have to tell him…"

———••◉••———

Mark practically leapt from his chair at the sound of a knock at the front door. If he opened that door and Greg was standing there, he was going to blow his brains all over the front porch. He clutched his shotgun as he approached the door, begging God for it to be Greg. He could easily claim self-defense. Greg would also be trespassing on private property. He took a deep breath before pulling the door open.

Aden jumped back at the force of the door swinging open, scaring the daylights out of him.

"Whoa, calm down there! What's gotten you so upset?" Aden asked as he watched relief flood Mark's gaze.

"I thought you were somebody else," he replied before motioning him to enter.

Aden took two steps through the doorway before he caught a glimpse of what Mark was holding.

"A shotgun? What the hell is going on? Am I missing something? Em ignores me for weeks, finally calls me and is crying on the phone, and when I show up, you have a shotgun at the door. Come on, Mark. What the hell is going on?" Aden demanded, his emotions being pulled in ten different directions. What had happened? Who did Mark think was at the door and why would that person's supposed arrival warrant a shotgun greeting?

Mark sighed heavily as he pushed the door closed, making sure to lock it securely.

"Aden…Emily needs to be the one to talk to you…not me. Just be ready, be open…and don't let her go," Mark stated before heading into the living room to place his twelve gauge by the coffee table.

Something wasn't right. Aden was beginning to feel truly frightened. Mark's words seemed sad yet angered, pained yet confused. Aden feared that he was going to be told something he did not want to hear.

Emily's stomach dropped to her feet when she heard footsteps outside her bedroom door. Aden was here. It was time to tell him everything no matter how scared she was or how much the memories pained her when she spoke about them. The thought of Greg touching her made her physically ill. The memories of what happened haunted her every night when she tried to sleep. Greg was all she could think about. Every corner she turned, she feared he would be standing there waiting to grab her. Every time the sun set and the lights went out, she thought she saw him lurking in every shadow-darkened corner. She wanted to feel safe, but she was afraid that she wouldn't have that luxury for a long time.

"Em?"

She jumped at the sound of Aden's voice on the other side of the door. This was it.

"Come in," she stated softly, hoping maybe he didn't hear her so she would not have to follow through with the conversation.

Aden entered slowly, his eyes falling on her immediately. He wanted to run to her and hold her, but she looked terrified sitting on her queen-sized bed, half her body under the covers. She looked so small, frail, and most of all, scared. There was a look in her eyes that he had never seen before. There was something missing. Her smile was gone, her skin was paler than usual, and there was something else that he couldn't put his finger on. As he studied her for a moment longer, it dawned on him what was missing. The light in her eyes that always made them dance and sparkle like the sun reflecting off the ocean waves was gone.

"Emily…sweetheart, I missed you," he stated with a genuine smile.

Her heart heavily fell from her chest when she saw him. He looked absolutely beautiful. All he was wearing were a pair of jeans and a blue T-shirt, his long hair pulled back in a ponytail. He was the epitome of perfection. How did she deserve him? He deserved much better than her.

"I missed you too," she whispered as she locked her gaze with his. She wanted him to hold her, love her, but she knew she wouldn't be able to handle it.

Aden moved over to sit at the foot of the bed. He couldn't see any signs of injury at first until his eyes adjusted to the light. All he could see were deep bruises marring her upper arms and her throat. Were his eyes playing tricks on him? He reached out to cup her cheek in his hand instinctively.

Emily immediately pulled away from his touch as if it had burned her. That was Greg's hand reaching out for her. He was trying to feel her and touch her. She cried softly as she shook her head violently, demanding the images to go away.

"I'm sorry...I...I'm sorry," she apologized repeatedly. She didn't know what else to say.

"Shhh, it's okay. Don't apologize. Tell me what's going on, Emily. I can't help you because I don't know what's wrong. I don't have a clue what's going on. Why are you afraid of me? Why can't I touch you?" Aden begged as he scooted a bit closer to her.

Emily took slow deep breaths, willing her tears to stop. She had to tell him otherwise he was going to keep thinking that he had done something wrong.

"Aden...something horrible...happened," she whispered as she stared down into her lap.

"Tell me, sweetheart! Tell me what happened," Aden begged, his desperation evident on his face.

"I'm afraid...that you won't love me anymore...or that...you won't believe me," she stated as sobs threatened to choke her.

"I'm going to love you forever, Emily...I promise. And of course I'll believe you. Never think that I would doubt you," Aden insisted as he slid a bit closer to her, needing to feel her body near his.

"It...it's about Greg...Mr. Riley," she spat as her chest heaved up and down with her sporadic breathing.

"What about him?" Aden asked with confusion.

"He raped me!" Her sobs completely overtook her, threatening to drown her.

Aden's eyes widened at her words as his entire body began to shake. His stomach flipped, making him nauseous as his head began to spin. Greg Riley had raped Emily. He forced himself on her and forced her to have sex. He thought he couldn't breathe. He was almost positive that his entire body stopped functioning.

"Oh my God," Aden mumbled. "Oh God." He couldn't restrain himself. He reached out for her and felt tears choking him when she fell into his arms in complete hysterics.

"I should've never let you go work out with him alone... never! This is all my fault. He's gonna die, Emily. As God as my witness, he'll pay for this, I promise. It's okay, baby. Everything is gonna be okay. I have you now, safe in my arms. You're gonna be okay..." Aden cooed as he held her tightly, making sure not to harm her. He was cautious of her bruised arms and neck, not wanting to further traumatize her or add to her pain.

"I love you, and I'm going to be here every step of the way," Aden promised as he squeezed her.

Emily felt as though her heart had finally exploded. Aden still loved her, and he wasn't mad at her for what happened. She couldn't help but smile through the tears as she clutched onto him with all her strength. She didn't know how she was going to heal after what Greg had done but she vowed at that very moment that she would try with all her heart, willing her mind to forget.

Mark sighed heavily as he listened to Emily cry from outside her bedroom door. He trusted Aden, but he was still going to refuse to leave his daughter's side for more than a few moments. His daughter's safety depended on his diligence and his awareness of the world around them. One false move and Emily could be hurt, kidnapped, or worse. He shuddered at the thought of Greg getting his hands on her. The way he went after her in the police station, grabbing at her, trying to kiss her, made his stomach heave, his blood boil. How was he going to keep her safe?

Emily took slow deep breaths, trying to calm herself after the turmoil of emotions began to cease. She was awestruck that she had just told Aden the truth of what happened, and he was still beside her, still holding her tight as if he never planned on letting her go.

Aden lifted Emily's face, cradling her chin between his pointer finger and thumb.

"I love you, Emily. I never plan on letting you go. I'm always gonna be here for you," he stated with such love and sincerity in his eyes, causing her tears to start anew.

She let her eyes fall shut, taking in the feeling of him being near. She could feel his hand on her face, his thigh resting against hers, his other arm wrapped around her body to keep her safe. Then suddenly his lips were on hers, soft and sweet. But no, is that Aden? No, it's Greg! He's kissing her again. He's holding her and she has a chance to escape.

"No!" she screamed out suddenly as she pushed and pulled away from him. Her eyes flew open and all she could see was Greg. He was smiling at her as he reached for her, whispering sickly to her that everything was going to be all right.

"Em, calm down it's me!" Aden called out, trying to make his voice audible over her screams.

Mark burst into the room at the sound of her cries and shrieks, only to find Aden deflecting her flailing arms as she scrambled away from him. She tossed herself to the floor and scurried away as fast as possible, only to run into Mark.

"Emily, calm down girl! It's only Aden! Greg's not here, he's not here!" Mark cooed to her as he knelt down to pull her against him.

"I'm so sorry, she was calm, and I just tried to give her a kiss. That's all, I swear!" Aden defended as he stared down at his cowering girlfriend.

"Sometimes she's even terrified if I touch her and I'm her father. It's not your fault. She might be this way for a while. I just wouldn't try much physical contact unless she initiates it. That's what the nurse at the hospital said, no matter how painful," Mark suggested as he held his quivering daughter.

Emily slowly chanced a glance behind her and felt sorrow erupt within her very soul when all she saw was Aden and the pain in his eyes. All Aden had done was try to kiss her, and what did she do? She had pushed away the love of her life. She had screamed as if he was trying to hurt her. But she swore on her life that she had seen Greg. She'd felt the hatred and obsession wafting around her, strangling every breath from her body.

"Aden," she whispered as her reality clarified, "I'm so sorry...I...I'm sorry."

Aden immediately dropped to the floor beside her and pulled her close as she reached for him. How was he going to help her heal? How could he even get close after what Greg Riley had done?

"Everything is gonna be okay..." he whispered to her, desperate to believe his own words. "Everything is gonna be okay."

Emily sat in the front seat of her father's truck on Monday morning staring at the school.

"I'm afraid," Emily whispered as she turned to face him. "What if something happens?"

"Steve will be with you every moment of the day. Don't you worry. He won't be getting anywhere near you," Mark reassured her as he pulled her tight against his side.

"Ready to go?" Steve asked as he stepped up to the window.

Emily smiled her welcome in his direction. Steve meant so much to her. He was like the uncle she never had. His head was freshly shaved and his goatee perfectly trimmed. She silently thanked God that her life was being protected by men such as her father and Steve. They could protect her with their eyes closed and their hands tied behind their backs. But Greg was no small opponent. He was just as large as her father, which terrified her, making her entire body quiver with dread. But she didn't want to miss school and risk destroying her grades even more than they already had been.

"Yeah, I'm ready," she replied. She hugged and kissed her father good-bye before climbing down from the truck with Steve's help.

"Stay close to me. Wherever you go, I go," Steve stated firmly as he led her toward main building.

"Well, well, the slut has finally arrived!"

Emily turned toward Sally's voice and glared heatedly at her as she and her friends made their way by.

"I knew you couldn't keep your hands off Mr. Riley for long. Geez, did you really need an A that bad in gym? Girls, we better get out of her way so we don't make Emily late for her quickie with Mr. Riley in the gym."

Emily stared with utter confusion as the girls laughed and made their way into the building.

"What the hell? What are they talking about?" she asked with alarm as she glanced between Steve and the building the girls had entered. "And how the hell do they know anything about me and Mr. Riley?"

"Hey, Em!" Jetta called to her from the front doors of the main building.

"Hey," she greeted as she made her way up the cement steps, her mind attempting to absorb the situation around her.

"Listen, I need to tell you what's going on. There's been some nasty rumors floating around this morning, and we need to put a stop to it. People are saying that..." Jetta looked around cautiously before whispering, "that Mr. Riley and you had sex. I don't know who is talking shit, but we need to figure it out."

Emily simply stared at her with complete horror. The downfall of being from a small town with a large high school was that it didn't take long for people to start talking. Not only did she have to suffer from her own damaged mind after what happened, but now she was going to have to deal with the looks, stares, and whispers from everyone and also the harassment from those who liked Mr. Riley.

"I…I don't know if I can do this," she whispered to Steve who stood behind her for support.

"If you wanna leave, we'll leave now," Steve offered.

She took a deep breath to steady herself before shaking her head in refusal.

"I was raped by him…that's the truth," she blurted to Jetta. Her friend almost passed out or threw up by the look of her reaction.

"Wh…what? Oh God," she exclaimed before pulling her into a tight embrace.

"I'm so sorry! Oh my God, this can't be happening," she whispered with disbelief.

Emily held back her tears as best as she could as she wished it truly was all a nightmare.

———❖———

Two classes down and no sign of Greg. So far she had been looked at with sympathy, disgust, shock, and disbelief from the many students who walked by her. Her friends had stuck by her while everyone else simply clogged up the rumor mill with more lies.

"Hey, Emily! How come Mr. Riley is getting all the action? First, Aden, now Riley? Who's next?"

Emily squeezed her eyes closed, trying desperately to ignore his words. Tyler Jones was on the football team with

Aden. She knew that this was just the beginning. When the rumors cleared up and everyone knew she had not had sex with him, that he had raped her, the harassment would get worse. Without Greg's training, the football team would never keep in shape. They would fight to keep him, but she would fight to be rid of him.

———◆◆◆———

Greg sat in his office, his mind racing with so many ideas and plans. He wasn't quite sure which one to follow through with. All he knew was that he needed to touch her. He was still pissed off about her filing charges, but no one had mentioned anything to him at the school, so regardless of her efforts, they were fruitless. He had meant what he said. Anytime he wanted her, he could have her, and no one would stop him. He wanted to head over to Emily's next class which was English, if he wasn't mistaken, and pull her out to have some time together.

"Greg?"

He looked up to find the principal of the school, Jack Mathers entering his office.

"Hey, Jack, what's going on?" he asked as he stood. "Come to congratulate me for the football team's victory last week? I deserve it more than their coach, for God's sake."

Jack stood a bit uncomfortably, staring at his long-time friend.

"Not exactly, Greg. We have to talk about something," he stated, his hands folded in front of him.

Greg quirked an eyebrow, eyeing him strangely. Something seemed off, and he was not sure what it was.

"About what?" Greg inquired as he leaned against his desk, arms folded over his chest.

"There's been some allegations brought against you by Emily Connors," Jack stated, wording his sentence carefully.

"Oh, I know. Poor girl was attacked but not by me. She was probably so terrified, she wanted the safest target. I hope she's doing all right. We have the best cops in the county, so I don't doubt they'll find the guy who did it."

Greg was talented at playing the innocent character. He could make anyone believe anything, but it didn't seem as though he was having much luck convincing Mathers.

"Greg, look. The committee had a meeting. In light of the ongoing investigation, we have to place you on suspension. We have no other choice," Jack stated, his words firm and final.

Greg's eyes widened.

"You're suspending me because of some screwed-up teenager that lies with every breath she takes?" he shouted as he moved around to the back of his desk.

"Don't say anything else, Greg. I don't want to have to repeat anything in court," Jack warned. "We have to ask you to get your stuff together and leave. We'll know if you can come back when this is all over and done with."

Greg watched with building rage as Jack walked out the door. He had thought Emily would drop the charges because of her fears, but apparently he had misjudged her. He had to talk to her. He had to shake some sense into her.

"Oh, I'll leave, but not before I talk to her," Greg muttered as he stormed out of his office. If Emily wanted to piss him off, then she would have to suffer the consequences. He made his way through the hallways, searching for the right classroom. His annoyance level escalated when the bell rang, releasing the students from their current classes. The last thing he wanted was for students or faculty to see him around her. The rumor grapevine in the school was on turbo, so he didn't doubt that everyone had heard Emily's lies. She needed to be spoken to then maybe she would see the error of her ways. He was about to round the next corner when the sound of Emily's voice halted his movements.

"I'll be right back. I have to use the bathroom," she stated to Steve, who was glaring a hole through a teenage boy who walked by laughing.

"I'll go with you," he replied insistently.

"No, come on, Steve. Everything has been fine. There's people everywhere. I just have to pee and then I have math class," Emily stated with growing weariness. She was sick and tired of having to worry and look over her shoulder. Greg wasn't stupid enough to come after her with Steve there.

"Fine," he stated reluctantly. "Make it quick."

She walked down the hall then turned down another hall to the left.

Greg watched her as she walked by him. He remained hidden in the doorway of a darkened classroom, waiting until the bathroom door closed behind her.

Emily sighed as she tossed her backpack beside the sink. She quickly used the bathroom before moving to the sink to wash her hands. She savored the warm water running over her skin and the smell of the floral hand soap. This was the smallest luxury she knew she would be enjoying for a while. Her father never left her side and neither did Steve. She was extremely grateful to have them by her side, but she couldn't help but miss her freedom. If there was a trial, it was going to be hell, and with Greg's freedom and life at risk, she knew he would try and shut her up even if it was just to save his job.

"So no peace for you for a long time," she told her reflection as she dried her hands with a paper towel. She jumped suddenly when the bathroom door was shoved open then quickly closed. Her eyes stared into his through the mirror in complete shock. His were flaming with such anger and desire that she felt immediately lightheaded. Emily opened her mouth to scream, but Greg was quick on the draw. He clamped his hand over her mouth and pulled her body against him.

"Are you trying to get me fired? I told you to keep your mouth shut about us, but I guess you were so excited that you just had to tell. I'm on suspension now because of your mouth."

The fact that he was whispering made him seem even more menacing. He spun her around to face him, hand still firmly over her mouth.

"You have to learn what happens when you disobey me. I told you *not* to say anything, but you did. You have to deal with the consequences," Greg practically growled.

She whimpered in pure terror as her body shook violently. She should struggle. She should scream. She should try and get away. But her body was frozen. She couldn't move. All she could do was stare into his cold, angry eyes.

Greg pulled her back toward the far end of the bathroom where the floor space opened. He swept her feet out from under her once again and Emily knew what he was intending.

"No!" she screamed from under his hand. Her words were only muffled cries as he shoved her down onto the floor then began pulling at her clothes. She bucked her hips, shoved him away, tried kicking at him, whatever she could do to make him stop. She could see Greg's anger rising by the moment, but she refused to lay there and be raped again. She paused momentarily when she saw him struggling with the button on her jeans. His eyes left hers to look down in hopes of achieving his goal, and Emily took advantage of his distraction. Emily balled her hands into fists and came out swinging, striking Greg wherever she could. All she knew was that she had to get away.

"Damn it!" Greg shouted as he tried to avoid her little fists. He quickly removed his hand from her mouth and swatted her hands out of the way roughly. Just as Emily opened her mouth to scream, Greg's hand swung without a second thought, slapping her across the face with a bit more strength than necessary.

Emily cried out, her head spinning from the force of the blow. She weakly continued to struggle as tears streamed down her face. There was nothing she could do to stop him. He pulled at her shirt, tearing it down the middle before yanking her jeans down her legs, but she was too dazed and confused to put up a fight.

"This is your own fault, girl. This is all on you," he stated angrily, his chest rising and falling as he tried to catch his breath from the struggle. Greg reached between her legs to feel her warmth against his fingers, moaning at the incredible sensation.

"Better be ready for me, girl or this is gonna hurt," he warned as he unbuckled his belt then worked on his button and zipper. Greg's head shot up when the bathroom door opened and a young girl stepped inside. In a single moment he knew he was caught. Her eyes were wide as she stared at both Greg and Emily. There was no way to deny what that girl was witnessing. He had no other choice but to get out of that school as fast as possible. Greg pulled Emily up by her hair and clutched her against him as he glared a hole through the girl.

"Get out..." he snarled, causing the girl to take off out the door.

"I'll be back. We'll finish at your house, in your own bed. This is not over, Emily. There won't be a trial. You are mine! And soon I'll have you all to myself and you won't be going anywhere. No one can keep you from me. I love you," Greg growled before forcing her to kiss him, forcing her mouth open for his enjoyment before he shoved her back to the ground.

Emily cried out as her head smacked against the tile floor. Her eyes drifted shut as she heard the bathroom door open then close with Greg's exit.

———◆◆◆———

"Someone help!" Elizabeth shouted as she ran through the halls, trying to find someone. She didn't know Emily that well, but she couldn't let Mr. Riley do what he was doing. She rounded the corner and saw the tall guy with the shaved head that had been following Emily all day. He was in a deep conversation with the principal.

"Emily needs help! She's in the bathroom and Mr. Riley, the gym teacher, is hurting her!" Elizabeth shouted as she made it to them.

Steve heard the young girl's shouts and immediately took off toward the restroom. He kicked open the door and felt as though the air was knocked out of his lungs. Emily lay on the floor unconscious with her shirt torn open, jeans pulled down, a dark bruise marring her face.

"Call an ambulance!" Steve shouted as he hurried to her side. He unbuttoned his over-shirt and laid it over her body to keep her covered.

"Everything's gonna be okay, Em. You're gonna be all right," he whispered as he brushed her hair from her face. The bruise looked even more horrifying up close. This was his fault. This was on him. Mark was going to kill him when he found out he let her leave his side.

"I'm so sorry, Emily."

14

"WHAT THE HELL happened?" Mark exploded as he burst into the emergency room entrance.

Steve dodged out of the way as Mark made a beeline for the front desk.

"I want to see my daughter, Emily Connors, right now," Mark demanded, scaring the receptionist half to death. She opened the doors for him to enter then pointed him toward her room with Steve hot on his heels.

"God…" Mark stated on an exhale when he entered her room. Her face was marred with a large bruise on her left cheek and eye. She was sitting up in her hospital bed, staring toward the window. He didn't know what to do. He had no idea how to keep Greg from hurting her. Being by her side at every moment was his best plan, and it still failed to keep her safe. There was only one way they could be sure Greg couldn't go near her, but that would land him in prison. He moved closer to her, not wanting to frighten her. She finally turned when she felt his presence.

"Please don't be mad at Steve, Daddy! I wanted to go by myself. I thought it would be okay. I'm sorry," she cried as she hung her head in shame.

Mark sat on the bed beside her and pulled her into his arms as she wept. He couldn't take her pain anymore. It had to stop. Her childhood, her high school life had been destroyed by one man's obsession. How was he supposed to mend the pieces? How could he put them back together? A mental image of Emily laying on the floor of the school bathroom entered his mind the way Steve had described it. His stomach churned with the possibility of what had happened or what could have happened.

"Emily…did he rape you again in that bathroom?" Mark asked slowly, not wanting to upset her even more than she already was.

She took a deep breath to respond, but only a whimper came out. She tried once more to form her words, to regain her control.

"No…he touched me…he forced me to kiss him…I remember him pulling my jeans down…but no, I don't think he did. He pushed me, and I hit my head on the floor so a lot of it is blurry," she recounted quietly.

"You have a mild concussion, sweetheart. You're gonna be all right. And that man is going to die," Steve stated softly from behind Mark, his anger and intent evident.

"You're gonna have to stay in the house, Em. You won't be able to leave unless I'm with you or Steve is. For the majority of you're time, I want you inside. Greg can't get in that house, so you're guaranteed to be safe," Mark stated regretfully as he saw the sadness pouring from her eyes. The poor girl had been raped by someone she'd trusted, someone Mark had trusted, and now she was going to be a prisoner in her own home.

"I guess I have no choice," she whispered as she gingerly wiped away her tears. She was convinced that as long as he was free, she would never be safe. Only when he was behind bars would she be able to walk, run, or just breathe without fear of running into him. Emily jumped suddenly when her father's cell phone began ringing in his pocket.

"Sorry, baby girl. Hello?"

"Mark, it's Jack Mathers from Kinley High. How are you?" Jack greeted carefully. He could hear the anger and agitation in his voice just from that single word.

Mark stood from the bed and kissed Emily's forehead softly before heading into the hallway to take the call.

"He'll be right back," Steve said reassuringly as he adopted Mark's seat.

"What's going on?" Mark asked gravely. He didn't like the uneasiness he heard in the man's voice.

"Well, I have some news. The school has been due for a new security system for a long time. We recently had a few of them updated like the cafeteria and certain offices," he began explaining.

"What does your equipment have to do with me?" Mark asked with annoyance. Emily needed him by her side. He did not have time for casual phone conversation.

"Well, the new cameras were supposed to be installed in the gyms and weight room next month, but I was just informed that they were installed almost two months ago to run for a month or so as a trial to make sure they worked properly..." Jack stated.

Mark's heart began a hasty beat as the man spoke.

"What are you saying?" Mark asked, praying he heard what he needed to hear.

"Ummm...well," he began nervously. "We have Greg Riley raping your daughter on video tape."

Mark practically dropped his phone at the man's words. There might not have been any evidence left on Emily's body besides her bruises, but the bastard had been caught by a camera no one knew was there.

"I'll be down to pick it up. I have to get it to the detective handling her case as soon as possible," Mark stated with a slight amount of joy. The man was going to rot in prison. The thought overjoyed him, but the downfall was that Emily would be forced to watch that tape in court to prove to the jury that Greg Riley was a monster. The thought of seeing the tape with his own eyes made his stomach churn. He thanked Mathers before hanging up the phone and heading back into her room.

"I have some good news, darlin'. There was a security camera in the weight room that no one knew about. It was being tested. It was recording when Greg hurt you," Mark stated as he held both her hands in his. "That bastard is gonna go to jail, and he'll never be able to touch you again."

Emily felt a slight amount of relief. They now had the evidence they needed, but what made them think Greg would stick around and wait to be arrested? He was sick in the head, but he certainly wasn't stupid. She smiled up at her father, the sadness evident in her eyes.

"I hope so, Dad. I really hope so."

—◆◉◆—

Emily sighed heavily as she reclined in the bathtub. She was home after an extra day in the hospital. Doctors insisted on keeping her for one more night to be certain her concussion was not going to be a problem. Emily had pleaded for her father to take her home, but she knew she had to stay. She shook away the negative thoughts, taking comfort in the knowledge that she was home now. Safe and sound in her own room, in her own bathroom, in her own tub. She picked up her phone when it signaled that she had a text message, and she smiled when she read Aden's loving words. She replied to him, telling him how much she loved him and how she couldn't wait to be in his arms without being afraid of him. She set her phone aside so she could dunk her head under the water, not wanting to ruin her phone. If all went well and Greg was locked up soon, she could put all of this misery behind her and work on healing. Another ding from her phone let her know that she had another message, but this time it was from an unknown number.

"Is the water warm?" the message read.

"What?" she mumbled as she read it again. "Probably wrong number." She closed the message and set her phone aside once more. Her hands were getting wrinkled, so she decided it was time to get out. She pulled the plug to let the water drain away before stepping out to grab her towel hanging on the back of the door. Her phone made the indication ding once more as she rubbed her hair dry then wrapped the towel around her body.

"Now what, unknown number," she muttered as she opened the newest message.

"You are the epitome of beauty."

Emily couldn't help but smile after reading it. It had to be Aden texting her from a blocked number, sending her sweet words like a secret admirer.

"He's so cute," she giggled to herself as she flicked off the bathroom light before heading into her bedroom to dress. She barely made it to the closet before her phone began ringing, the call being from the unknown number.

"Hello, my secret admirer," she answered sweetly, waiting to hear Aden's voice on the other end of the line.

"God, I could eat you up. You look absolutely delicious in that towel. Why don't you drop it a little bit? Maybe show me a little more of what's mine?"

Emily couldn't move as she listened to his words. Her stomach heaved as her body began to tremble. If he knew she was in a towel, then that meant he could see her. She tried to shake off her fear but couldn't quite accomplish such a feat.

"Leave me alone," she whispered as she squeezed the phone tightly in her hand.

"Never...you are mine! Get that through that pretty little head of yours," Greg growled threateningly.

She stepped up to the sliding glass doors but saw nothing besides the field and then the tree line in the close distance.

"If my head is so pretty, why did you give me a concussion?" she asked as she stepped out onto her small balcony.

"Em, I didn't mean to," Greg stated, his voice apologetic.

"Oh, but you meant to slap me? Is that what you're saying?" she replied as she scanned the area, trying to spot where he was hiding.

"I didn't want to, but you wouldn't let me touch you! What was I supposed to do? You pissed me off, baby. I'm sorry," Greg stated as he sat down on a large fallen tree with a heavy sigh.

"You're not sorry. If you were truly sorry, you would prove it...come to my balcony," Emily demanded. She knew that the cops were tossing his place any time now and they obviously wouldn't find him there, so if she could lure him close to the house, then her father would be able to get the job done.

"Why? So your Daddy can blow my head off from the comfort of his own home? I'm not stupid, girl. We'll be together soon enough. So are you gonna drop that towel or what?" he asked as he watched her.

"Go to hell," she stated slowly and clearly. "If you try and come near me, I won't stop my Dad or Steve from shooting you. Hell, I might just do it myself," she stated matter-of-factly.

"Oh really? God, I love your fire! It's so damn sexy. I can't wait for us to make love again. You'll like it…you'll love it…and when I have you all to myself, I will make you enjoy it. You'll cry for more whether you like it or not," Greg stated with a sick chuckle.

"Why, Greg? You could probably have any woman you want that would be with you willingly. Why do you have to torment me?" she begged, needing to know why he chose her.

"Because you're perfect. You're beautiful, smart, funny, kind, sexy, sweet. I get excited when I think about seeing you. I love you, Emily. I'm never going to let you go. I can't… you're everything I've ever wanted," Greg said breathlessly as he watched her leaning against the rail of her balcony. Her damp locks were waving gently in the breeze, her hair matching the color of the changing leaves. Autumn was on its way bringing those crisp evenings and cool day breezes. He wanted to share them with her. He wanted her to realize just how much she meant to him.

Emily hated the words he was speaking. Those were the things that every girl wanted to hear. Those were things Aden always said to her. Those were not words that should be spoken from her rapist.

"I hate you and I never want to see you again. I love Aden and I always will. Leave me alone and never come back," she threatened, wanting this ordeal to be in the past. She heard Greg's laughter which sent chills of dread throughout her body, raising goose bumps on her skin.

"I love you too, sweetheart. We'll be together soon. I have to disappear for a little while, but I promise I'll come back for you. It may be a little while, but I will come back," he stated before his voice deepened to a low growl. "I promise, Emily."

She did a full body shiver as the line went dead. She was given little comfort in the knowledge that he would leave her alone for a little while because she knew he would keep that dreadful promise. He would come for her, and there would be nothing she could do to stop him. She didn't want to try and outsmart him nor did she want to try and best him with any kind of strength. The only protection she had was Steve and Mark. There was no chance the police department would catch him. They were simply never around at the right place at the right time. She just didn't know what to do. Greg was never going to stop until he got a hold of her. And once he did, she was never going to escape. She would never graduate and go to college. She would never know what it would be like to get married and have a family. She would be trapped by Greg for a long time or even worse, forever. She shook her head to rid her mind of those horrendous thoughts. Her body became aware of the sudden chill in the air, the goose bumps multiplying over her exposed flesh. She hurried inside then closed and locked the balcony door, not wanting to take any chances. She needed to feel safe and secure despite her knowledge that a simple door would not stop a man of Greg's size.

"Dad!" she shouted as she moved around her room to gather her clothes. She quickly dried off and dressed as she heard her father's thudding footsteps hurrying up the stairs.

"What's wrong, honey?" he asked as he pushed open her door.

"Greg called me. He has my cell phone number. He's in the woods watching me. He said he's leaving for a while but then he'll be back for me. So tell the cops that he won't be home when they get there," she stated frantically as she finished zipping and buttoning her jeans.

"Son of a bitch," he growled as he pulled all of her curtains closed. "I'll call Michaels and tell him. Are you okay?"

She immediately hurried over to him and wrapped her arms around his waist.

"I'm okay," she confirmed despite the lingering fear that hovered in her heart. "I just want this to stop. He keeps saying he loves me and wants to be with me forever. Why? Why can't he just find someone his own age that will actually wanna be with him?"

Mark squeezed her tighter, held her closer as he stroked her hair.

"I don't know, Em. He's sick and I don't care if he ain't right in the head, I'll kill him if he comes close to ya," he promised. "I just want you to be safe. I feel like no matter what I do, I keep failing at that."

"No, Daddy. He just…he keeps tricking us, and I keep screwing up. I was attacked in that bathroom because I wanted to go without Steve. It wouldn't have happened if I just let Steve go with me. He would have never come near me," she stated as she snuggled her face against his chest, loving the comfort she felt. Her father had been her rock her entire life, her one consistent stability. She thanked God that she had him now when she needed him most. "Please don't let me go. I don't want him to take me away."

Mark squeezed his eyes shut, willing the tears away as he felt her body shaking from her sobs. The bastard had torn his daughter apart. Instead of thinking about what dress she was wearing to the prom, she was cowering in her room, wondering when her rapist was going to attack her again. There was a simple solution that would guarantee that Greg would never touch here again, but he couldn't bear the thought of being away from her. Greg Riley should die for what he did to Emily, but he wouldn't die by Mark's hands, not when he had Emily to lose. He loved her with all of his heart. That girl was his shining star, the main reason why he worked so hard to keep his motorcycle shop thriving. He always wanted to give her everything, the best of the best from clothing to education. She never asked for anything like normal teenagers. She never pitched a fit if things didn't go her way. Mark was committed to his daughter's happiness, and there was no one in the world who deserved happiness more than her.

"As long as I'm here, he'll never touch you again. I promise," Mark stated as he rocked her gently in his arms.

Emily took slow, shaky deep breaths as she held him tightly. She knew he would protect her no matter the cost, but the simple fact was that he could not be with her every moment of every day. Mark meant his promise, but it was not one that Emily would hold him to.

Emily tapped her pen against her notebook as she stared off into space toward the nearest bookshelf. Steve and Aden were sitting at the table with her in the library, monitoring the passersby. Aden and Emily had study hall during the same period and as seniors they were able to spend study halls almost anywhere. Her eyes scanned over a shelf of books, identifying the new and old from the wear and tear of their spines. Her eyes focused on one that seemed like the newest out of them all, but she flinched when she read the author's name, Greg Cooper.

Only my eyes would choose to look at that book, she thought sarcastically,

"What's wrong, baby?" Aden asked as he looked in the direction her gaze had previously been.

"Nothing, I just looked at the wrong book on the shelf," she replied as she reached out to take his hands in hers.

Aden held them tightly, wanting to reassure her that she was safe. He was thankful that Mr. Riley was suspended, but he never had the chance to feed him his fist. He hoped he would get that chance at one point in time or another.

"Hey, Aden. Are you seriously still with her after what she did to us?"

Aden turned to see one of his buddies, Zack, standing behind him. Zack was the running back for the school's football team. That's how the two had met their freshman year. He stood and pulled Zack a few feet away to hush the conversation from Emily's ears.

"Listen, Riley raped my girlfriend. Everything she's said has been the truth. Riley is a liar and a rapist. I don't give a shit what happens. Get your head out of your ass and open your eyes. Nothing has been done to you or anybody else except Emily. I'm not leaving her, ever. So get over it and leave her alone," Aden stated threateningly. He didn't care if Zack was almost his height and his build nor did he care that they were close friends. No one was going to mess with his girlfriend.

"Who the hell do you think you are? Aden, come on. Bro's before ho's, man! She's making up shit 'cause Greg doesn't want her. She flirts with him every chance she gets. Don't let her ruin his career and our chance at winning the state championship just because she wants to be a whore. Hey, Emily, how about a quickie in the bathroom like you gave Riley?" he shouted over to her.

Zack grunted loudly as Aden's fist collided with his jaw, sending him up against the wall behind him. Aden immediately continued on the attack, pummeling him with fists and elbows until he hit the floor.

"Aden, stop!" Steve shouted as he pulled him away. "Calm down, son."

"You son of a bitch," Zack muttered as he held his bloodied nose. "Don't you ever come near her again!" Aden shouted, lunging back in Zack's direction.

"Hey!" Steve shouted as he pulled him back. "Listen, Emily needs you. So get outta here and take her with you. Security is probably on its way 'cause the woman behind the desk just grabbed the phone. I'll tell them what happened. Now go!" Steve stated before pushing him toward Emily.

Aden hurried to her and took her hand.

"Come on," he stated as he grabbed her backpack along with his. They hurried out of the library then down the stairs but headed for the back door instead of the front to ensure they avoided any security.

Steve watched with a heavy sigh as they hurried down the stairs. Aden held her hand in his, their fingers laced. He had her pulled protectively close to his side before disappearing from his sight. That boy loved her, and he knew Emily would be safe with Aden while he took care of the scum who was making his way to his feet. Steve slowly stalked toward the kid, backing him up against the wall.

"Listen here, boy. You have two choices. You can tell security that Aden hit you first and start unnecessary problems or you can let them know that you started it and play it down as best as you can. If you value your body the way it is, then I suggest you do the right thing. It'll definitely be hard for you to play football if I break both your arms and your legs. And don't you ever...*ever* speak to Emily that way again. Greg Riley raped her on the weight room floor as she cried for somebody to help her and here you come along, making her feel violated all over again. So keep that mouth of yours shut, do you understand me?"

Zack nodded vigorously as he stared into Steve's eyes. He didn't know what to say. He wasn't sure what to think anymore. All he knew was that he did in fact value his body parts being intact and unbroken, so he intended on taking the man's insisted advice.

"Got it."

15

"EMILY, THE GIRLS are here!" Mark called to her. He was tying up the garbage to prepare to take it outside when he saw two sets of headlights driving up the driveway.

"Okay," Emily replied as she tossed her pen and notebook on to the coffee table before sliding off the couch and heading toward the door. She paused as her hand reached for the doorknob. All she could picture was Greg standing on the other side of that door. He would smile down at her and lick his lips as he studied her right before lunging at her.

"It's okay, darlin'," Mark whispered in her ear as he reached out to hold her wrist in his hand. He guided her hand to the doorknob and with a deep breath, she carefully turned it and pulled it open. Mark sighed with slight relief as he felt her entire body relax under his hands when she saw Jasmine, Kim, and Jetta heading up the porch steps.

"Hey, gorgeous!" Jetta greeted as she slung her overnight bag over her shoulder.

"Hi! Oh, wait, you weren't talkin' to me, never mind," Jasmine stated. "We know you weren't talkin' to Kim."

"Jasmine!" Kim exclaimed, playfully offended.

Emily smiled as she laughed for what felt like the first time in months.

"Come on in, girls," Mark greeted as he opened the door wider and stepped aside.

"Hi, Mr. Connors," Jetta greeted as she walked inside.

"Hey, Dad," Kim stated as she crossed the threshold only to be shoved by Jasmine.

"Hey, Pops," Jasmine greeted as the other girls laughed. Once Kim caught her balance, she threw her pillow at Jasmine's head, even causing Mark to laugh.

"You deserved that one, li'l lady. And quit with the Pops name, I ain't that old yet," Mark stated with a chuckle before closing and locking the door behind her. He immediately typed in the five-digit code into the security system, which locked the house up tight. No one was getting a hold of his daughter. There was slight comfort in the fact that the girls were having a sleepover that night. It made it quite unlikely that Greg would try anything as long as they were there keeping Emily busy and occupied.

Jetta watched Emily as she stood there with her arms wrapped around herself and a faulty smile resting on her lips.

"All right girls, I'm not gonna talk to you like you don't know what's going on. You know that Emily has not left this house except to go to school, and we know what happened there. You are to stay in this house. You can go anywhere and do anything as long as it's inside this house. We can't take any chances," Mark instructed as he glanced at his daughter. She just looked so sad. The pale hue of her skin made the bruises on her neck and cheek stand out prominently, which intensified his need to keep her inside that house.

"Got it," Jetta stated, speaking for all of them.

"Good, now go have fun," he replied before moving over to kiss Emily on her forehead.

"Come on, let's get this party started!" Jasmine exclaimed as she looped her arm through Emily's, trying desperately to lighten the mood.

Mark watched as the girls hurried up the stairs toward Emily's room. He could only hope that the girls could take her mind off the hell that had been defined as her life for the past few months.

"So what should we do first?" Kim asked as they all set their bags down at the foot of Emily's bed.

"I'm kind of hungry," Emily stated quietly as she glanced around her room, just to see if anything was out of order since she had left.

"Ya hear that? She's hungry, people. So I'm thinking we order some pizza, chips, and soda and get fat!" Jasmine suggested excitedly, making Emily smile.

"I'll ask my Dad to order for us. What kind do you guys want?" Emily asked as she grabbed a pad of paper and pen off her bedside table.

"Let's do one cheese, one pepperoni, and how about sour-cream–and-onion chips," Jetta suggested, knowing those were Emily's favorites.

"Guys, get whatever you want. You don't have to get what I want," Emily stated as she sat on the edge of her bed.

"Yes, we do, girl. And if you don't like it, too bad!" Kim replied making Emily laugh.

"Okay, okay, let's order the food before we starve," Jasmine stated, winking in Emily's direction.

Emily jotted down everything they wanted and reluctantly took the money Jetta handed her then headed down to the living room.

"Daddy, can you call and order pizza for us?" she asked as she approached the couch.

"Sure, baby girl. What do you girls want?" he asked as he reached for the phone beside the couch.

Emily sat down beside him and handed him the paper then the money.

Mark gave her a confused look when the money entered his view.

"Who's is that?" Mark asked.

"Jetta's," Emily replied.

"Tell her if she don't put that back where she got it from, she's gonna get it," he playfully threatened. "Go ahead back up. I'll bring it up when it gets here."

Emily snuggled closer to him for a moment as he kissed her forehead.

"I love you," she stated before kissing him on the cheek then standing and heading toward the stairs. "I love you too, darlin'," he replied as he watched her hurry up to her room. So far, she seemed just fine, but he was not about to let his guard down. He was not about to let that man get his hands on her again. He lifted the phone and dialed the pizza place, trying to keep a positive attitude that Greg Riley was somewhere in Timbuktu. After all, he did have a warrant out for his arrest, and every police department in the state was watching and waiting for him to pop back up on the radar.

⊷⊷⊷⊷⊷⊷

"So how are you and Aden?" Kim asked as they all got comfortable on the rug. They had hooked up Emily's CD player, which had been shoved under her bed, and it was now playing upbeat songs. Besides cheerful music, the nightly agenda had plans for only comedy movies, nothing scary or reflective for Emily.

"Okay, I guess. Must be hard for him to have a girlfriend who can't stand to be touched by him," she stated as she fidgeted with the corner of her bed comforter.

The girls all stopped to stare at her, knowing there was no way to avoid the topic anymore.

"It's okay, Em. We don't have to talk about it," Jetta stated as she rubbed her friend's arm comfortingly.

A knock sounded at the door, startling them slightly.

"Pizza's here," Mark called through the door. "My hands are a little full."

Emily quickly stood and opened the door for him, smiling when she saw his face. He had let his hair down, and a few strands were hanging in his face. Emily smiled as she tucked them behind his ear so he could see.

"Why thank you, my girl," he stated before kissing her forehead then walking into the room to place the food on the floor near her friends.

"Thanks, Mr. Connors. And next time, I'm paying," Jetta stated with a glare making Mark laugh as he tossed her a small package of napkins.

"I'll think about it," he replied before heading back out the door. "Have fun, girls."

Emily gladly accepted Mark's tight embrace he pulled her into, the comfort wrapping around her just like his arms.

"Go ahead, Em. Try and not worry," Mark whispered before exiting the room.

She moved back over to sit with the girls and reached for one of the pizzas.

"Maybe eating is what I need to do," Emily stated with a laugh.

"Amen to that," Jasmine agreed as she opened the other pizza box.

Emily flipped open the lid and immediately froze. On top of the pizza was a piece of paper with her name scrawled across it. She didn't want to touch it but then her curiosity wouldn't allow her to leave it untouched. She could only hope that it was from someone else other than the person she feared it had been sent by. She took a slow deep breath to calm her heartbeat. She felt short of breath as she reached out with a shaky hand to lift the piece of paper.

"Em, are you okay?" Kim asked, turning the girl's attention to her. "What's that?"

"I…I don't know yet," she replied, her voice barely a whisper as she unfolded it.

> *Emily,*
>
> *I know we haven't been able to see each other ever since I got to be with you in the bathroom but everything is gonna be alright. I love you so much, baby. I miss being able to touch you…kiss you…oh but soon enough. You will belong to me again. No one can keep you away from me…no one…*
>
> *Love,*
> *Greg*

Emily felt tears flood her eyes as she read the last sentence. Was she ever going to be safe? Was she ever going to be able to live her life without being threatened or having to look over her shoulder?

Jetta gently took the paper from Emily's hands and quickly read over it before tossing it aside and pulling her friend into her arms.

"You're safe, he can't get in this house. That's why he sent this crap in a pizza because he knows that he can't get in here," Jetta stated confidently, trying to comfort her as much as possible.

"What the hell is his problem?" Kim asked as her and Jasmine scanned the letter.

"I don't know…I want to know why he wants me so much. He knows I hate him, but he just won't leave me alone."

Jetta held her tighter, knowing that what had happened to her is probably the worst thing that anyone could do to another person.

"You don't have to talk about it if you don't want to," Jasmine stated softly, giving her the option to keep her pain inside if that's what she wanted to do.

"No…I want you guys to know. I want you to know everything," she replied as she carefully pulled away from Jetta. She steadied herself, taking deep breaths to keep herself calm.

"Tell us, Em," Jasmine stated softly, encouragingly.

"It happened months ago, but I remember that day like it was today. We…we were working out in the gym just like we did every Saturday. Everything was normal, was just fine until Greg…Mr. Riley said that I owed him. Do you guys remember when he got us out of trouble with Principal Mathers?"

All the girls nodded, remembering the fight in the cafeteria.

"He said that I owed him for that because he helped us get out of trouble. He had me backed against a wall with his hands like this so I couldn't move," Emily continued, holding up her hands to show them how Greg had her trapped.

"What the hell did he want you to give him? Money?" Kim asked with confusion.

"That's what I said! I told him I don't have money to pay him back, so I don't know what to give him," She replied before swallowing. "That's when he said he wanted a kiss... my payment to him was a kiss."

"Are you serious?" Kim exclaimed.

"What happened when you wouldn't?" Jetta asked, assuming that she fought like hell against degrading herself.

"I...I tried to change the subject. I tried to head toward the door, but he just pushed me back into place," she replied as her body began to shake slightly.

"Then when you still wouldn't?" Jetta asked.

Emily glanced up at her with the most pain and heartache that she never knew was possible to feel. How was she supposed to tell her what happened without her thinking it was all her fault? Would she blame her? Would she then not believe her about what happened? Maybe she should stop talking and not continue with her morbid tale.

Jasmine elbowed Jetta in the rib and glared heatedly at her. She could see what Emily was about to say, and the pain she saw in those emerald eyes was practically unbearable.

"I...I did kiss him. He said if I did, then he would let me go," Emily whispered as she wrapped her arms around herself.

Jetta squeezed her eyes shut and turned away momentarily before reaching out and rubbing her arm comfortingly.

"I'm sorry, Em. I didn't mean it the way I said it. What happened after that, sweetheart?" she asked, encouraging her to continue if she wanted to.

"He...he pushed me against the wall and that disgusting kiss seemed to last forever. I had no choice but to kiss him back because he kept shoving his tongue down my throat... but then he finally stopped, and he did let me go. I ran to the doors, but they were locked when I tried to open them. I demanded that he let me out, but he just said he needed me...he couldn't let me go. He kept coming toward me...I was so scared, I didn't know what to do," she explained as she pulled her knees up to her chest.

"I can't even imagine," Kim whispered, shaking her head slightly.

"I tried to run but he picked me up, threw me over his shoulder, and carried me over to the other side of the weight room. Of course, it was the side furthest from the door. He put me down, I tried to run one more time, but he grabbed me tightly, basically locking my arms behind me. He took out my knees and laid me on the floor then got on top of me," she continued, feeling tears well in her eyes.

"You can stop if you want, Em," Jasmine stated quietly.

"No…let me finish. I kicked and I screamed but it was Saturday, practically no one was there. He held me down while he pulled down my pants. First he just…touched me. Then he held my arms above my head, pulled open my legs no matter how much I fought…and he raped me. He kept grunting and telling me how amazing I was and how incredible I felt under him. I was crying. I cried out for Dad and he said that my Daddy can't help me. He kept saying he loved me…acting like I wanted it. When he finished…I wanted to die…I kept showering and bathing, but I never felt clean. I still don't…especially after what happened the other day," she explained before showing her friends her wrists and neck more clearly.

Their eyes widened when they got a better look at her neck. The handprint bruise was so vividly outlined, the large size matching the size of the bruise on her face.

"Maybe none of this would have happened if I didn't kiss him. It's my fault that he did this," she whispered as tears slowly streamed down her cheeks.

"No, it's not, Emily. You did the only thing that was giving you a chance to escape. What he did is his fault and no one else's," Jasmine stated emotionally. "Once they find him, he'll never hurt you again. He's gonna spend the rest of his disgusting life in prison for what he did to you."

"They'll never catch him. If he wants me, then there's nothing that will stop him from getting his hands on me. He'll keep coming back for more. He'll keep trying to get me until he either kidnaps me…or who knows what else," Emily replied before wiping away her tears.

The girls didn't know what to say. They could tell her that everything was going to be all right, but they knew they did not have a clue what was going to happen.

"Your father is always going to be here to protect you. I don't know why Mr. Riley is doing this, and I don't care because all I know is that he's hurting my best friend. Your father will stop him. He's not going to let that dirt bag take you away or any of that. And we may not be as big as your dad, but I'll guarantee that we'll all go down fighting for you," Jetta stated passionately before pulling Emily into her arms. Kim and Jasmine moved over to them and enveloped both girls in their arms as Emily let the tears flow from her eyes that threatened to drown her.

She shouldn't have had them come over. The fact that Greg gave a note to the pizza guy to put inside the box meant that he was outside. She had no right to put them in danger. She should send them home where they would be safe, but she loved having them near. She felt comforted by them, encouraged by them, and they were good at helping her forget the misery around her.

"Let's cut this out. This is a time to celebrate. Emily and Aden's two-year anniversary is coming up. So let's dance!

Let's choreograph and let's try again to teach Jetta how to dance," Jasmine stated as she stood and moved over to change the disc in the CD player.

"No, no, no, last time we did that it was a disaster. I'll just be the DJ and work the CD player," Jetta stated as she released Emily and tried to back away.

"Oh, come on! Never hurts to try twice," Kim pleaded as she hopped to her feet then pulled Jetta up to her feet by her hands.

"Let's do it," Emily stated as she too made it to a standing position. She wiped her tears away before pulling her hair back to tie it into a ponytail.

"You heard the girl. Let's do it!" Jasmine exclaimed before blasting the most upbeat hip- hop song she could find.

⋅•⋅⬦⬤⬦⋅•⋅

Mark immediately perked up from the couch in the living room when he heard banging coming from Emily's room. He jumped over the back of the couch then started to charge up the stairs but quickly halted. He listened carefully for a moment then breathed a heavy sigh of relief when he heard music and laughter followed by more banging. The girls were dancing and at least one of them falling by the sound of it.

"Poor Jetta," he muttered with a chuckle before heading back over to the couch. He picked up his book and tried to continue reading, but he knew he would simply sit there and continue listening to ensure the girls' safety. The house was alive with the invisible digital security system, keeping the house locked up tight. No one was getting in that house to hurt Emily or anyone else as long as he was around.

16

EMILY STARED OUT the window of her bedroom, watching the leaves drift slowly from the trees to the ground. The air was crisp and refreshing as it slipped in from the cracked window. Autumn was kicking in, dissipating the remaining heated days of seventy and eighty degrees. She didn't mind. This was the perfect weather for her. Not too hot but not yet too cold. She sighed as she flipped open her cell phone once again. Still no message. Football practice at the school had ended an hour ago. He had promised to text her as soon as they were finished, but she was still waiting.

"Maybe now that Greg's gone, Coach needs to keep them longer," she thought rationally as she stood from the window seat. She made her way out of her bedroom then down the stairs, only to find her father throwing on his jacket and lacing up his boots.

"Dad? Where are you going? It's Saturday," Emily asked as she made her way over to him.

Mark sighed as he stood and took her in his arms.

"I'm sorry, Bobby called and said some guy is giving him a hard time and wants to see a manager. Why don't you grab a coat. We won't be gone but a minute."

"Actually, Aden's done with football practice and should be here anytime now. I'll be fine. I'm sure he'll pull in not long after you leave," Emily replied as she fiddled with her cell phone in her hands.

Mark sighed heavily, not liking the idea of leaving Emily home alone, but he checked his watch and saw that she was right. Aden showed up at their house every Saturday after football practice like clockwork. He still didn't want to leave her alone, but there had been no sight of Greg for weeks and for a majority of that time Emily had been confined to the house. He felt horrible that she was trapped in her own home but until Greg was caught, he would do whatever kept her safe. He stroked her hair, holding her close as he willed himself to walk out the door.

"I'll be back as fast as I can," Mark stated before kissing her once more then heading out the door, locking it securely behind him.

Emily listened to the silence around her. It was momentarily intimidating before it became soothing. No noise meant that she was alone. Being alone meant that she was safe. She headed into the living room before flopping down on the couch, not quite knowing what to do with herself. Her eye caught the pile of mail on the coffee table that her father must have brought in earlier that morning. She sifted through it, pausing for a moment to study the cover of the newest dance clothing magazine she received. She tossed the bills on the other side of the couch, set her magazine beside her, then studied the last piece of mail. She held an envelope with only her name written across it. No return address and no stamp, which meant that it was placed in the mailbox by hand, personally. There was no denying who it was from. She took a deep breath before tearing it open then unfolding the paper.

> *Hey my girl,*
>
> *I miss you like crazy. We haven't made love in so long, it's killing me! How's school? I hope your holding up alright without me. It's hard for me to be away from you too. I haven't been to my own house in a while either. That one is your fault. Why couldn't you just be quiet about us? We were gonna be just be just fine until you brought your Dad and the damn school into our relationship. But I forgive you. You and I will be together soon enough. I love you, Emily. I know you love me too. You think you love Aden but that's just a phase. You'll get over it soon, then I'll come get you and we'll be together. So are you wearing it yet? If not, I'm sure it's because you want me to put it on for you. Soon, baby…*

real soon. I have to end this letter but I want you to
remember that I love you and you are mine...no one
else's...and you know it.

Love Always,
Greg

Emily stared down at the paper in her hands, unsure whether she wanted to throw up first or tear the paper into shreds. She took a deep breath before pushing up off the couch then hurrying up the stairs to her bedroom. She closed the door behind her before tossing the letter on to her bed then venturing into her closet. She shoved clothes then shoes out of the way until she found the large cardboard box in the back. She pulled it out then dragged it over to her bed before taking a seat. This had not been Greg's first letter to her. If her counting was accurate, it was number twenty-seven. She pulled open the box then lifted a smaller box from inside. She opened it then placed the newest letter inside along with the other twenty-six. Inside the cardboard box were countless gifts Greg had sent her over the past few weeks. There were teddy bears, chocolates, love cards, and those were only the G-rated items. He had also sent her lingerie, stories he'd written about them having sex, and hundreds of photos of her. They ranged from pictures of her at school, with her friends, to her dancing in the backyard and close-ups of her bathroom window while she stepped out of the shower. She slowly reached inside the box, taking slow deep breaths to keep herself calm.

Over the course of the past few weeks, the slightest noise had made her scream and run for her father, so she had taught herself to breathe deeply and slowly when she felt as though she may lose control. It helped keep her feet on the ground and to avoid panicking. Once she had realized it worked, she had used the tactic ever since. She lifted a small velvet box into her hand and simply stared at it.

So are you wearing it yet?

The words wafted through her mind as she continued to stare. She didn't know why she was even touching it, but she felt compelled to open the box and look inside. So she did. Inside sat a large diamond ring that sparkled it's greeting to her. The band was white gold…her favorite. How had Greg known that? She had no answer. It felt heavy in her hand as she slid it from the case. She should put it back and go back downstairs but she needed to understand Greg. He couldn't have raped her for no reason. Why had he chosen her? Why did he want her? Why was he hell-bent on having her when he could have any woman he wanted?

"Why me?" she whispered as she slid the ring onto her left hand ring finger. She was sickened to find out that the ring fit perfectly. It glinted back at her as she wiggled her fingers. She couldn't deny that the ring was absolutely stunning. Why did she put it on? Why didn't she just throw it away the moment it came in the mail? She once again had no answers. Maybe it was for leverage or maybe it was because it still pained her that someone she had been so close to had abused her in a way she had never dreamed possible.

"I'll always hate you for what you did to me," she whispered to the ring, as if Greg could somehow hear her through it.

She jumped suddenly when her phone began ringing from the window seat where she left it.

"Hello?"

"Em? It's Zack, please don't hang up on me! I know I was an asshole to you, but you have to listen," Zack begged on the other end of the line.

"No, I don't have to listen," she replied matter-of-factly. Zack's words still made her shiver with both anger and disgust.

"Yes, you do! Aden is hurt! We screwed up one of our plays at practice. They're taking him to the hospital now, and I know you'd wanna be with him so that's why I called," Zack stated as he smiled. He could tell that Emily would be on her way.

"I'm leaving now. I'll be there soon," Emily stated, her words panicked as she ran to her bedside table to grab her shoes. She flipped her phone shut then shoved it in her pocket before running out of her bedroom, down the stairs, then right for the front door. She snagged her jacket from the coat rack then grabbed the Ford F-150 key off the hook in the kitchen beside the refrigerator. She didn't have her license yet, but Mark had put the key there just in case anything were to happen, and she had to get away in a hurry. She made a dash to the door and quickly typed in the five-digit code to disarm the security system before pulling open the door only to run face first into a large body.

"Well, where are you going in such a rush?" Greg asked as he shoved her back into the house.

Emily lost her footing and landed on the floor on her backside. She barely felt the pain through the shock as she stared up at him, awestruck. Her eyes shifted to the security keypad to the left side of the door. All she had to do was hit the alarm button, but with Greg's large frame standing in the doorway, she knew her chances of making it close enough were slim to none. Regardless of her odds, she had to try.

Emily leapt off the floor and launched herself toward the door with her arm outstretched toward the keypad. She felt her fingertips graze against the buttons, but Greg's reflexes were too quick. He easily grabbed her and shoved her back, landing her right back on the floor.

"Did you happen to get a phone call just now? Well, Zack misinformed you because practice ran over today, but Aden is just fine. His phone has been misplaced unfortunately so don't bother trying to call him," Greg stated as he stepped inside then closed and locked the door behind him.

"You…you went through all that trouble just to get me to open the door? How could Zack do this to me?" Emily whispered as she backpedaled slowly.

"I guess he didn't appreciate being threatened by Steve in the library. You know, high school boys tend to hold grudges and serve payback. I guess you've just been served," Greg stated with a chuckle.

"Yeah, I'm sure you had nothing to do with it," she replied sarcastically.

Greg followed her, studying her body as she moved slowly, skillfully along the hardwood floor. He felt himself harden in his jeans. He wanted to take her right there, but he had promised her they would make love in Emily's own bed.

"I missed you…" he stated sweetly as he watched her slowly rise to her feet. As Emily held her hands up in a defensive manner, something caught his eye. There was a large sparkle on her finger. Greg's eyes widened and a smile spread across his face.

"You're wearing the engagement ring," Greg stated as he moved toward her.

Emily's heart fell into her stomach when she realized that she had been so caught up in getting to Aden that she hadn't taken that damn ring off. Maybe she could use this to her advantage. Maybe if he thought she wanted to be with him, then he wouldn't hurt her. Was she capable of that kind of deception? The thought of him touching her made her ill, but all she had to do was buy herself some time until her father returned home.

"I...I wanted to see what it felt like," she replied softly as she stepped behind one of the leather chairs in the living room. All she had to do was keep her distance from him and keep him calm.

"So, how does it feel?" he asked, eager to hear her answer. The large diamond looked beautiful on her delicate finger.

"I...I like it," she replied as she forced a smile on her lips.

Greg's smile slowly faded from his face as he studied her. Her body was shaking slightly, she had stepped behind a piece of furniture as a barrier, and the smile on her face never reached her eyes. He had seen her smile genuinely so many times with her friends, her father, and when she danced. The smile she was giving him was fake. She didn't want him. She was lying to him.

"You like it? Really?" he asked with artificial excitement before he let the darkness encompass his features. "Do you think I'm really that stupid? Do you think that I'd believe that you would go from wanting me to burn in hell to wanting to be my wife?"

Emily cried out when he lunged toward her, shoving the large leather chair aside as if it were a beach chair. She looked back momentarily at the sound of a large crash. The chair had landed directly on top of the glass coffee table, shattering it to pieces and distracting her for the moment

Greg had needed. He grabbed the back of her shirt and shoved her forward, propelling her on to the stairs.

"I thought you were done misjudging me? I thought you were done underestimating me? I guess not! That may not be good for you, but it's great for me, sweetheart," Greg growled as he subdued her, her back pressed against the staircase.

"Please, please don't hurt me!" she begged as she ceased her struggles.

"Oh, I won't hurt you. This is meant to feel good, not hurt," he stated with an exasperated laugh.

She cried out as he yanked her up and tossed her over his shoulder as if she weighed nothing.

"I promised you we'd make love in your bed, so let's go keep that promise."

"No!" Emily screamed as she squirmed in his grasp. She swung her leg down toward him over and over, trying to hit the spot she knew would drop him.

"Bitch!" he growled as her foot struck him between the legs, forcing him to his knees which lowered Emily enough to stand on the steps. She swatted and kicked at him until his grip faltered. She took off up the remaining stairs the moment he released her then dashed into her bedroom before shutting and locking the door behind her. She was trapped. She looked around the room for a weapon as she ran to the phone, but nothing seemed logical or effective enough to harm Greg Riley, a man who was built like a brick wall. She immediately dialed 911 as Greg began banging on her door.

"I swear to God, if you don't open this door, you won't live to graduate high school, Emily. Don't test me!" Greg growled as he jammed his shoulder into it, the frame cracking slightly.

"911, what is your emergency?"

"Somebody, please help me!" she whispered harshly. She immediately and carefully placed the phone under the bed where Greg wouldn't spot it and prayed they would not hang up. She quickly made it to her feet just as Greg's foot kicked the rest of the door clean off its hinges.

"Please just leave me alone! Please!" Emily begged as she backed away. She had nowhere to run. The windows were locked and only Mark had the key. There was no way she had enough time to get into the bathroom and lock the door and Greg was blocking the only way out.

"I think you enjoy this. I think you piss me off at every twist and turn to try and make me chase you. Do you like this?" Greg asked before pretending to lunge at her, making her flinch violently.

"No! I don't! I want you to leave me alone and get out of my life. My life is in shambles because you're obsessed with me!" she screamed as she backed away toward the far wall.

Greg's anger began boiling over. All he saw was red as her words flowed through his mind.

"When we first met, you flirted with me, wore tight little outfits when we worked out together. You were the one that wanted me! You're a damn tease! You wanted me! You can deny it all you want, but no matter what you say, you're body says different..." Greg growled as he inched closer and closer.

Mark shook the man's hand as he handed him the keys to his fully repaired Harley Davidson. The man was ecstatic and that always brought a smile to Mark's face. He loved motorcycles and working around them, owning a shop to repair them had always been what he wanted. He waved as the man took off on the Harley just as his phone began ringing in his pocket.

"Hello?"

"Mark, it's Detective Michaels. Are you home?"

"No, I'm just leaving the shop, why?" Mark asked, his entire body becoming alert.

"The phone tap on your home phone line has paid off. A 911 call was just made from the house. Me and a few officers are on the way, get there now!" Michaels practically shouted.

Mark was already on his bike before Michaels had finished his sentence. He shoved his cell phone in his pocket before taking off from the shop, needing to get home before anything happened to Emily. He couldn't help but fear that something already had.

Emily cowered against the wall as Greg inched closer. She squeezed her eyes closed tightly imagining she were somewhere else, safe. She felt his body press against hers and she did the only thing she could. She lifted her knee to hit him in the crotch but Greg jammed his knee between her thighs before she could achieve her goal.

"That's starting to get really old. But now you'll have to make it up to them and make them feel better with that pretty little mouth of yours," Greg growled as he yanked her off the wall.

"Help! Somebody help me!" she screamed at the top of her lungs as she kicked and flailed, trying desperately to escape his grasp. She cried out when he threw her down on to her bed then climbed on top of her.

"Isn't this what you always wanted, baby?" Greg taunted as his hands roamed over her body, rubbing and groping her wherever he pleased. "I know you want this. Just let it happen or things are gonna get damn rough!"

"Go to hell!" she screamed in his face before turning her head and biting down on the hand that was near her shoulder.

"Ow! Knock it off!" Greg shouted before slapping her across the face. He watched her as she fell back, her eyes closing and opening, trying to focus after the blow. She reached up dazedly to cup her bruising cheek in her hand as she tried to refocus her vision. His entire body shivered. He needed her. He needed to completely consume her. There was no one there to save her this time. There was no phone for her to run to, no door to run out of, and no window to climb through. She was trapped and the mere thought of her naked beneath him, pleasing him before he satisfied her was enough to drive him mad. He grabbed her shirt and tore it down the middle with ease. Emily was still dazed so her struggles were almost nonexistent.

"God, you're beautiful," he whispered on a husky exhale as his eyes devoured her whole. He could barely see her luscious skin through her lace bra but it was enough to excite him beyond his ability of control.

"No…" Emily whispered. She began to regain her focus when she felt her jeans being tugged down her legs. She was suddenly aware that she was laying beneath him in only her bra and panties, her body almost completely exposed to him.

Mark hurried up the porch toward Detective Michaels and another officer who had beat him there by mere moments.

"Unlock the door, we'll head inside. You stay out here," Michaels instructed.

"Like hell I will," Mark stated as he quickly unlocked the door then pushed it open. The first thing his eyes fell on was the mayhem. His favorite leather chair was flipped over, the coffee table smashed into millions of shards of glass.

"God…" he whispered as he slowly crept inside behind the two men. His head snapped toward Emily's bedroom when he heard her cry out in pain. The son of a bitch was in her room, and he was hurting her, hitting her. Mark knew he couldn't barrel up the stairs and into the room in case Greg was armed. Mark's negligence could cost Emily her life.

As they made their way quickly but silently up the stairs, Mark could hear the things Greg was saying to his daughter. Things that made his stomach fall to his feet.

"Please…don't," Emily cried as she lifted her hands to push against his chest.

Greg laughed at her futile attempts.

"Mmmm, it feels good when you touch me. Now you better be a good girl and give me what I want. Don't make me hit you again. Next time, you might not be awake afterward," Greg stated, his final words practically a growl.

"Leave me alone!" she screamed when she saw him working on the button and zipper of his jeans. "Please don't make me! I swear I'll do anything, just not that!"

"Oh, I'm going to and you're gonna do it whether you like it or not," Greg shouted as he climbed up to straddle her chest which pinned her arms to her sides. "If you bite me, I swear to God, I'll teach you what the true meaning of pain is."

Emily struggled beneath him as he exposed himself. She tried to kick at him, but the angle was too awkward and her arms were rendered useless. She clamped her mouth shut and turned her head away just as Greg grabbed a fistful of her hair and pulled her head toward him.

"Freeze! Hands in the air! Let her go, Riley!" Detective Michaels shouted as they burst into the room, weapons drawn and pointing right at Greg's head.

Greg locked eyes on Mark's and smiled as he slowly slid off his former friend's daughter, making sure to rub his exposed manhood against her before standing. He slowly moved toward the window to the right of the three men standing in the doorway as he zipped and buttoned his jeans back up.

"On your knees! Hands on your head!"

Mark bolted into the room the moment Michaels shouted that he was clear.

"Daddy!" Emily screamed as he pulled her off the bed then into his arms.

"It's okay, baby girl! It's gonna be okay," Mark cooed as he held her in a death grip against him. He sat down on the edge of her bed and sat her in his lap before sliding off his T-shirt and slipping it over her head.

"You're covered up. Everything is gonna be okay. I'm here now," Mark whispered in her ear as he held her tightly.

"Greg Riley, you are under arrest for the rape of Emily Connors. You have the right to remain silent. Anything you say can and will be used against…"

Michaels was interrupted mid-Miranda warning when Greg caught him with a right hook, dropping him immediately. The other officer didn't last much longer once Greg kicked out his knee then slugged him into unconsciousness.

Greg made it to his feet slowly, his gaze never wavering from Mark as he made certain to position himself between the door and Emily and Mark.

"She's mine. Now hand her over, and I won't hurt you," Greg demanded as Mark stood from the bed.

He shoved her behind him defensively as he stared at the man he once looked at as his brother. His body was trembling. He wanted to kill him. He wanted to make him suffer the way he had forced his daughter to suffer.

"You're lucky you are even breathing right now, you son of a bitch! Little girls turn you on? Huh?" Mark shouted as his hands balled into fists at his side.

"Emily is no little girl, Mark. That sexy thing is a full-blown woman," Greg stated with a soft chuckle, the hunger for her shining in his eyes. "Have you ever seen a little girl with luscious D-cup breasts and legs that could make any man drool?"

"You sick bastard..." Mark growled as Greg slowly moved closer to them, boxing them in against the wall. "I swear to God if you get any closer..."

"You'll what, Mark? Huh? You swear that you're gonna protect her, but you never do! I'm the one that treats her the way she deserves to be treated. She needs to be cared for, and I can do that. I'm gonna take good care of you, baby," Greg stated, his last words directed toward Emily who peeked out from behind her father. "Go screw yourself," Emily spat as she glared her hatred through to his core. "I should, should I? But I'd rather enjoy screwing you!" Greg shouted before lunging at her.

Mark immediately shoved him back and came out swinging. He caught Greg with a right hook, jab to the stomach, then caught an uppercut from Greg.

Emily watched in horror as the two battled fiercely, throwing fists and elbows left and right.

Greg hit his knees as he stared up at Mark, his lip bloodied. He was holding up his hands defensively just as Mark swung for another right hook. Greg suddenly came up with his arm right between Mark's legs, all while staring over at Emily. Mark hit the ground hard as he doubled over in pain, leaving him unable to get back to his feet and leaving Emily standing there wearing only his shirt to cover her body and with no weapon to defend herself.

"Now, come here!" Greg shouted as he stalked toward her, his intentions becoming much more threatening to her life when he slid a pocketknife from his back pocket.

Emily felt her blood run cold as he flicked the blade open with expert skill. She looked over at her father and saw he hadn't moved much from Greg's cheap shot.

"Greg, please…don't hurt me anymore," Emily begged as her back hit the wall. She was cornered with no chance of escape.

Greg lunged at her, shoving her hard against the wall as he pressed the frigid blade against her skin.

"Now you're gonna come with me, Emily. Because if you don't, I will leave you with a precious gift that you will see every time you look in the mirror," he growled as he moved the blade up to press it against her cheek. "Don't make me ruin this pretty face."

Emily's eyes were wide with terror as she stared into his cold, smoky eyes. She had no choice. She could try and distract him to buy herself time for her father to recover, but she feared trying Greg's patience. By the wild look in his eyes, he seemed ready to snap at any moment, so she did the only logical thing she could think of to do. She carefully leaned forward, only mere inches to prevent him from cutting her face, then pressed her lips to his.

Greg immediately stiffened and froze where he stood as he felt Emily's lips caressing his. He wasn't sure whether fear was driving her actions or if it was want. But when she lifted her hands to cup his face, he finally received his answer. She wanted him, and whether she liked it or not, he was going to take her away from her father so she truly would be all his. She would probably fight at first, but he would teach her how to obey him. Greg lowered the knife from her skin then tossed it aside before sliding his fingers into her hair then down to cup her face in his hands as well.

"I love you, you sweet little witch," Greg whispered once he parted their lips.

Emily stared into his eyes which were once angry and unfeeling but now she saw a sparkle and her greatest fear was confirmed. Greg truly meant it when he told her he loved her.

She opened her mouth to speak, not quite knowing what she was about to say, but she never had the chance. Her father suddenly yanked Greg away from her and locked him in a choke hold as he dragged him away.

"Get outta here, Em!" Mark shouted as Greg struggled fiercely for release.

She could only stand there and stare at her father and Greg as they struggled. She could hear Mark shouting for her to run, but she was frozen in place. She had to snap out of it. She had to get help before Greg had the opportunity to truly hurt either of them. Emily ran over to an unconscious Detective Michaels and grabbed the two-way radio clipped to his belt.

"Hello? Help me, please! We need help at the Connor's house, it's 327 South Grove Road. Greg Riley knocked out Detective Michaels and another officer, he's fighting with my dad, and he's trying to abduct me! Please hurry!" Emily stated in a rush of words as she tried to catch her breath.

Greg slugged Mark with an elbow to the ribs which faltered his hold. He immediately shoved him away then pounced on top of him, throwing fists like a madman.

"She's mine! She loves me and she just proved it! Did you see your daughter kiss me? Her tongue in my mouth? She wants to be with me! Not you!" Greg shouted as Mark tried to block the blows.

"Stop! Get off him!" Emily screamed as she jumped onto Greg's back, wrapping her arms around his neck. She knew she couldn't hurt him, but she had to try to help her father.

"Damn it, girl. Let go!" Greg shouted as he stood from Mark. He tried to shake her off, but she wasn't letting go so he grabbed her head and flipped her over on to her bed. He grabbed her throat and pulled her up before shaking her violently.

"Pick one! Me or him! You can't have both!" Greg shouted as he shook her again. She couldn't breathe and she was losing focus from the way he was shaking her. She clawed at his hand, but he was not letting go until suddenly she could breathe again.

Mark jabbed Greg in his right kidney before kicking out his knee. He threw a vicious kick to his lower back before pounding away with punches and kicks as Greg lay on the ground, attempting to fight back but failing. Mark finally stopped his movements, breathing heavily as he stared down at the bloodied man at his feet.

"You'll never touch my daughter again, you son of a bitch," Mark growled before walking over to Detective

Michaels who was beginning to stir. He yanked the man's gun from his belt then headed back over to Greg.

"This is done...*you* are done. Burn in hell for putting my daughter through this and for ruining her life!" Mark shouted as he aimed the gun right at Greg's heart. He stared down at him with such hatred, knowing that this was the only way to protect his daughter once and for all.

"Daddy, no!" Emily shouted as she hurried over to him and grabbed his arm.

Mark stared down at her with disbelief. Was she protecting him? Did she want him to live even after everything he had done to her?

"Are you trying to protect him, Emily?" Mark asked, his voice practically a whisper from the shock he was feeling.

"No, Daddy, never. But please, don't sink to his level. Don't prove to him that you're as much of a monster as he is," Emily begged as she looked deep into his eyes, hers pleading.

Mark sighed heavily as he turned his attentions back toward Greg. No matter how much he hated the man laying at his feet, he knew Emily was right. He couldn't kill him. He wanted to fill Greg's body full of lead and watch him die, but he knew he couldn't. Emily needed him. He was all she had left, and he had no right taking himself away from her. He lowered the gun with a heavy sigh before turning to pull his daughter into his arms.

"It's over...it's all over," Mark whispered.

Emily clung to him tightly as she watched Detective Michaels and the other officer rush to flip Greg over and cuff his hands behind his back. She could tell he had cracked or broken ribs by the way he growled as they pulled him up to his knees. She felt tears stream from her eyes as he stared at her with such anger and love.

"I'll come back for you," Greg mumbled before spitting on the ground at Mark's boots. "He'll let you go someday. That'll be when we're together...I promise."

"No...you won't. You're going to be in jail for a long time for what you did to me...and that is something that I promise," Emily stated firmly.

Greg growled and struggled against his restraints as Detective Michaels and the other officer dragged him out of the room.

"I love you!"

Emily squeezed her eyes shut at the sound of Greg's shouts then buried her face in her father's chest. She prayed to God it was truly over. They still had to drive Greg to the police station and book him, so he had a lot more time to figure out an escape.

"He's not going anywhere but prison, baby girl."

It was as if he could read her mind. She could hear Greg shouting from outside now, no longer in the house. She slowly slid away from her father and made her way out of her bedroom then down the stairs toward the front door. She stood in the doorway and stared at Greg as he was dragged toward the police car in the driveway, despite his struggles. She watched as he spat again toward the house only this time it was blood instead of spit.

"I love you, Emily! Please don't do this to us!" Greg practically screamed as he locked eyes with hers.

She felt her body beginning to shake as fear crept back into her heart. But suddenly, she felt her father's hands on her shoulders. She felt his support and his love surrounding her entire body.

"I'm okay, Daddy. I'm still scared, but I know it's over. He can yell and scream all he wants," she stated before turning and looking up into her fathers eyes. "It's over, Daddy. I'm so sorry for all of this."

Mark felt tears prick his eyes as her small hand reached up to run her fingertips over the bruise on his face and the cut on his lip.

"None of this is your fault, sweetheart. Everything is gonna be all right now," Mark replied as he gently pulled her into his arms.

"Mark, we should get Emily to the hospital to make sure she's all right," Detective Michaels stated as he made his way toward them after locking Greg up in the police car.

Mark looked down at his little girl and saw the fresh bruises on her face, her neck, and her wrists. He could punch himself for not thinking more clearly.

"Of course, let me grab her some sweatpants and me another shirt and we'll head out in the truck."

Emily stared through the back window of the car. Greg simply stared at her, his face a mask of pure rage. He was saying something over and over. At first she couldn't read his lips but as he continued to repeat it, she finally identified the words *I love you*. Her lips quivered as she felt tears filling her eyes. She took slow deep breaths to calm herself, willing the tears away as she stared deeply into his eyes.

"I *don't* love you," Emily whispered, being sure to exaggerate her lips so he could understand her. She watched as a pained look entered his eyes and, for a brief moment, she almost felt sorry for him. This was a man she had looked up to. This was a man she felt completely comfortable with. And then he had become the man who haunted her every dream. He had become a man who she knew lurked around every corner just waiting to grab her. But now he was the man she would put in prison. She knew there would be a trial, and she knew he would be convicted because of her testimony. She would not feel guilty. She refused to feel anything but relief. She stared at him as she slid the diamond ring off her finger, finally, then tossed it on to the ground. Greg's eyes grew even more fierce, almost psychotic as he stared down at it then up at her.

"Here you go, sweetheart," Mark stated as he handed her a pair of her sweatpants. She slid them on as Mark put on a shirt and pulled his keys from his pocket. "Let's get you to the hospital and get you checked out, Em."

Emily held on to her father's arm as they headed toward Mark's truck. She couldn't pull her gaze off Greg who was fighting to get the handcuffs off. He was screaming for her, begging her to love him.

"Don't look at him," Mark insisted as he turned her head away from him. He watched Greg for a moment, wondering what made him become the man he was. Regardless of the reasoning, he had no right ever laying a hand on his daughter. Nothing else mattered anymore besides Emily's safety. Once Greg Riley was in prison, Emily would be safe, and he would never lay a hand on her again.

17

Eight months later

THE BREEZE WAS cool against her warm face as she reclined against the large trunk of her favorite weeping willow tree. She smiled as she listened to the shouts and laughter coming from behind her. It was the day after Emily and Aden's high school graduation, and her entire house was full of friends, family, and even pets. She could smell the grill, which was alive with her father's famous hamburgers and hot-dogs that no one seemed to make like him. She giggled when the sun came out from behind a small cloud, letting the sun trickle through the branches to dance over her freckled skin.

This was peace. This was her new place of tranquility. This was, once again, truly her home. It had taken almost a year for her world to be pieced back together after everything that had transpired. Emily had testified against

Greg at his trial, and when she heard the verdict, her heart had almost stopped. Greg Riley was found guilty of second degree sexual assault, endangering the welfare of a child, and third degree assault which sent him to jail for fifteen years. Greg's lawyer had tried for a psychological defense, claiming that Greg did not understand the consequences of his actions. Luckily, the jury had seen right through his last innocent act. When Emily had taken the stand, his lawyer had tried to poke holes in her story and even tried to make the jury believe that she had wanted Greg, and that they were romantically involved. Emily had then gone into a complete rage. She started describing to the jury exactly what happened with blunt and straightforward words, just like her lawyer had told her.

"Don't be sarcastic, don't be cryptic. Say penis, vagina, intercourse, don't dumb down what he did to you. It's going to hurt to say things like that, but it will make the jury see through to the black, disgusting heart he has,"

That advice had been her gold mine. Once she began, Greg immediately started telling her to stop, yelling for her to shut her mouth. Emily stared right into his eyes before she had continued.

"You raped me! I never loved you, and I never will love you! I am going to hate your pathetic existence until the day…you…die!"

Not a moment later, Greg had flipped over the table he was positioned at and charged the witness chair.

"You little bitch! I'll fucking kill you! You belong to me! You're never gonna be safe!" He had shouted at the top of his lungs. He had made it mere inches to her before the guards were able to take him down with Detective Michaels' help. As they tried to drag him away, Emily's lawyer had been hell-bent on a confession.

"Feel better, Mr. Riley? Do you feel like a big man?" she had taunted.

"She's mine! You'll never protect her from me!" Greg screamed as he had struggled in the guards' grasp.

"So you did rape her?" she asked matter-of-factly.

"I fucked that girl better than anyone could! I gave her what she needed, I gave her what she wanted! I made her mine! I'm gonna make love to that girl for the rest of our lives! She's not safe from me!" Greg screamed before they had dragged him through two wooden doors out of the courtroom.

Emily shook her head to come back to focus as the images faded away from her mind's eye. She then smiled when she remembered being excused from the witness chair, walking out, and immediately being met by her father's tight embrace. She could practically still feel the hug, feel his strength and support surrounding her. But now she could feel the joy of all the people celebrating in her backyard, swimming in the pool, eating all the junk food laid out on the large rectangular table.

"Well what is a beautiful woman like you doing all the way over here?"

Emily smiled and turned to look up.

Aden returned the smile as he leaned down to squat beside her.

"Just taking a second…taking everything in and letting some things go," she replied as she leaned her head against his available thigh.

He placed a soft kiss on her temple before situating himself to sit beside her, his arm over her shoulders and her head against his chest.

"It's always healthy to set free old ghosts, old demons. It's how you move on with a fresh and free heart," Aden stated as he leaned his chin against the top of her head.

"I've done just that, my love," she replied as she tilted her head back to look into his eyes. His lips looked so inviting, but she had not kissed him since the day before Greg had raped her in that gym. She had been kissed by him once, which had resulted in her screaming and cowering in fear. She had given him little quick pecks on the cheek and maybe one on the lips when Aden was not even prepared to kiss her in return. She wanted to kiss him, really and truly kiss him just like she used to.

"I have something for you," Aden stated, breaking her thoughts up.

"What is it?" she asked as he reached into his back pocket. He slid away from her then pulled himself to a standing position before offering her his hand and pulling her up as well.

He took a slow deep breath as he slid the gift from his pocket, rubbing the velvet box against his fingers to ease his nerves.

"Emily, I love you so, so much. After everything that's happened, I never want to be away from you again…not even for a minute. You are my angel, and I plan on loving you for the rest of my life," Aden declared before slowly lowering himself to one knee.

Emily's eyes widened as tears welled in her emerald orbs.

"Aden," she whispered as she covered her mouth with both hands.

He smiled as he reached up and pulled down her left hand and held it gently, lovingly in his grasp.

"Emily Connors, will you be my wife?" Aden finally asked. His entire body was shaking as he waited for her answer.

She was completely and utterly shocked as she watched him open a small box to reveal a white-gold diamond ring.

"Aden…I…" she whispered as she tried to calm her breathing as well as her tears.

"You don't have to answer me right now, baby," he quickly stated as he stood back up. He removed the ring from the box then carefully slid it onto her strong, beautiful finger.

"I want you to take your time. I want you to heal completely. We're gonna keep going no matter what. Only answer when you know that you're ready, Em. I've been saving up for that for a long time, so I think I can wait a while longer for an answer," he encouraged as he held both her hands in his.

Emily stared up into his eyes and felt her breath leave her lungs at the sight of such love, passion, and support. Her brain was screaming to say yes, but there was a lingering feeling that she was not the same person that she used to be and was now no longer good enough for this man. But with the way Aden was looking at her, the way his eyes seemed to see only her, made her realize that her uneasy feelings were not worth feeling. She needed to give him an answer. She couldn't let any final fears take away the greatest opportunity of her life.

Emily reached up on the tips of her toes to wrap her arms around his neck. She studied his eyes, those perfect shining eyes, before pulling him down to press her lips against his.

Aden was momentarily shocked by the feeling of her body pressed against his and her lips caressing his. He thought that he absolutely had to be dreaming. But as Emily parted her lips to invite him in, he knew he was wide awake. He enveloped her in his arms before dipping her to the right. Their lips and tongues caressed in a passionate dance that had not been performed in so long, too long.

She could feel him holding her tightly as they kissed one another. She felt an explosion of confidence and love being undeniably seared into her heart. There was no fear, not an ounce, as he took control of the kiss and deepened it even more. All there was, was the beating of their hearts and the sweet excitement pumping through their veins, reassuring them both that the ghosts were gone. Emily's demons had been cast out and only strength and peace now resided in her heart.

Aden slowly ended the kiss, wanting to see her eyes to ensure she was not frightened. He smiled breathlessly when he saw her eyes sparkling and her lips smiling.

"My answer is yes, Aden," Emily declared.

"Thank God!" Aden exclaimed before sweeping her up in his arms and twirling her around. As he held her tightly, he made a silent promise to himself, to God, and especially to his new fiancée that he would never let anyone hurt her ever again.

Mark closed the lid to the grill and set aside the tongs he had just used to roll the hotdogs over. He turned to look for Emily, noticing that he had not heard her voice in a little while. His eyes scanned over all the family members and friends trying to locate her.

"What's with the face, ya look lost," Steve commented as he approached his close friend.

"Have you seen Em?" Mark asked as his eyes continued to search.

"Right there," Steve stated as he pointed out toward the weeping willow.

Mark froze as he watched Emily and Aden kiss. He had not seen them kiss like that since before that dreaded day.

But this time, something was different. He did a full body shiver when the sun glinted off something on Emily's finger. Aden had actually done it. He had asked Mark for Emily's hand in marriage, but Mark thought that event would have been years down the road. He watched her laugh and smile as Aden twirled her. He knew he couldn't be selfish and take her away from him, no matter how much he wanted to keep her close. He never wanted to let that little girl out of his life.

"Well I'll be damned, the kid did it," Steve commented before finishing his bottle of beer. He glanced over at Mark and saw that familiar look in his eyes as he stared.

"Hey, man, listen. She's always gonna be your daughter. She loves you more than anything. She ain't just gonna walk out of your life. It'll be a while before they can get out on their own and get on their feet."

"How am I supposed to just let her go? Give her to another man?" Mark asked as his fists clenched. There was no way he was shedding a tear in front of Steve over the fact that his daughter was now engaged.

"You don't have to let her go. She's always gonna be in your life. You saved her from that bastard. You raised that girl from the moment she was born. There's no way she'll ever walk out of your life."

<hr />

"Let's go tell my dad. Then after we tell him, we need to make sure he knows that I'm not leaving him. I love my dad so much, Aden. This doesn't mean that…you know, that you replace him, does it?" Emily asked with worry.

"Never, baby. I could never replace your dad. We're gonna be working on getting out on our own for a little while. Not too long, but we're not taking off anytime soon," Aden reassured.

"Okay," Emily replied as she took his hand. "Let's go tell him."

Mark watched as they started heading in his direction. His eyes locked with his daughter's and they both smiled at one another. Her eyes stared adoringly at him, sending all of her love through that smile and those eyes.

"Maybe she won't be taken away from me again," Mark whispered.

"You're not losin' a daughter, you're gainin' a son," Steve encouraged, which brought a smile to Mark's face.

"That's true. Well here they come. Time to give at least a little bit of her away," Mark stated quietly as Emily and Aden made their way over.

Emily squeezed Aden's hand tightly as she glanced up at him then back toward her father. She loved both of these men more than life itself. Mark had saved her from that monster and Aden had saved her heart. They were both her heroes. Her heart swelled with the confidence that they would never let that ghost, that evil demon, come back to haunt her.

Turn the page for an exciting sneak peek of

If You Only Knew
sequel to Stephanie Oneilstraight's

What You've Done to Me

Prologue

Greg Riley grunted as he pulled himself up, the single metal bar struggling to hold his body weight. A thin layer of perspiration glistened on his skin, his body continuing to heat as he worked himself hard. He had to be in top shape for this day. This was the day he had waited three years for. He remembered his first day in jail like it was yesterday. He'd intimidated every guard that came his way but only one dared to try his anger. One guard by the name of Ken Rammond. The man had known the facts of Greg's case, so he had known why he was in prison and had decided to try and use that toward his advantage while he had led Greg down the hallway toward his cell. Unfortunately, he had learned not to test Greg Riley's anger. The man's last sentences ran through his mind as if a voice was growling in his ear.

"You're gonna rot in here you son of a bitch. I really hope we get someone else in this cell bock that is bigger than you so you can know how it feels to be raped. I bet that girl is so happy that you're behind bars."

Greg had kept his composure for the most part. He had remembered that causing trouble would pull him from his overall goal, but the man's final words had thrown him over the edge.

"You're a baby rapist, you bastard. You're gonna rot in hell!"

Greg had launched himself at the man, grabbing him by the shirt collar before repeatedly slamming him up against the concrete wall. No one was about to refer to Emily as a baby, and no one was going to insult him in that fashion. Greg chuckled as he pulled up on the bar then lowered himself at a faster pace. The man had been in a coma ever since, and Greg had made solitary confinement his permanent home. Since then, every waking moment had been filled with nothing but exercising. His body mass had expanded substantially since he had last seen Emily's beautiful face. If only she could see him now. She would no doubt be impressed. Prison was meant to take the evil out of the people trapped inside. It was meant to teach them a lesson for what they had done. But not for Greg Riley. Three years in prison so far had only taught him about his love for Emily. His heart ached for her as every day ticked by minute by minute. His sentence had been for fifteen years and so far, only three had gone by. How was he supposed to live for twelve more years without her? There had been times in the past three years where he had pondered his feelings for her, wondering whether he loved her for just her pretty face, or if he truly loved her for her heart and soul. Could it be possible? Her face was one of an angel, her body that of a seductress. It could be easy to mistake lust for love.

"Never," Greg muttered before letting out an animalistic growl as he worked the pull-up bar more vigorously. His biceps bulged as he lifted all of his body weight over and over. These years had turned his muscular, toned body into pure stone. His body fat had dropped to an almost nonexistent percentage. Oh yes, Emily would definitely appreciate his improvements, if only she would come to visit him. He had to keep confidence that his lawyer would pull through, that she would think of something. Greg finally released the bar, his large frame landing with a prominent thud. He turned slowly in a full circle, studying his cell. Solitary confinement was meant to be torture, but to Greg it was simply relaxing. He enjoyed being away from others. It gave him the opportunity to concentrate his thoughts on Emily. He momentarily felt tears sting his eyes as her face wafted through his mind, but he refused to let them fall. He would never be so weak. He would stay strong for Emily, no matter how long it took for them to be together.

Greg sat down on his cot with a heavy sigh as his body slowly began to cool from his strenuous exercise. He slowly reached underneath and extracted a small piece of paper from under the mattress. He opened it for what seemed like the thousandth time in the past three years and carefully read over the words scrawled across the lined paper.

"You're so incredible. Your body is like a mountain of muscle. I want to run my hands over. I never thought I could feel this way, but I always think about you. I imagine you are watching me while I dance. I can't wait to see you in gym class on Monday. I love you."

Those words made his heartbeat pick up tenfold. His lawyer had to come through for him. She just had to. Greg's head jerked up suddenly at the sound of the solid metal door being unlatched. Once open, a large guard came into view, an angry look adorning his features.

"You are one lucky son of a bitch, Riley. We've just been given orders to release you. Your lawyer is tying up loose ends with the warden. You'll receive any belongings that you gave up your first day here, but for everything else, you're on your own."

Within a span of two hours, Greg Riley had released, one of the guards mentioning that his release had been processing for months. As the large barbwire-topped gates parted, allowing him his first steps of freedom, he tilted his head back into the brightly shining sun and breathed in the summer air deeply. He was free. He was almost skeptical as to whether he was dreaming or if he was truly awake. He smiled suddenly as he saw his lawyer's car coming around from the other side of the prison. He was definitely going to have to thank her for all of her hard work, but there was one favor he would ask of her and that was for her to explain how she had gotten him released. He knew slight details, but he wanted to know the whole sweet story.

CPSIA information can be obtained
at www.ICGtesting.com
Printed in the USA
BVOW11s1916070716
454465BV00002B/2/P

9 781683 019923